Best wishes Carmel,
James Mc Carthy

The
Coffin Maker

James McCarthy

PNEUMA SPRINGS PUBLISHING UK

First Published in 2012 by:
Pneuma Springs Publishing

The Coffin Maker
Copyright © 2012 James McCarthy

James McCarthy has asserted his right under the Copyright, Designs and Patents Act, 1988, to be identified as Author of this Work

Pneuma Springs

British Library Cataloguing in Publication Data

McCarthy, James.
 The coffin maker.
 1. Ireland--Fiction. 2. Suspense fiction.
 I. Title
 823.9'2-dc23

ISBN-13: 9781907728440

Pneuma Springs Publishing
A Subsidiary of Pneuma Springs Ltd.
7 Groveherst Road, Dartford Kent, DA1 5JD.
E: admin@pneumasprings.co.uk
W: www.pneumasprings.co.uk

This book is dedicated to
Carmel and Richard

1

'Ah-ah, that was a sore one.' He hit his knee on the revolver stuck with duct tape to the underside of the dash when he reached forward for the remote control to open the gates. He should move that pistol somewhere else, but it wouldn't be as easy to grab when he needed it.

This gun, a Glock 17 had a reputation for reliability, and it was a hell of a lot better than his previous gun which he bought in England as a deactivated firearm. A dodgy gunsmith in Dublin fitted a new firing pin, and that restored it to working order. It didn't come with any safety guarantees, and he was sure one day it would blow up in his face. He was glad to be rid of it.

It was near midnight, and it had been a long drive in the hearse back to the island, although he had some luck on this trip, the customs officer didn't search the coffin. He felt tired, and it would be a relief to take off his undertaker's uniform; everything black except a white shirt.

He pressed the red button on the remote control, and the wrought iron gates creaked open. When he got time he would spray WD40 on the pivots. It wasn't exactly a hard task, but recently he had become careless about maintenance jobs like that.

The green button on the remote for closing the gates didn't work anymore. He'd shut them later.

He drove forward and the security lights came on, lighting up the house and, behind it, the coffin showroom, the workshop, morgue and crematorium. On the other side of the yard, the Chapel was in darkness.

In the showroom window, he had four different priced coffins on display, like grand pianos with their lids open. He had watched a TV documentary on American funeral parlours, and he copied this method for putting them on show.

The neon sign over the showroom read: 'ACHILL ISLAND FUNERAL UNDERTAKERS. Hand crafted coffins a specialty. Owners Pat O' Donnell and Son.'

That sign was up there over 50 years, when his father first started the business. Pat missed him since he passed away as a sounding board for all the difficult decisions he had to make about the business.

He halted outside the morgue, switched off the engine, and got out. He might as well shut the gates, and he walked back across the yard. Before he got there, two SUVs with North of Ireland registration plates drove in. They stopped alongside him with the blast of heat from the engines.

Three men in boiler suits carrying machine pistols got out. This didn't look good. He had read somewhere that new boiler suits didn't leave any crime scene evidence.

'What can I do for you gentlemen?' he asked pretending there was nothing strange about armed men in boiler suits calling to his undertaker business at midnight.

A short man with a beer belly stepped forward. The front of his boiler suit bulging out was making him look pregnant.

'Are you Pat O'Donnell?'

'Pat O'Donnell junior. My father died a few years ago.'

It wasn't the time for a smart answer like, 'who is asking,' 'or what is it to you.'

'We want a coffin.'

'You've come to the right place. What size.'

'Your height.'

'Average then.'

Pat had heard that in this situation, it was a good idea to talk to your captors, if that's what they were. He thought about making a run for it, but his knees were shaking so much that he wouldn't get far before they shot him.

'I have to take his Lordship out of the hearse first. That's what I call the male corpses, and the females are all princesses.'

This was the time for elaboration to try to get some of his power back. Followed closely by Chubby, surely that was his nickname, he opened the mortuary door and switched on the lights. The inside looked stark and clinical with whitewashed walls, marble tops and stainless steel furnishings. He pulled on a white lab coat stained with embalming fluid that looked like blood and searched around for a face mask. Hanging on a nail, he found a mask used for spraying red paint and he put it on. A pair of red gloves completed the outfit. He was being theatrical, and he hoped it would unnerve them.

He pushed the heavy-duty trolley used for moving caskets, from the morgue to the back of the hearse, opened the tailgate and slid the coffin onto it.

'His Lordship needs some air.'

Time for more drama, he removed the lid of the coffin slowly as if he was afraid something would jump out. The head of the corpse had fallen sideways during the journey, and he walked around the coffin a few times before he bent forward and straightened it.

'Don't touch anything, there could be bugs about.'

The gunman stepped back. He was doing all right in unsettling him, but these men were dangerous, and he didn't know how many more were in the SUVs. No one offered to help nor did he expect it as he pushed the coffin into the morgue and onto the chain rollers. They started automatically and moved the coffin along to the refrigeration cabinet. He could have put the lid back on the coffin but decided to leave it open for effect. He closed the cabinet doors.

Next on the agenda was a coffin for the thugs. It didn't look like they would pay for a hand crafted one. He selected a cheap Polish import and pulled it down from the rack. Normally, it would need preparation like padding, polishing, attaching handles and a name plate, but he would forgo that chore to get rid of Chubby and his mob as quickly as he could.

'Will this one do?'

'Get on with it,' Chubby said in his deep Northern accent.

'Will you take it in one of the Jeeps?'

'Put it in the hearse and take whatever you need to dig a grave.'

'The digger is in the cemetery down the road. I can tow it behind the hearse.'

'Dig it by hand and get a move on.'

Chubby was getting impatient, and it was better not to push him too far. Pat poured embalming fluid into the coffin before he put it into the hearse. That would give off the stink of death and sicken anyone travelling with him. Alone in the hearse, he would have better chance of escaping from this lot, although the hearse wasn't exactly a racing machine. The heavy diesel engine he had fitted to give more pulling power for taking coffins from England made it even more sluggish.

He hadn't dug a grave by hand for a decade or more since he started in the undertaking business. They had employed gravediggers in those days, and he worked with them for a time, as his father insisted he should experience all aspects of the undertaking business.

He had stacked spades, picks, and shovels under the coffin platform of the hearse in case the digger broke down. That never happened. Chubby climbed into the passenger seat and sat rigid, holding the barrel of the gun in his hands and the butt between his knees. It was the way Pat had seen soldiers carrying weapons in jeeps on the TV. Maybe he'd had military training. Pat reversed the hearse into the roadway.

'Where are we going?'

'Colony cemetery.'

'Do I need my embalming kit?'

'Drive.'

It was an unusual place to go. The community hadn't used the cemetery for hundreds of years. Maybe this lot wanted to exhume remains. He drove towards the cemetery followed by the two SUVs. The smell of the embalming fluid would have overpowered him if he hadn't been wearing a mask. Out of the corner on his eye, he saw Chubby holding a hand over his mouth and nose.

'Go faster!'

'At this hour, a speeding hearse would attract attention.'

'Stop.'

Chubby jumped out, vomited on the roadway and walked around for a few minutes taking in large gulps of air. He hoped Chubby would opt to travel in one of the SUVs.

2

'Give me that mask,' said Chubby, roughly gabbing Pat's mask and trying to yank it from his face.

He took the extra mask from the glove compartment and gave it to Chubby who had difficulty getting it to seal across his nose. In Pat's experience once exposed to the sickly smell of embalming fluid it somehow stayed in your nose for hours.

Eventually, they drove over the crest of the hill leading to Dugort village, and the spectacular view of silver strand framing the sea emerged. Pat slowed slightly. He usually enjoyed the scene. His passenger showed no interest; he wasn't here for the view. Over to their left the outline of St. Thomas's church surrounded by the cemetery was bright in the moonlight.

'Park behind the church,' barked Chubby.

The jeeps pulled in behind them. Years ago, the caretaker had secured the cemetery gates with a chain and padlock and after his death no one could find the key. It had remained unopened since.

Normally Pat scrambled over the wall when he needed a name from the headstones for one of the John Doe corpses he brought from England, but he wasn't going to tell them about that. Chubby looked at the chain and padlock for a few seconds and went to the rear of the SUV and searched around until he found a bolt cutter. He cut through the rusty chain and the gates squealed open with a sound like chalk on the blackboard Pat remembered from his schooldays. That was one sound he hated. Back at the rear of the Jeep, Chubby hauled out a chain and a padlock from under a tarpaulin and hung it on one of the gate pillars.

'Up you go to the top corner and bring the digging tools with you,' he said, walking towards the graves.

Pat swung the spade and shovel on to his shoulder and, carrying the pickaxe in his hand, trekked after Chubby. One of the land rovers followed them grinding away in a low gear, driving over graves and leaving deep rutted wheel tracks, like they were competing in an off-roader.

'Dig here,' said Chubby, when they reached the remotest part of the cemetery. Pat surveyed the area for a few minutes. Overgrown with weeds and shrubbery it wouldn't be his first choice for digging a grave.

'I need to go back to the hearse for a tape-measure and the coffin,' he said, leaving the tools on the ground.

'No more play-acting. You knew you needed them before you left the hearse, get on with it.' Chubby raised the gun and pointed it at him. For a moment, it seemed as if he was going to shoot.

Escorted by a gunman, he walked back to the hearse, pretended to search around for a while before he took the tape-measure from the glove compartment and slipped the Glock pistol into his pocket. The empty coffin was light and with Pat at the front and the gunman at the rear, they carried it up to the grave site.

He pegged out the grave, six feet six long by three feet six wide, and he started to dig, carefully cutting the green sod into chunks for replacing on top of the grave. With the top layer away, the ground was a mixture of soil and sand. Deeper down, he'd find heavy earth and rock. With each push, the shovel went deep into the sandy soil, and soon he had a high mound piled up on the graveside.

He hadn't done this much physical work for a long time, and he was soon wet with sweat and breathing heavily. All he needed now was a massive heart attack, and they wouldn't even need to shoot him. Maybe that's what they were hoping for. The three gunmen had taken up positions, lying flat on the ground behind gravestones with their guns pointed at him. What was it all about? Had somebody decided to get rid of him? And why Northern gunmen?

The Jeep door opened and a fourth man stepped out. Pat stopped digging to take stock of him. He looked different from the others, wearing a suit, tie and polished brogues. He stood still, and looked around the cemetery and out to sea. Then he moved from grave to grave, bending down to examine the headstone names and carvings, as if he was about to make rubbings of them. Just another addition to the mystery of why the hell they were here.

Pat resumed digging. It wasn't long before he uncovered a large tree root. It was from one of the poplar trees growing outside the perimeter wall, there for hundreds of years. They were everyone's idea of a cemetery tree, and it was a pity to cut the roots and maybe damage the tree, but he couldn't avoid doing it. He had encountered tree roots in graves before, mostly when he opened existing graves. It was something he kept from relatives, but it wasn't unusual to find the roots entangled in the skeletons of their beloved ones.

He needed an axe and he would incur the wrath of Chubby for going back to the hearse again. He climbed out of the hole. A few feet deeper, and he wouldn't be able to do that without help, or a ladder. Chubby ran over the graves towards him, bent double commando style. The charade looked ridiculous.

'Get back in there.'

'I need the axe from the hearse to cut that root.'

'Be quick about it then.'

He returned with the axe and took his time cutting through the root, but he couldn't pull it out. Something was holding the point of it in the clay. If he had the digger, it would make short work of it but ifs and buts were no use to him now. Time was his friend. He would dig around the root slowly with the spade and that would make the job last longer and give him an opportunity to think about his situation and maybe make a run for it. He started digging again.

'Hello, what do you give a man who has everything, a coffin and a grave?' Pat jumped startled by the voice. Rotund and jovial, the man in the suit was standing on the graveside looking down at him. His polished shoes covered in clay no longer shone in the moonlight.

'I'm Billy Saunders. I'd say you're a local man?'

If this man was collaborating with the other to kill him, it appeared, he didn't know much about him.

'The family has been here since the eighteen thirties.'

'I'm from East Belfast myself, and I traced our family back to the Scottish lowlands. They came over during the plantation.'

Pat didn't give a damn where he or his family came from, the highlands or lowlands or wherever else. Neither did he need him standing over him like a ganger. Common sense dictated, play along, and he might learn something from him. He seemed more approachable than any of the others.

'Have you lived away from the island at all?'

Here, we go a question and answer session on the gravedigger's life. Before he had time to answer, Chubby came over and placed an empty beer crate upside-down near the open grave.

'Sit on this, Major.'

'Thanks.'

What did he mean by Major? Were they some kind of an army? Probably better not to ask that questions. Just get away from them as soon as possible.

'My father sent me to Dublin for embalming training. I have a small undertaking business up there now,' said Pat.

He omitted the details of his UK business; this man didn't need to know everything about him. Indeed, no one needed to know about his other work, not even his confessor if he had one.

'Tell me about embalming.'

Typical, just about everyone he met asked about embalming or cremation. There must be a primal instinct for blood and gore. Now might be a good time for an urban legend. Pat stopped digging, lent against the side of the grave and rested his hands on top of the shovel.

'When I was training in Dublin, there was a story going around about one of the morticians. He was an arrogant so-and-so. He came to work each day with a prime steak, cooked it in the morgue kitchen and sat with the bodies to eat it. The lads had enough of him and decided to teach him a lesson. One of them sliced up two fresh human kidneys full of disease and gave them to him as beef. He cooked and ate the kidneys and spent the rest of his life trying to repeat the dish, it was so good.'

Pat threw up a few shovelfuls of earth to please Chubby.

'That's a good one all right. We had one in Belfast about the pet alligator its owner flushed down the toilet. He grew up to monster size in the sewers, specialising in eating people, although I never heard of anyone he had gobbled up. The sewer workers refused to go down there, and they went on strike. To get them back to work, they got extra pay, and an armed spotter to go down with them to watch out for the monster.'

The major seemed friendly enough, and he might get a chance to ask him what this was about. Pat decided to keep up a conversation.

'There are loads of stories about rats, and they are a problem for undertakers. They can burrow down into coffins and eat the flesh of the remains and gnaw the bones. They even chew through concrete and steel. That's the way they grind back their two concave front teeth, if they didn't, the teeth would grow into their bottom lip and kill them or so I have heard but I don't believe it.'

'I know a bit about rats. I worked as an exterminator for the Belfast City Council for a while, and you are never more than ten feet away from a rat wherever you are. The sewers going up to toilets are full of them. Sometimes they come into the bathrooms up through the toilet bowl, and then you have a problem. In America, they have special traps to stop them doing that. We couldn't get rid of them, even though we put all kinds of poisons down there. We had one man who wouldn't wear a protective suit. He died of that disease you get from rat's urine, I'll think of the name of it in a minute, and that's no urban tale.'

'It was careless, like smoking at petrol pumps.'

'Some get away with it but a lot don't. Veils disease, that's what they call it.

'We had another tale going around in the North. You might have heard it. Long after closing time, two drunks were taking a short cut home through the City cemetery in Belfast. They saw a spade and shovel on their friend's grave. No doubt left there by the gravediggers when they finished work for the day.

"I see Andy is having a work done, probably getting in the phone and television," said Billy swaying from side to side.

"He was a great man for a bet on the horses, and he liked to watch the races on the TV," said Billy, doffing his cap to no one in particular.

"It's a bit late tonight, but we'll ring him in the morning to see how he's getting on," said Sammy.'

'That tale takes a lot of beating,'' said Pat. He had heard it before, and all the characters in the tale were local. It was interesting how these stories spread from parish to parish and eventually reached from one end of the country to the other. Always told by someone who knew someone who knew the person it happened to.

The Major looking out to sea seemed thoughtful and asked, 'Is there much fishing going on here?'

'Some deep-sea fishing for sport but not much else since the EU cut down on quotas. Not like the old days,' said Pat, who felt no great compulsion to discuss island life with him but in this predicament, he'd keep talking.

'In the past they fished at night for salmon and by first light they had them boxed and packed in a van ready to send to the Dublin fish market.

'In early August, when I was a lad it was great to stand on Purteen pier and watch boats coming in weighed down with herrings. When they forked them into boxes their silver fins glittered in the sunlight. They made fish boxes in those days from wood and banded them with metal strips, now they make them from plastic. It's progress I suppose, and we are not far away from plastic coffins.' The Major sat in silence for a long time listening to the sound of the waves breaking on the shore and the rustling of the warm breeze in the leaves.

The Major finally broke the silence,

'I still want to hear about embalming,' he said. Pat wondered if this would be a goodtime to ask him about why they were here.

3

'With practice there's not a lot to embalming.'

He started digging again but he couldn't talk and work at the same time, he could do it in his younger days, but not now. The side of the grave was damp and cool when he rested against it.

'It's easier if you get the bodies fresh. I put a cannula into a major artery and drain the blood, what's left is a bony skeleton and baggy flesh. Then I pump in the embalming fluid and the body, more or less, fills out again. If you pump in too much, it might start to leak out through the eyes, and you could have a 'crying statues' scenario on your hands.'

Pat stopped talking and started to square up the corners of the grave with the spade. He needed to get them as near right-angled as he could to feel satisfied.

'The face is the important bit, to make it more lifelike you might have to fill out the cheeks with cotton wool, especially if they wore denture. When a person is dying, relatives take out the dentures and the face collapses and become fixed when rigour sets it. I thought about using expanding foam to blow the face out again, but I'm not sure about that. My wife, when she was here, set the hair and made up the faces. I have to get in a hairdresser now.'

He was working again and trying to shut out thoughts about his wife Marie. He didn't want to think about her.

'My wife Maisie died a few years ago.' The Major's voice faltered, and he went silent for a while.

'How long does that stuff keep the corpses from going off?'

'Don't know. All the undertaker wants is to have the face looking good for the family and keep the smells away.'

Pat had watched a TV programme on Stalin, his body remained intact and on show to the public for over sixty years. The Russians changed the secret embalming fluid every year and as far as he knew, they never revealed the chemicals used. If he managed to get out of this, he might ring the Russian Embassy and ask about it, although there were more pressing items on his to-do list.

'With all the bugs about you need to take a long shower after you're finished.'

'I couldn't do that work,' said the Major.

'There are men for every job, although I wouldn't fancy going down the sewers.'

They were silent, and the only noise was scraping sand on steel as he dug deeper into the bottom of the grave.

'I wish I had grown up in a place like this, remote and peaceful,' the Major said.

'We were too far away from everything, the good and the bad,' said Pat.

'The bad is always there.'

The Major sounded resigned and defeated. That's if he was reading him right. Each time the shovel hit a rock the vibration went up through his arms, and his fingers tingled. It was like getting an electric shock. He would need practice in digging graves by hand again, and it was a relief that he didn't have to. This was the last one he would ever do, and even guns wouldn't force him into this again. From now on, it was the mechanical digger or nothing.

He decided to stick to his plan and keep up a conversation with the Major.

'I went to school on the island in the Franciscan Monastery, the big building we passed on the way here.'

'I saw the belfry lit up as we drove passed,' the Major said.

'When I left school, I went to work with my father and he sent me for proper training in Dublin. The big city was an eye-opener.'

'I always lived in a big city; Belfast.' The Major sounded vague and mechanical as if his mind was somewhere else.

16

'I have another part of the business in Ringsend in Dublin. I have a man working for me up there and he looks after most of the work. They wouldn't give me planning permission for a crematorium.'

It was difficult to know if the Major was listening or not. He started to speak again.

'I think of her, Maisie, every day. You never get over it.'

The rock Pat uncovered was too heavy to lift on the shovel, and he hunkered down, clasped his arms around it and lifted and rolled it out of the grave. Breathless, he stood still for a few minutes. It was stupid to do that; he could have put his back out.

'That's like lifting the stones in the World Strongest Man on the TV,' said the Major.

'That was an awkward brute, and my back's not the best. I should have smashed it with the sledge hammer first.'

The Major stood up and looked out to sea.

'The sea is so calm with the moon shining on it.'

It was the only thing that was calm; Pat's mind was in turmoil as he tried to figure out what action he should take. The strangeness of digging a grave for an unknown recipient in the middle of the night was surreal, to say the least. Was there any possibility that they would let him go when he finished digging the grave? Common sense was telling him that it was unlikely. There was always the possibility that it was for him. Few events in life end the way you want them to. He would prefer cremation.

'That's the Atlantic Ocean you know and it's a different story on a stormy night,' said Pat, determined to keep this man engaged in conversation until he learned more about all of this crew.

The Major sat down and started talking again.

'The sea was our backdrop in the Harland & Wolfe shipyard. That's where I served my apprenticeship to welding.'

Pat didn't know much about the North of Ireland. It was like a foreign country to him, although he heard a tale or two about it.

'I had a big dream that when I retired that I would build a steel motor sailor and sail the world with Maisie. She loved to travel but my life took a different turn.'

He was looking down at the ground, probably thinking about what might have been. It sounded like his life had diverted from the main line into a siding. Big deal, join the human race, few lives worked to plan.

'My people were working-class from East Belfast. Good living people, Christians. I went to Sunday school, learnt the Gospels by heart and sang with the Salvation Army.'

It didn't make any difference to Pat who he sang with; it could have been the Hare Krishnas for all he cared. He didn't want to be this man's confessor or have anything to do with him. Suddenly, the Major's jovial front disappeared, and his mood got darker. Dispirited and shoulders drooping, he looked like a man who had reached the end of whatever road of life he was on. He started muttering. What he was saying was just audible.

'I'm dammed. I'll spend my eternal life in Hell. We kidnapped those poor people off the street and fuelled by drink and drugs, we tortured and murdered them. I was a ringleader. There is no mercy and no salvation for me.' He started crying quietly, a man in agony over a past he couldn't escape from.

4

Horrified by what the Major said, Pat stopped digging and steadied himself by placing his hand against the side of the grave. He dropped on one knee into the damp earth and closed his eyes to try to shut it out. He had read about the Shankhill butchers and other loyalist marauding gangs trawling through areas of Belfast looking for victims. They took their captives to lock up garages in the East of the city and tortured them for days before killing them. Theirs was a terrible death. Thank God these terrible events were over, and he never expected to come face-to-face with any of it, especially not on his home island. The Major was still muttering and whimpering.

'I could have cried when they closed down the yard, it was a great place to work. There was always a passenger liner in for refit and that's where we ate our lunch up in the staterooms. We didn't have to climb any stairs. The lift operators used to swing us up, ten at a time to the first-class deck.'

Pat tossed up another shovelful of shingled soil onto the bank. The pebbles in the mix made it heavy to lift, but they were always in the soil near the sea.

'Such riches, there was nothing for us but the best in those days. In the social club, I could take part in almost any pastime, and of course, there was always the opportunity to dance the night away. The bar was open seven nights a week and I could have gone in and drank any time. We had some great sing songs. When the troubles started, I joined a paramilitary group in the yard and worked my way up through the ranks to Major. There was always religious strife in the shipyard.'

'We terrorised and murdered, I will take my guilt to the grave. I took my eyes off the Lord. It was my damnation, my damnation,' said the Major, lifting his head.

'It was but I don't need to hear any of this,' Pat said, but the Major wasn't listening. He had stopped talking and Pat felt relieved that he had shut up, and hoped he wouldn't start up again. He had no sympathy for him. All he felt was anger towards this torturer and murderer, and he didn't care whether he was hearing him or not. He should just swing the spade and take his head off. It was tempting but he couldn't. This Major was one bad piece of work. Did he and his gunmen plan to torture and kill him as they had done with so many others? He would use the Glock pistol to defend himself before that happened. The images of torture and death he was conjuring up in his head scared him. He needed to put this nonsense out of his mind and replace it with something that wouldn't distract him. A true story about what happened a long time ago on the Islands came into his head.

He'd concentrate on that story and forget about the whinging Major. In the early 17th century, a landowner from the mainland put his cattle over there to graze on the uninhabited small island next to Achill. He employed a young man called McDaid, and his mother to look after them. After three years, he returned to the island to inspect his stock, and he didn't like their condition. McDaid objected to the way the landowner was verbally abusing his mother and in a fit of rage hit him over the head with a spade and with blood flowing from the wound, he thought he had killed the landlord. He fled from the island in a curragh and made his way to County Fermanagh where he had relatives.

Pat had to stop digging. He was no longer used to this work, and the rough spade handle rubbing against his palm had raised a blister. The red welt, filled with fluid, was painful, and if he had a safety pin, he would burst it. He didn't have any sticking plaster in the hearse either; anyway, he wouldn't get much sympathy from Chubby if he stopped digging. He tore out the lining of his pocket and wrapped it around his palm. It didn't help much, but it was better than nothing.

He started digging again. Years passed and although McDaid wanted to go back to Innishbiggle, he remained in County Fermanagh afraid that the authorities would hang him for murder if he returned home. He learnt a trade, tailoring. By chance, he was sitting on a fence one summer evening when two stocking salesmen stopped to talk to him. By their accents, he knew they were from near home, and he enquired about his mother and the landlord. Both were alive and well. McDaid returned home and he travelled the islands as a journeyman tailor for the rest of his life. He always wore a blue suit and from that he derived his nickname, the blue tailor. He was a gifted songwriter and to this day, the islanders sing the songs and poems he composed both in Irish and English in the Island pubs. The Major started talking again.

'We made our own machine-guns in the shipyard; they weren't that hard to make. We had the skills, the machinery and the right metals there to hand. I was a reserve constable and the leader, and the others were ex-army or police. We drove around the streets of Belfast at night looking for victims to haul into the Land-Rover and take back to a garage in Newtownards. It wasn't Christian or even human what we did to those poor men and boys. I have nightmares about it.' The Major got up from the beer crate, looked out to sea for a while and then sat down again.

Pat kept digging. He was down about three feet and there was still a bit to go. He knew he was going slower, tired by the physical effort; he climbed out of the grave and lay down for a rest on the dew damp grass.

'Get back in there and dig, you stupid bastard,' shouted Chubby, shattering the strange silence that hung over the graveyard. Pat looked up, and from behind the headstones the thugs had the red laser night sights of their guns trained on him. He got to his feet and looked up at the mountain behind them. It was tempting to make a run for it. He would lose them easily on the mountain, but there was the problem of getting over the perimeter fence, before they shot him. A world-class sprinter wouldn't manage it. He jumped back into the grave and started digging slowly.

The Major was talking again, not as loud as before and more jumbled.

'From the shipyard I went into the prison service. It wasn't hard to get in with my paramilitary background. They sent me to Long Kesh to look after the loyalist in the H-Blocks.'

Pat exposed a root, thin and white like the tentacles of an alien life form. He cut through it with the spade and a watery liquid dripped from it, probably poisonous, better not to touch it with his hands.

'Everyone treated the prison officers like dirt; the lowest of the low. Belittled by their seniors in the prison service even the detainees berated them and sometimes physically attacked them. I was different - no one treated me like that. A Major in the paramilitaries received respect. The loyalist in the H-Blocks obeyed my every command. If they didn't, my enforcers took care of it; either beat them up or shot off their kneecaps for insubordination.'

'Real nice work if you can get it,' said Pat sarcastically but the Major was not listening. It was as if his hearing had shut down.

'I didn't need an appointment to see the Governor. I just walked into his office to talk to him. He knew that I had the power to make life difficult for him; to start a riot among the loyalist prisoners anytime I felt like it. I took as much time off from work as I wanted and a lot of that time I spent driving around Belfast looking for people to lift.'

'A great way to spend your time,' said Pat angrily, using a flat stone to clean the build-up of clay from the shovel blade.

'I brought the sound of the Lambeg drums into the H-Blocks. We smuggled in drums and uniforms, and the loyalists prisoners got permission from the governor to march around the yard on the twelfth day. It was the only time they could go wherever they wanted outside the cages.'

Pat usually skipped the bits in the papers about Northern Ireland, but he had read something about the H-Blocks. Loyalist detainees had tried to escape by breaking out of their cages and using a human pyramid to try to climb over the perimeter fence. The prison officers discovered the plot before any of the detainees could escape. Was it possible the Major had informed on them? He would have had an ulterior motive to preserve his status as the top man in the prison.

'Long Kesh was where I turned my life around. An evangelical minister came in one day to talk to the detainees about getting saved. The session was in the prison chapel. I was in charge of the one or two detainees who came to hear him. He was an American, and his special ministry was bringing prisoners to the Lord. He had preached in the toughest prison in the world.'

The spade blade was shining in the moonlight. When he had started digging, it was rusty but with use it had brightened up. It wouldn't have looked any better if he had used a grindstone on it.

'I felt challenged by what the preacher said and half way through his sermon, I started to cry; the gift of tears. I was the first up to the altar when he called us forward to give our life to Jesus. When he prayed over me, I fell backwards unconscious; slain in the spirit.'

Pat didn't understand this mumbo-jumbo, but whatever it was, it had affected this killer.

'The next day I said a few words in some ancient language that I couldn't understand. I was speaking in tongues. I knew then that the power of the Holy Spirit had saved me, and that I would do everything I could to stop the murder and mayhem that I was part of. I became an informer.'

5

Pat stopped digging and looked up when he heard the noise of the SUV door opening. Good Lord were there more of them? He hadn't counted on that. A tall young woman stepped out. She walked in their direction, stepping gingerly from grave to grave in high heels. As she came closer, he could see she was clutching a white handkerchief, and her eyes were red from crying. She stopped a short distance away from them.

'Hi, I'm Pat,' he almost stretched his hand out of the grave for her to shake. A good-looking young woman, he was automatically assuming that she meant him no harm. Nonetheless, with the mess they were in, it didn't sound like the right greeting.

'I'm Teresa,' she said without looking at him. It felt like the end of the conversation. She didn't address the Major or take an interest in him. It appeared, she didn't even know him. Her presence added another piece to a jigsaw that already had too many. What other surprises were in the SUVs? The Major was staring at the circle of red laser light shining on his breast pocket. Pat traced it back to the gun Chubby, half-hidden behind a gravestone, was holding. The Major was talking.

'I was a changed man. I never murdered another person. I told it all to a friend of mine, a sergeant in the RUC, and he persuaded me to stay with the group and inform on them.'

'You animal, you lifted my uncle, and they wouldn't let us open the coffin to see him; he was so badly disfigured.' Teresa was sobbing and dabbing her eyes with the handkerchief. The Major wasn't listening; he was talking again almost smugly.

'I did that for three years, and I saved many lives.'

'That makes it all right then,' said Pat without looking up from digging. The Major still wasn't listening.

'The sergeant was a sensitive man. He read his bible ever day, and I think he was more suitable to church work. They found him dead with his service pistol beside him.'

The Major stood up and moved the beer crate around until it was sitting on leveller ground.

'He couldn't take it. Maybe I should never have told him about the way we tortured those people we killed. It must have preyed on his mind.'

'You're not that thin-skinned, just another day's work for you,' said Pat, sick by what he was hearing. The Major hadn't finished yet. 'They gave me another minder. I didn't know him, and I didn't trust him but I was too far involved at that stage. I think he leaked that I was an informer.'

Teresa was on her knees beside a headstone, her shoulders lifting and falling with each sob. He felt like telling her to get up. The long grass on the grave top would destroy the knees of her fancy trouser suit.

'I argued that it was a dirty tricks campaign when I was hauled up before the Paramilitary Council. Someone was trying to smear me. I got away with it that time. With peace coming, I thought that was the end of it, but it wasn't.'

He looked over in Chubby's direction.

'They came after me a few times, but I still had my service revolver to protect me. That's all over now, I made my peace with the Almighty, and I'm ready to go.'

Pat didn't see it coming. An enraged Teresa ran at the Major and pushed him; he lost his balance and toppled into the grave. He landed on top of Pat and knocked him over on to the handle of the shovel. With the crunching sound of wood on bone, the pain, and blood flowing down his shirt-front, Pat knew he had a broken nose.

Chubby came running over, the laser light from his gun bouncing around the cemetery like a strobe light.

'Cut it out. Get back into the SUV.' He gestured towards Teresa with the barrel of the gun. The laser flashed across Pat's eyes, and it was so bright that he thought Chubby had blinded him.

'I'm OK Sergeant. Leave her alone, she has nothing to do with any of it,' said the Major. Covered in mud, he climbed out of the grave and walked towards Chubby. Without responding, Chubby retreated.

'Are you all right, I'm sorry. I didn't mean that to happen,' said Teresa. In the tussle with the Major, she had broken the heel of her shoe, and she was finding it difficult to balance.

'I'll be fine when I get out of this nightmare.' He held the back of his hand against his nose to try to stanch the flow of blood.

She handed him a tissue, and he used it as a plug. All that did was to redirect the blood into his throat, but at least he could spit it out and continue working.

'I'd say it's a broken nose,' said the Major trying to brush the mud from his clothes with his hands. If looks could kill, with the way Teresa was glaring at the Major, he was a dead man already.

The large root that had balked Pat's progress since he started digging, was still there. He wrapped his arms around it and, using his weight, pulled. It came out suddenly, and he fell backwards into the wet clay. He would feel comfortable and secure cosseted in the mud, if only the reality of his situation would go away.

He would have stayed lying there longer if he hadn't seen the human arm entangled in the end of the root. Stripped of flesh, the hand and arm were intact apart from the marks on the bones where rats had gnawed at them. He got up quickly spat out blood and started to untangle the arm. The bones were long and probably belonged to a man, although they were quite thin. He lifted the arm carefully and laid it on the grass next to the grave.

'Come and see this,' said Pat, calling Chubby over. The gunman waited for a few minutes before slowly walking over to the grave, pointing the gun straight at Pat.

'What now? I've just about had enough your nonsense.'

They used this grave before. I need a body bag from the hearse for the remains.'

'Go and get it, and be quick about it,' he said, turning to Teresa. She looked to Pat for help.

'No, I'll get it myself.' He didn't wait for a reply, and Chubby didn't challenge him as he walked passed him to the hearse. Pat pulled out a body bag from under the coffin platform. He rarely used them, except for collecting the scattered remains of road accidents. They were good for that job; liquid proof, body fluids didn't leak out of them.

He stretched out the body bag at the graveside, and before he could get to the arm, the Major had lifted it and placed it gently in the bag. He stood over the grave, ready to place the next piece of the remains into the bag. Could be he thought doing service to the dead was amends for the terrible crimes he committed. Pat was loathe to involve him in anything. He was thinking about how to stop him when the shovel scraped on metal; he had uncovered a brass plate. He cleaned the dirt off it with his sleeve to make the writing legible. He spoke the words as he read them.

'Here lie the remains of those from this parish who died of famine fever. Dated; 1848.'

'It's a famine grave. There's no way of knowing the number buried here,' said Teresa, standing on the graveside looking in.

6

'We're not going to find out. I've stopped digging. "Respect the dead," my father always said.' Nevertheless he felt they would force him to keep digging. He would need to go carefully and not cross Chubby on this one.

'I don't know much about the famine,' said Chubby.

'Why does that not surprise me?' said Teresa, hunkering down to stare into the blackness of the grave.

He had uncovered a famine grave and he couldn't even imagine how many people, men, women and children they buried here. In his long association with graves, Pat had never had an experience like this and he didn't expect to have another one, any time soon.

'It's unforgivable, that at the time the potato crops failed, Ireland exported enough food to feed everyone in the country.' She stood up but was still looking down at him. With anger, the pallor had gone from her face.

'What food was going out of the country?' asked Pat. He had spread the body bag on the bottom of the grave and was scraping clay from the sides to cover it over.

'We were sending cattle, grain, bacon but not live pigs to England.'

She sounded smart and educated. How did she fit in with this bunch of thugs?

'The Ottoman Sultan offered to send ten thousand pounds to help the starving people of Ireland. Queen Victoria was only sending two thousand pounds and she asked the Sultan not to send more.

Pat stamped down the clay at the graveside with his feet. It provided a flat surface for the coffin to rest on. He toyed with the idea of putting the brass plaque on top of the grave, it might be better to leave it where it was. Undertakers were a superstitious lot; he was always the last to touch a coffin before filling in the grave.

'The Queen didn't want people to know that she hadn't been generous to her starving subjects in Ireland. The Sultan obeyed her wishes and sent a thousand pounds, but he secretly sent two ships filled with grain to Drogheda.' Teresa sat on the nearest grave.

'Her majesty, the Queen, would never do anything like that. She would never be any man's debtor,' said the Major. He had lost the thread of the conversation and was confusing Queen Victoria with the present Queen, Elizabeth. They ignored him.

'The Choctaw Indians in America sent seven hundred dollars to help victims of the Irish famine. An astonishing act from people who were so poor themselves. They had their own 'trail of tears' some years before the Irish famine,' said Teresa.

'What was that about?' asked Pat.

'I think it was in the eighteen thirties, the US government persuaded the Choctaws to move from their homelands to the new Indian Territory. That was a walk from the deep south of the US up to Oklahoma. Thousands died on the trail from starvation, and disease,' she said, her eyes closed either to aid her memory, or else from the horrible picture her imagination was painting of it.

'I didn't know any of that,' said Pat. They were silent for a time and Pat prodded the spade into the side of the grave, pretending he was digging.

'Was the island badly affected by the famine?' she asked.

'We lost half of the people during the famine. They either died or emigrated.'

Down as deep as the height of the spade handle was Pat's rule of thumb for measuring the depth of a grave. This one was far short of that, but he didn't want to disturb any more of the remains than he had to. Chubby wouldn't notice what depth the grave was.

He didn't like talking to educated people. They soon found his weakness. If she knew he was stupid, how would she feel about him? His teachers used to say that he was a slow learner, and then they'd say, "he can learn if it's explained slowly to him." During his schooldays, before dyslexia, had a name, others pupils thought him stupid. Some tried to bully him, chanting "you are thick." With his fists, he could handle any of them and after a few fights, they stopped tormenting him.

Brother Bonaventure delighted in telling his pupils that those in the first row of the class would go to university and get big degrees, doctors, lawyers. The second row, for example, would get into the civil service, the banks, and in the back row were the future bookies, auctioneers/estate Agents, shop keepers, trades people and all sorts of clever conmen and money makers. They would end with fast cars and the most desirable young women. Well, he was in the back row and while he didn't have a fast car, he got the girl he wanted and unfortunately lost her again. That was another story. Now Teresa was asking more questions.

'Where did they emigrate to?'

'They went everywhere: America, England, Scotland, Canada, Australia, New Zealand and other places.'

He didn't know how long he could keep Chubby thinking he was still digging. It was important to fool him for as long as possible. There was no doubt that Chubby intended to use the grave for one or all of them. Escape was uppermost on Pat's mind, though he still had no plan.

'Is this a famine cemetery?' asked Teresa, half covering her face with her hands.

'Never heard it called that, but it might be. What kind of grave are you sitting on?'

She leant forward to get a better view of the writing on the headstone, although he felt it wasn't necessary with the brightness of the night. The near-daylight was more of a curse than a blessing. If it was darker, he could make a run for the boundary wall and try to get away.

She read from the headstone.

"Here lie the remains of lay preacher, Mr. Robert Anderson,

30

Colony Village, who died of famine fever on the 4thApril 1841.

Even though I walk through the valley

of the shadow of death,

I fear no evil, for you are with me;

Your rod and your staff, they comfort me.

Rest in peace."

'A mixed religious community? She looked towards him as if expecting an explanation.

'Around the famine time, an Irish speaking minister from County Meath set up a community on the island to convert people,' he said, wondering how he was going to outwit his captors. Nothing was coming to mind.

Pat looked up, and they still had the laser beams from the sub machine-guns pointed in his direction.

'Did he get to make many converts?' she asked.

'For food, they changed religion and changed back again when times got better. The Rev Nangle hired two ships in Liverpool and filled them with yellow meal for the island. At the start, he bribed people with the meal to get them to change religion, but later in the famine, he gave everyone food.'

'Did they not fish?'

'They had to sell their curraghs to pay the rent. They ate seaweed, but it wasn't enough to keep them from starving.'

The Major was showing no interest in what was going. Pat wondered if he could trust this young woman and, maybe, together they could plan something to get out of this mess.

7

The Major was talking again.

'We holidayed on Achill every year, I don't know for how many years. After the twelfth day, we would come down and stay for two weeks. It coincided with the Glasgow fair fortnight and there were always a few Scot lads holidaying with us. The locals didn't take one blind bit of notice of us.'

Pat's shouldered ached from scraping down the sides of the grave, but it made a convincing noise. Any time now Chubby would notice that he was adding nothing to the heap of earth at the graveside and might come over to investigate.

'We were all loyalists together, with the same religion and like views on what was happening to our country. We stayed in touch over the years, and eventually we started travelling in a group to the island. Then the troubles started, and we banded ourselves into a private army in Northern Ireland to save our country. The name of our group wouldn't mean anything to you, so I'll leave it out. The Sergeant over there came along with the troupe. He trained us on the hill behind us here, running up and down until we exhausted ourselves. In later years, every man had a side-arm with him,' said the Major looking over in the Sergeant's direction.

These thugs knew their way around the mountain. He was wrong to think that he could escape from them once he got on the mountain route.

'It was great training under their noses in the Free State, enemy country. In the daytime, we climbed the mountain at running pace and at night, we went up in full kit. By the end, we were fighting fit. Aha, they were the days, when you could trust the word of the brethren.'

'It didn't surprise me, when they came back to the island for this job,' said the Major.

Pat had one digging tool left in the hearse that he could claim he needed to complete the job. He hauled himself out of the grave and shouted over to Chubby, 'I need the crowbar from the hearse.'

Chubby didn't answer but gestured towards the hearse with the laser beam. Pat took it as a 'Yes' and walked slowly across the cemetery to the hearse. He hauled the steel crowbar, six feet long and two inches in diameter, from under the coffin platform. The crowbar was heavier than he remembered, but he hadn't used it for a decade.

In an instant, the warm sweat on his body turned icy cold, and he shivered. What a time to pick up a bug from the corpses after all the years he had worked with them without getting any infections. His mind was starting to play tricks on him as well. He could have almost sworn that he heard the clomp of a horse hoof and a scraping sound as it dug into shingled surface on the laneway behind him. He would need to take hold of his senses. He glanced around and to his surprise, straining up the hill towards him, was a horse and cart loaded with coffins. Weary mourners were walking behind the cart, some holding on to it for support. Remnants of starving people, emaciated with extended stomachs and large lifeless eyes in skeletal faces. The driver, sitting on the shaft of the cart was holding the reins loose in his hands, shoulders hunched and chin buried deep in his chest, too weak to lift it up. Good Lord it was a sorry sight.

The horse did not need any guidance; he knew his way to the cemetery. As the cortege came closer, Pat could smell the decaying bodies in the rough wooden coffins, and hear the horse snorting, and grating metal on metal as the cartwheels rotated on dry axles. The priest was walking before them with a silver crucifix in a white cloth held to his chest. The Anglican Minister beside him was holding a bible in his hands. Above all the other noise was a mournful mantra coming from the mourners, and it took him a moment to recognise it; the rosary prayers in Irish. His Irish wasn't the best, but he translated it easily,

'Hail Mary full of grace the Lord is with thee, blessed art though among woman and blessed is the fruit of thy womb Jesus…

The perimeter wall around the graveyard had vanished and the headstones were standing stark against the heather of the mountain. The horse obediently turned into the cemetery and stopped,

'Where to?' asked the driver, lifting his head and turning around.

'We opened one at the top,' said a man from the mourners in a low voice.

'Get on with ye,' shouted the driver sharply to the horse, and he shook the reins a couple of times. The horse got going and plodded up the path through the graveyard. It stopped at the grave Pat was working on. This was unreal; an enactment burial of famine corpses. The cold had gone from his body, and he was feeling normal. Who would believe such a tale? The island community would think he had lost his reason. Four men lowered the coffins, with care, into the grave and Pat jumped when the women mourners let out a terrible wail, like the screech of a thousand banshees. His father had told him about it, the *caoin,* a lament for the dead practiced in the old days. The priest held up his hand for silence and handed the crucifix to an altar boy and started reading from a prayer book.

'Man thou art but dust and into dust thou shalt return.'

The rest was in Latin, and he didn't understand it. He wasn't a mass server when he was at school; the teacher said he wasn't smart enough to learn the responses. The priest gathered a handful of soil and shook it into the grave. He stood respectfully aside while the minister, in a cultured Protestant voice, read from the Bible. With the grave refilled, the priest shook the holy water and the *caoin* started again. Grim faced, the priest and minister walked together from the cemetery but the joy of the Lord was absent from their faces. They stopped close to Pat.

'Is the fever spreading in the settlement?' asked the priest, he took the stole from around his neck, kissed it and folded it.

'It's spreading like wildfire. It's terrible to see little children suffering,' said the minister choking with emotion.

'It's wiping out whole families. Soon, we won't have enough able-bodied men to open graves. I'd better get few more mass graves dug,' said the priest.

'Rumours are spreading in the settlement that it's a plague from the Lord. I'm countering with the truth,' said the minister, and they moved out of earshot.

The cart passed him. The wheels were squirting water out of the ruts in the track, as they went along. Horse carts were before Pat's time, and he hadn't seen one working before. The wheels sloping inwards were wobbling around on the axle and making a grating nose with each turn. A good dollop of axle grease would cure that. Maybe they didn't make it any more? His father told him stories of how Pat's undertaker grandfather used to prepare the horses and carts for the day ahead. The helpers removed the cartwheels, and coated the axles with grease. They then cleaned the harnesses with saddle soap, and polished them. His grandfather had great affection for the horses. He fed and watered them before each burial. He dismissed any helper caught abusing the horses in any way.

The cart passed within a few feet, but the driver seemed unaware of him. They were like actors in different dramas. Chubby shouted and broke the spell,

'Get back here.'

The mirage, if that is what it was, cracked like a mirror, chunks disappearing as if into a mist. He shivered and hoisted the crowbar on to his shoulder and struggled up the hill. He dropped the crowbar close to the open grave. His shoulder hurt, and a bloodstain had appeared on his shirt where the bar had rested. He jumped back into the grave, picked up the spade and started scraping again. He was running out of time to think of an escape plan.

The Major had got rid of any signs of his repentance and he was sitting up and alert, eyes darting around the cemetery, as if he was searching for something, he addressed Pat,

'Young man, I know you don't trust me, but after you're no further use to them, they'll shoot you.'

Pat looked up. He was trying to figure out what the Major was up to, something he would use to his own advantage.

'I'll cause a distraction and while their attention is on me make a run for it. It's your only chance and before the Father in heaven, I'll be doing one decent thing,' said the Major, standing up and walking in Chubby's direction.

'Sergeant, we go back a long way. I trained and promoted you. You know me. We have seen action together. These others are nothing, upstarts, but they have turned you against me.'

The Major stopped, the laser lights shining on him. Teresa stood up, looked at Pat and, balancing awkwardly on one foot, kicked off her good shoe ready for action.

'No, don't run, they'd shoot us before we get far. I bet, in the upheaval the Major would try to get away in the SUV,' said Pat as he climbed out of the grave.

The Major took a step closer to Chubby and Pat jumped when he heard the rat-tat-tat of machine-guns. Blood spurted from the pinpoints of laser light shining on the Major's body, and the force of the bullets spun him around, and he dropped face down on a grave. He was dead before he hit the ground.

A silence, apart from the sound of the incoming tide splashing on shore, descended on the graveyard. What next? Pat's mind was racing, would it do any good to appeal to Chubby? He had nothing to do with any of it. He didn't know much about Teresa, but he felt sure she was innocent of any wrongdoing. Her involvement with his lot of thugs was a mystery.

'Haul him into the grave, we don't need the coffin,' said Chubby. Pat walked over to the grave and looked down at the Major's body. Blood was leaking from it and pooling around him on the ground.

'I've thought of a better use for the coffin,' said Chubby. The laser lights swung around and rested on Teresa.

8

Pat knew what he had to do. He had heard the message often enough from the instructor on the four-day simulated army training course in Tiglin forest in Wicklow. It was expensive but with the turn his life had taken he needed to know how to use guns.

"When facing the enemy is not the time to think about the do's, and don'ts and the might have been. When you attack, have one thought in mind: eliminate the opponent."

That was the training session approach, but the real world was different. He had never fired a shot at anyone in his life. If he was going to shoot at them, he needed to think of these gunmen as murderers, and he and Teresa would die if he didn't act.

With his thumb, he released the safety catch on the Glock pistol. It gave a loud click. Had they heard it? His heart felt like it was about to explode, and a pulse was beating in his ears. Sweat was running down his forehead and into his eyes. He wiped his forehead with the back of his hand. The gunmen hadn't heard.

"Aim for the largest target, the chest and don't wait to see the result, fire at your next target," the instructor had said. Pat curled his index finger around the trigger and without taking the gun from his pocked aimed at Chubby's legs. The noise was deafening and, ignoring his training, he watched Chubby drop his machine-gun, and fall backwards. The bullet had lodged in his thigh, and Pat motionless, continued to stare until his training kicked in. He fired at the second and third murderer, and they screamed as bullets hit them. In the dim light, as far as he could see, he had shot the first one in the knee and the other one in the hip. Teresa fainted and lay in a heap beside the open grave. He didn't have time to attend to her; he followed through on his training.

"Disarm the enemy after you shoot them. If injured, with weapons by their side, they could still be dangerous. Confiscate their weapons."

Pat approached them cautiously. They didn't resist when he grabbed their machine-guns, and dumped them into the open grave. Teresa was sitting upright and looked groggy.

'Are they dead?' she asked fearfully.

'No injured, but they would have killed us, if I hadn't acted.'

'What do we do now,' she asked looking up at him.

'We need to get them to a hospital.'

He kept the pistol pointed at Chubby and walked towards him. Chubby was holding his thigh where the bullet had lodged, and his trouser leg looked soaked it in blood.

'Can you drive?' Pat asked, still holding the pistol ready in case Chubby had a hidden weapon.

'I don't know.'

'I'll put on a tourniquet. I can do first aid. Give me your belt,' Teresa said to Chubby.

He loosened his belt and handed it to her. Pat didn't have any training in that type of work. It wasn't necessary for any of his clients, although at times he would benefit from it for himself. Cuts and bruises from coffin making were a regular event, and he wouldn't be the first to cut off a limb with a power tool. His father, a careful craftsman, had a stump instead of a first finger following a run-in with a power saw.

Teresa wrapped the belt around Chubby's thigh and tightened it until the flow of blood went to a trickle.

'Hold the belt tight until I tell you to let it go,' she said to Chubby, and straightened up from kneeling beside him.

'Let's check on the other two,' said Pat still holding the pistol ready, but it was unnecessary, there was no defiance left in either gunman. One of the thugs had his eyes closed, and he was moaning quietly. His knee was a bloody mess of torn flesh and bone. The other one was holding his hip where the bullet had lodged.

'Please help me,' he said. Teresa knelt down near him and said in a reassuring a voice, 'We'll look after you.'

'I'll get an SUV,' said Pat. He ran across the graveyard, jumped in and turned on the ignition. He waited for the diesel engine warming light to go out before starting the engine. It fired with the familiar diesel knock, and it sounded loud enough to wake the island. However, nothing stirred apart from the gentle movement of the trees and the sound of the sea. He parked as close as he could to the thugs, and pushed down the rear SUV seats until they were almost flat. He removed the two pillows from the coffin and placed them on the seats, that was as near as he could go to convert the seats into beds. The two wounded criminals screamed with pain as Pat and Teresa helped them into the SUV and on to the makeshift beds.

'Right, your turn to move,' said Pat as they helped Chubby, who wasn't as badly injured as the others, into the driver's seat.

'Do you know the way to the hospital in Castlebar?' asked Pat, holding the door of the SUV open and getting ready to bang it shut.

'I do,' said Chubby, grimacing with pain as he held the clutch pedal down with his injured leg.

'Loosen the tourniquet a bit in about half an hour. If it's still bleeding, tighten it up again,' said Teresa. Chubby nodded his head, and Pat banged the door shut. Chubby started the engine, and drove across the graves and on to the roadway. He was going to have a painful forty-mile drive to Castlebar and out of their lives.

'I'll tidy up here a bit,' said Pat going over to the Major's body, and looked at it for a moment. He rolled him over on his back, caught hold of his legs, and dragged him to the graveside. With Teresa's help, they put him in a body bag and rolled it into the grave.

'I'm going to the hearse for an artificial grass mat,' said Pat.

Teresa sat on a grave, looking exhausted, she didn't say anything. He covered the grave with the grass mat, and to a casual observer, there was no evidence of an opened grave. With Teresa at the foot and Pat at the head of the coffin, they carried it back to the hearse, and pushed it into the back.

'Will you drive the SUV they left behind?'

'I have never driven anything like that before,' she said standing up and taking a look at the parked SUV outside the cemetery gate.

'We can't leave it here. It's no different to driving a car, the gears and everything are the same.'

Teresa reluctantly climbed in.

'It's so high up like a truck.' Her feet didn't reach the pedals, and he had to move the seat forward.

'It's just fear. You'll be OK once you start driving it,' he said. She didn't seem convinced.

'Take it out on to the main road, and wait for me. I'll lock the gates, and then go ahead in the hearse.' The SUV kangaroo hopped a few times, and then it moved slowly to the road. At the speed she was driving, it would take them to next year to get back to the funeral parlour. He collected the tools and replaced them under the coffin platform before locking the gates. He drove up beside the SUV and waved to her to follow him. Her speed increased and when they turned into his house, she was keeping pace with him. Considering that she was driving an unfamiliar vehicle, and the trauma she had been through, it was an impressive performance. He parked the SUV in the hearse garage and locked the door. If seen by the locals, its North of Ireland registration plate would be a topic for discussion, and he didn't want that.

'That's enough for one day. I'm going to Dublin again in a few days, and I'll give you a lift. I can put you up here until then,' he said as she followed him to the front door of the house.

'That'll do fine. Can I use your phone to call my mother?'

'No problem. The prefix for Belfast is…' He went ahead of Teresa into the front room to where the phone was. He left her to make the call but with the phone stuck on the loudspeaker, he could hear everything she said.

'Mama, this is Teresa.'

'Are you safe? Where are you, I'm worried sick?''

'Achill Island and I'm fine.'

'What, how did you get there?'

'You know the Major I talked about. His own comrades took us here and shot him dead. It was terrible; they forced the undertaker here to bury him.'

'I told you not to take the job in Reid's.'

'They are good to me, Mama. I'm at the undertaker house. He's going to give me a lift to Dublin in a couple of days, then I'll take the train home.'

'Take care of yourself. I'll be praying for you.'

'I will and I'll ring every day mama.'

'Bye for now Teresa. I'm so relieved to hear from you.'

'Bye mama.'

9

Pat didn't want her to know that he was outside the door listening so, when he heard her moving, he rushed up the stairs to get out of the way. He didn't like eavesdropping, but in his defence, he didn't know anything about this young woman. She didn't seem like part of the Major's killing machine but he only had her word that she had no involvement in it. Her innocent face made it difficult to believe that she was up to no good. It reminded him of a quote his English teacher used a lot to the class. It went something like 'there is no art can find the minds construction in the face.' It was always Pat's problem at school writing down what the teachers said; the smarter ones had no problem with that.

He was standing on the landing when she emerged from the sitting room.

'I'm finished with the telephone; I'll pay for the call.'

'No need, I put them all down to the business, is your mother OK?'

'She's worried but I'll call her every day.'

'She knows you're safe. I'm fixing up a room for you but first I'll take a shower out in the morgue.'

'I'll sleep anywhere.'

'I have loads of space, it's no bother. You can have a shower up here yourself. There's a lock on the door.'

In the morgue, he removed his mud covered clothes and stepped into the shower. He had it installed with loads of jets and it reminded him of a car wash. The hot water tumbling down over his body and took away some of his stress along with the grime and blood.

Back in the house he climbed the stairs slowly to the landing, and turned towards the blue room. It had remained undisturbed since his wife, Marie, had last cleaned it and made up the bed. It was her favourite place, she had furnished it with blue carpets, curtains and bedspreads. Her presence was so strong in this room that it always brought back his sense of loss. He knew she would agree to give the room to this young woman for a few nights, it was part of what Marie was, generous to those in need. He couldn't bring himself to sleep in this room since her death and his bedroom was the small one at the back of the house.

He shut all of that out of his mind, stripped the bed and replaced sheets and pillowcases with fresh ones from the hot-press. With everything in place in the bedroom, he went downstairs.

'Tea is ready,' Teresa called from the kitchen.

'There's food in the fridge and there's drink in the cabinet over the cooker if you would like something stronger in your tea.'

'I'll try to eat although I'm not hungry,' she said.

Sitting at the kitchen table, he took stock of her. Even in her distressed state and her hair wet from the shower there were some questions he would have to ask her that couldn't wait.

'Why did those people pick my place? I never had anything to do with them.'

'Your lights were on, everywhere else was in darkness. Will they come back tonight?'

Her fear seemed genuine.

'With their injuries, you won't see those boys for a while.'

'I never want to see them again.'

He hesitated but now was as good a time as any to ask her,

'How are you involved with that lot?'

'I'm an estate agent and I went to East Belfast to collect the Major and show him a house in Bangor. It was bad luck that they came for him while I was there.'

'You were lucky that they didn't shoot you there and then.'

'They took me with them instead. They must have threatened the Major, and I suppose that's why he wanted to move house.'

'I wonder why they didn't kill the Major on his own doorstep and save them hassle?'

'I think they wanted him to disappear without trace.'

She got up to go to the toilet and he took the opportunity to take a bottle of Powers Irish Whiskey from the cabinet and pour a generous helping into her teacup, and into the teapot. It would help her to relax. His supply of alcohol was for offering a drink to the relatives when they came to use his services. He didn't take any himself and there was a good reason for that; he had eventually got around to saying it at an AA meeting,

'I am an alcoholic.'

When Marie died, he couldn't cope and the solution was the demon drink.

'A typical case.' That was how the counsellor described him, hiding bottles all over the house and morgue, and even in coffins. Sometimes he woke up in a coffin or sleeping in the back of the hearse. He kept on working throughout, and he couldn't remember half the people he buried during that time. He shuddered to think of the botched embalming he must have done during his drinking days, it was fortunate that he didn't have crying eyes or a face slip of a corpse in front of the relatives. It didn't bear thinking about.

The turning point was a young fellow, Jonnie, who wanted to train as an undertaker. He came on Wednesdays on a work experience course from Ringsend Tech, and while not the sharpest knife in the drawer, he was a willing worker. His background wasn't the best, his family in Ballyfermot had thrown him out for drug abuse, and he was living rough on the streets. It was a miracle, he had found his way to Ringsend Tech and his attendance there was apparently good. He was always the first to arrive at the premises on Wednesday mornings and, after a few weeks; Pat gave him permission to live in flat over the morgue. Jonnie was the first to notice that Pat was mixing up the brass nameplates he was putting on coffins and the shock of what he was doing drove him to seek help with Alcoholics Anonymous. He still shuddered at the thought of it, there were families out there who had buried the wrong person. The correct name was on the coffin but the wrong person was inside. Maybe the right procedure, even at this late stage, was to exhume the bodies and try to match the correct remains with the nameplates. It would involve hundreds of graves or even more than that. In truth he didn't know how many. It would involve teams of DNA experts and all kinds of other experts as well; the scandal of the year and it would put an end to his undertaking business although he didn't mind that much. He had discussed the problem with Marie and she thought that when Jonnie spotted the wrong nameplate going on the coffin, it was the first and only time it happened. Anyway he was not to blame, was he not an alcoholic at the time. Marie would be so supportive if she was alive, and he missed that, but he had to live with the uncomfortable realisation of what he might have done.

The first AA meeting he attended was in Adam & Eve's Church, Merchants Quay. He parked the hearse in a side street, and felt a bit worried about leaving it there, it was unusual for joy riders to steal a hearse, but they might vandalise it. Hopefully it would still be where he parked it and undamaged when he returned. He sat at the back of a room filled with people talking and laughing. He didn't feel like talking or laughing, and he needed another drink from the bottle of whiskey hidden under in the glove compartment of the hearse to steady his nerves. He was getting ready to leave when a man about his own age started to talk to him and put him at ease. That was the start of the long road back and indeed there were many slips on the way. That first night after the meeting he went into the nearest pub in Merchants Quay with a few like himself who were also sitting at the back of the group. However, the AA worked and he was sober for now, and he had no intention of going back to that life.

Teresa came back from the toilet. Trembling slightly, she held the cup of tea in both hands as if coaxing the heat from it into her body. He guessed delayed shock, and he kept refilling her cup hoping the whiskey would calm her down.

'I feel drowsy; have you have put something in my tea?' 'Whiskey, I thought it would help after what you have been through.' He reached up to the cupboard shelf, took down the bottle of Power's, and placed it before her on the table.

'You should have asked me first. I thought it was Rohypnol. And another thing I wasn't always an estate agent,' she was slurring her words, but she was calmer.

'Is that so?' He was being sociable, but he couldn't care less about her previous jobs. He had work to attend to, and she was an unwanted intrusion into his life, but there was no stopping her now, she was now in full flow.

'I had just finished college, and about to start a teaching job when my world turned upside-down. Those Loyalist butchers; they lifted my uncle, and bundled him into the back of a black taxi on the Fall's Road. They took him to a lock up garage in East Belfast, and tortured him for days before dumping his naked body in the Lagan. I don't know the tortures he suffered, the authorities brought him back to us in a sealed coffin, and they would not let us open it. I can only imagine what it was like.' She was sobbing uncontrollably and Pat didn't know what he should do. At this stage he normally offered grieving relatives a drink, and put his arm around their shoulders to show support for them in their grief. He did nothing, and after a few minutes she started talking again.

'I sometimes imagine him coming home from work, striding up the Fall's road with folded copies of the Irish News and the Belfast Telegraph under his arm. Smiling and greeting everyone he met, and humming 'My Lagan love'. He was a baker, and in his white working clothes, it was impossible to miss him. I had terrible nightmares after his death, and I was unable to settle into teaching, no matter how hard I tried. I knew that I would have to get away from Belfast and from Northern Ireland, and I didn't want to go to England. With fluent French, the obvious place to go was Paris, to teach English. I booked into a cheap hotel for the first week, and in that time I got a job teaching English to business people. I also moved into an apartment with two French girls. My life went on predictably for a few months; I was on the usual tourist trail of getting to know Paris, and trying to get my head back to some normality. Have you ever been to Paris?'

'I was there once,' said Pat, taking a sip of orange juice. He didn't tell her that it was on his honeymoon.

'The girls told me they were in the entertainment industry, and I envied their party lifestyle. They had a lie in every morning, and they were out all night with no shortage of money and escorts. My work got scarce as the months went on, and one of the girls suggested, I join them in show business, whatever that meant. I soon found out, they were dancers in Folies Bergère. I'll never forget the address, at 32 rue Richer in the 9th Arrondissement. At first, I was adamant that no matter what, I wouldn't have any involvement in that life, what would my mother think? But needs must, I was only getting a few days teaching now and again, and working most of the time as a waitress, a job I hated. The girls took me along to see the show, and apart from a nude in every performance it was not too bad, or so I told myself. At the interview they asked if I could dance and I told them about my Irish dance training from the age of four to the end of secondary school. I'm not sure that they knew much about Irish dancing but when I danced a slip gig they seemed impressed. The performers came from all over the world, and the camaraderie with the other girls was great. No matter what happened we were there for one another. At time I was the only Irish girl dancing in the Folies. I'm sure, like many other jobs it wasn't anything like I thought. Managed by a choreographer, we practiced our dancing routine in the afternoon and without a break, we went straight into the three hour live performance. It was exhausting work but I enjoyed it.'

'I heard of an Irish can-can girl all right, Miss Bluebell,' said Pat, and that's all he knew about her. He wouldn't have anything to do with it, on the island they thought that type of dancing was scandalous.

Teresa topped up her glass with whiskey.

'The first topic of conversation they had with me was about Miss Bluebell; she was Margaret Kelly, an orphan from Dublin, and she danced over there before and after the Second World War. She had a head for business. She created her own troupe of high-kicking dancers, and they were the famous Bluebell Girls. She selected only tall girls for the troupe; decked out in high heels, and feathery headgear, they dwarfed everyone else on-stage. The Bluebells are still dancing today in the Paris Lido.'

'What happened to her?' said Pat, bloated from drinking too much fizzy orange juice.

'She married a Romanian Jew and by all accounts, they were happy together. His name was Marcel Leibovici, and during the war, she hid him from the Gestapo across the street from the Police headquarters. The Gestapo knew she was hiding him somewhere, and even though they interrogated her many times she never revealed his whereabouts.'

'Few people could hold out against the Gestapo, they weren't exactly choirboys,' said Pat, going to the sink and filled his glass with water. He had enough fizzy orange for one night.

Teresa went on talking,

'Irish women are strong women. We were the first to emigrate to England the USA and elsewhere on our own, without men in tow.'

The whiskey was taking effect, she was slurring her words. Pat wished she would either fall asleep at the table or go up to bed, neither happened.

'Where was I? I'm losing track of the conversation. Oh yes, the Folies Bergère. I was naïve at the time, there was a lot going on in the background that I didn't know about. It took me ages to find out that their lifestyle came with a price. Addicted to drugs or drink or both, the girl's entire money went to fuel their habit. Rich businessmen set up some of the girls in apartments, and others, in their free time, were high-class call-girls. Welcome to the seedy world of show business. I didn't want any of it, except the dancing, which I enjoyed.'

She stopped talking for a moment and Pat, thought she was falling asleep. No such luck, she started up again.

'Henry was the cause of my problem; he was one of the musicians, the piano player for our practices and shows. He was from Morocco, and we started going out together. Eventually, we moved into our own grotty flat near gare de l'est station. Young and in love, I ignored the warning signs, he was a drug user, he had a never-ending supply of hash from home. Some he used, and the rest he sold on the streets. When the doctor told me the cause of my morning nausea was pregnancy, the thought horrified me. People would think it was a terrible to say that, but in my religious family, we never talked about pregnancy before marriage; a forbidden topic. Besides, I thought Henry was using a reliable contraceptive. When he came back to the apartment, I told him I was two months pregnant. Unconcerned, he shrugged his shoulders in the typical French way, and sat down to read the papers. That was the moment I realised that I was on my own, it was unlikely this man would stand by me. Later I learned that I was not the first, it was his calling card to prey on young foreign girls coming to the Folies Bergère, and when they got pregnant he left them. My situation was bad, I would soon find myself out of a job, a pregnant can-can dancer, and going back home was not an option.'

Pat wasn't happy listening to this kind of talk; it was more suitable for a priest rather than an undertaker. It was in part, his own fault giving her whiskey, but he thought it would have the opposite effect on her, relaxing her and getting her to sleep. Work was piling up in the morgue that needed his attention.

With her eyes focussed down on the table, she didn't look up when she started talking again,

'I made the worst decision of my life, it was against my background and rearing, I gave up my child for adoption.'

The only sound in the kitchen was her sobbing. Her whole body shook as the thoughts that haunted her every waking moment, came back to torture her. The baby she gave away was a girl and where was she now? What terrible thoughts was she thinking about a mother who gave her away to strangers? Sometimes in the mornings; between sleep and waking, a little dark-haired girl in a pink dress sat on the end of the bed smiling at her. She could see her now even though it was late at night, sitting there. She reached out to touch her, but she was gone. She tried to stand and Pat came around to her side of the table to help her up.

'It's maybe time for your bed?

'Yes, I'll go to bed.'

When she stood up, she was unsteady on her feet, and he held out a protective hand, but she didn't take it.

'I'll finish my story tomorrow, but if I can't sleep, I'll be down again.'

10

Pat waited a few minutes to make sure she was asleep before getting up and walking quietly to the kitchen door. He froze when it creaked as he opened it. He waited and listened but there was no sound from the upstairs bedroom. He stepped into the yard, and the morning air was sharp in his face, but it looked like the start of another sunny day. The weather on the island in autumn was like that, cold and misty in the mornings and then brightening up as the day went on. He walked briskly across the yard to the morgue and pushed the door open. The familiar smell of chemicals greeted him. The tang of Jeyes Fluid hung heavy in the air, an even stronger smell than embalming fluid. He felt relaxed in the morgue, everything in its place, and a place for everything, as he had left it.

He removed the John Doe body from last night from the freezer, and set it on the conveyor belt to the crematorium. This was the quickest way into the furnace, and a route not used when relatives were present. For them, the journey for the corpse was the more dignified trip through the Chapel of Repose.

They were getting more careless in the city morgue in Birmingham, where he picked up the John Doe bodies. This one was a Chinese male, and it would have had been difficult convincing the Customs officials that this man came from the island. He would have to speak to them about it. It was sad there was no one to claim the body; somewhere he must have a family. He had probably lost touch with them, ending up alone and finally dead on the streets of Birmingham. What was his story?

This was no time for reflecting on the ills of the world, nevertheless, he would say a prayer for this man. He should remember that as an undertaker, he was carrying out one of the corporeal works of mercy, burying the dead, or so his teachers had told him about his father work. He reached up to the bookshelf, and took down his father's Jerusalem bible. It was beside the only other book there: Chemicals used in Embalming that he had not read.

Marie, before they were so cruelly parted, was helping him with his dyslexia. She had gathered information on dyslexia courses, and had bought self-help books about it before she died. Afterwards, he hadn't the heart to pursue it further. He masked his handicap well.

The bible lay opened at the psalm with the black string marker lying across the pages. In truth, he didn't have to read the text. His father made sure of that by having him repeat the words until he knew them by heart, 'The Lord is my Shepherd, I shall not want…'

It was clever of his father to select that Psalm. Pat could use it at any funeral, and particularly at the interdenominational removals from the Chapel of Repose. He pushed the red stop button and the conveyor belt halted. He recited the Psalm slowly. It was the respectful thing to do. He started the conveyor belt rolling again, and the corpse disappeared into the roaring flame that would consume everything except a few bone fragments. He would crush them later when the ash had cooled down.

Next he removed the false bottom from the coffin. In Birmingham, they had tightly packed the inside with plastic bags filled with white gold; heroin. This much powder was worth millions of Euros. He lifted out the bags, one at a time, and crammed them into a holdall, careful not to puncture any of them. He didn't want a trace of heroin in the morgue that a sniffer dog could pick up. He had almost completed the work when the morgue door opened. Teresa came in; she stopped for a moment to adjust her eyes to the brightness of the strip lights. She gasped and raised her hands to her face, when she saw the drugs.

'O' my God, You're a drug dealer?'

'No, no, I'm not that,' he said, moving away from the holdall and towards her.

'Let me out of here,' she turned around, and ran quickly out of the morgue without listening to his protests. He went into the house after her, and was just in time to stop her running out the front door. It would cause some stir in the village if she told them that he was a drug dealer.

'Get away from me. I'm so unlucky to keep running into your sort.'

'It's not what it seems, I'm working with the Garda.'

'You're what? Pull the other one.'

'No, give me a minute to explain, and if you're not satisfied then go.'

'All right let me hear it.'

It was not the easiest story for Pat to tell, but she had backed him into a corner and there was no other way. He would have some explaining to do to his Garda handler. Apart from him, she would be the first outside the Garda force to know that he was doing undercover work.

'Oh where do I start?'

'Start at the beginning - that would do,' said Teresa.

'Right, we'll ring my Garda contact first.'

He picked up the telephone directory from the floor and looked up the number of the Pearse Street Garda station. When he found it, he handed her the directory and pointed to the correct number, 'dial the prefix 01 first, and when the Garda at the desk answers, ask for Detective John O' Neill.

'OK.' Her hands shook as she dialled the number and almost immediately a female voice answered 'Pearse Street Garda station. You're through to the desk, how can I help?'

'Could I speak to Detective John O'Neill?'

'Hold on and I'll put you through.' Except for an electronic buzz, there was silence for a few seconds before a male voice said, 'Detective O'Neill here.'

Pat took the phone from her and used the agreed code, 'Avalanche.'

'Is there anything wrong? You don't often call at this hour. Is there someone else there with you?' asked John O'Neill.

'More later, there's a dead loyalist in an open grave in the old cemetery, can you deal with it?'

There was a long silence before O'Neill answered. 'Some of the lads will collect the body and hand it over to the PSNI. They will leave it somewhere at the side of a road in Northern Ireland, and the politicians will have the usual arguments about who shot him. Is there anything else?'

'It's my work this time, three other loyalists are on their way to Castlebar Hospital with gunshot wounds,' said Pat, aware that Teresa was staring at him with a puzzled look on her face.

'How the hell are you involved in this? Anyway, the PSNI will get hold of them when they try to get back over the border. We have close cooperation with them.'

'It happened by accident, there's more. I have a girl here from Belfast. They abducted her,' said Pat looking over at Teresa.

'Can you trust her?'

Teresa gave him a wry smile.

'Yes–I'll look after her,' said Pat, grinning.

'Is the cargo intact,' asked O'Neill.'

'No problem, I'll let you know when they contact me about the drop.'

'OK, bye,' said O'Neill and the phone went dead.

The loudspeaker on the phone was on, and Teresa had heard the whole conversation.

'Do you not believe me know?'

'Yes, I do, are you a Garda?'

'No. If I tell you the whole story, it could threaten your life,' said Pat, aware of what had happened to his wife.

'What could be more dangerous than the streets of Belfast? I'm willing to take that chance,' said Teresa, moving closer to him. So near he wanted to reach out and touch her concerned face, with its alabaster skin framed in long dark hair. He forced the thought out of his mind. This was not the time or place.

'OK here we go. When I started up the undertaking business in Ringsend, I passed a hairdresser's on my way to work in the mornings. Since I needed someone to make the corpses presentable for the families to view, I called in one day, and that was how I met my future wife Marie. She didn't take easily to doing corpse's hair, but when she saw how happy her work made the relatives she continued with it. Eventually, we married and life was good.

'I got into all this when the biggest drug lord in the country, known as the big fella, wanted another way to bring in drugs. He hit on the idea of false bottom coffins and John Doe corpses. With contacts in the Birmingham City morgue, all he needed was an undertaker to take the loaded coffins into the Country.

'I told the Garda, and they asked me to work for the big fella, and find out as much as I could about him. The Garda suspect he might be a professional man, either an accountant or a solicitor or even a member of the force making millions on drugs, while his foot soldiers took the rap for it. I have to admit that I haven't had any luck in finding out much about him yet.'

'What you are doing is dangerous. If the big fella finds out you are working for the Garda you're a dead man.'

'I know, but I have a personal score to settle with him. One day, no different to any other day, two tough looking visitors called to the morgue. Choirboys they weren't, and they bluntly told me that their boss, the big fella, wanted consignments, they didn't say of what, taken in coffins from Birmingham. I said 'no', and as a parting present, they smashed up a few coffins.

'I went to the Garda. They took details, and while they were sympathetic, there wasn't a lot they could do, unless they caught the thugs in the act. I got threats by phone, and I ignored them. Then one night they started a fire in the backyard. A reminder to me what could happen to the morgue if I didn't comply with the wishes of the big fella, whoever he was. If I had listened to his threats and not been so pig-headed, my life wouldn't be as messed up as it is.

'The intimidation got more vicious, and they started to target our home. We lived in Ringsend. They threw stones through our windows, torched our car and put a lit paper through our letter box. The fire destroyed the hall and stairs carpet, we were luck that they didn't burn us alive. They even killed our dog. While they made telephone treats against Marie, I never thought they would follow them through.

'Pregnant; she went to see family in Co Meath and on the way back on the motorway to Dublin, a black 4x4 Jeep started to tailgate, driving within inches of her back bumper. It went on like that mile after mile, and she felt terrified. She called me on the cell phone, and I told her to go slowly, and I would call the traffic Garda, which I did. They got there too late. The 4x4 had driven Marie off the motorway and her car rolled down a twenty-foot embankment. When the Garda got there, Marie and our baby were dead and the Jeep was long gone. I'm sure they did that on the big fella's instructions. At that point, I decided to work with the Garda, doing whatever I could to bring him to justice.'

'That is awful, and I'm sorry that I was so terrible to you,' said Teresa putting her arms around his shoulders. The pain he felt the day they died was still there and his eyes filled up.

'What will we do next?' she asked, so close to him that she was almost talking into his ear. He noticed the "we," but it was his struggle and the last woman involved, his wife, was now dead.

'I'll put the coffin with the holdalls into the hearse, and when the big fella's men ring we'll head for Dublin. Then you can take a train to Belfast.'

'I'm not going anywhere. I'm staying until we sort this out,' said Teresa tightening her grip on his shoulders.

11

Pat slid the coffin filled with heroin into the hearse, and closed down the tailgate. His mobile phone rang and when he answered, a gruff voice said, 'Get going.'

'That's the call; we need to get moving,' said Pat

'Ok – I'm ready. How long will it take to get to Dublin?'

'About six hours. We're not expected to go fast with a coffin on board.'

With Teresa sitting next to him, he drove out of the yard and turned to the right across the bridge to the mainland, and on to Newport. It was reassuring to have Teresa there beside him, but he didn't know why she should have that effect on him. It wasn't exactly as if he knew her all his life and trusted her. The mountains and the sea of the island seemed to captivate her and lift her low mood. He was so familiar with the scenery that he didn't notice it any more, although now through her eyes, he was awakening to its beauty. It was a pleasant contrast to the weather stained brick houses of Ringsend where he spent most of his time. She spoke first,

'It's so strange travelling in a hearse.'

'It's the same as sitting in a van. You'll get used to it.'

'I read somewhere that people say what's on their minds in the confines of cars, just like in a confessional,' said Teresa sounding absent minded.

'I don't know about that. The ones I carry in the back there never say anything.' They both laughed.

'Sometimes it gets to you, travelling alone with a corpse.'

I remember watching a horror film on the TV and a few nights later I had to take a corpse over from England. I felt spooked driving along in the dark with only the corpse for company. It reached a stage where I was afraid to look around in case the corpse was sitting on top of the coffin looking at me.' He slowed to take the sharp corner into Newport.

'Is that what you have these CDs for - to distract you?' She picked up a handful of CDs from the dashboard shelf, and read some of the titles. 'Louis Armstrong - 25 Greatest Hot Fives & Sevens, Basie & Williams - Count Basie Swings, Nat 'King' Cole - After Midnight, Duke Ellington - The Far East Suite, Ella Fitzgerald - Sings the Cole Porter Song Book, Billie Holiday - Lady in Satin.' She put the CDs back, looked up quickly and with a sharp intake of breath muttered, 'O' My God, what is that?' She brought her hand up to her face and caressed her cheek with her fingers. He knew what had caught her attention - the twenty foot high gable end mural of a public hanging. He had driven passed that painting thousands of times without taking much notice of it.

'That's a memorial to Father Manus Sweeney. This is the spot where they hung him.'

'Could we stop? I would like to see it.'

'No problem.' Pat stopped the hearse and Teresa got out and stood looking up at the painting; examining it in every detail. Several people passed, obviously locals, as Teresa was more of an interest to them than the mural. Who could blame them; she looked tall and elegant standing there. Pat searched the glove compartment for the instant camera he knew he had stacked away somewhere. When he found it, he handed it to her through the open window. She took several pictures of the mural and then sat back in the hearse.

'That hanging happened a long time ago, in 1798,' she said adjusting her seat belt across her body and clicking it into place.

'I didn't know the exact year.'

'It's all written on the bottom of the mural. Father Manus Sweeney attended a seminary in France and he returned to the Island an ordained a priest. Banned from saying Mass, priests in Ireland in those penal days had to adopt various disguises to remain undetected. Father Manus ministered to his flock on the Island for years before the

Crown Forces eventually captured him and ended his life in such a public and barbarous way.'

'Terrible times,' said Pat, navigating the hairpin bends out of Newport.

'Bad things still happen to people. I wish all classes and creeds could live peacefully together,' she said, gazing at the road ahead.

'The world is a long way away from that,' said Pat, speeding up. He hated driving on these country roads; most of them were like this, up through the gears for the short straights and changing down to cope with the sharp bends. They were silent on the way to Westport and driving up Barley Hill Teresa saw an arrow pointing up a laneway to the Convent of Mercy. The white convent soon came into view on the top of the hill.

'That's the first convent we've seen since we left the island.' She was silent for a while before saying, 'I was in a convent for a while.'

'As a pupil?'

'No, as a nun,' she said, turning around to look at his reaction. He tried to hide his surprise but she must have seen it in his face. 'You're taken aback by that. It's usual for people to react in that way. They either think nuns are mystical and romantic or else the "living dead," like in the Marie Monk story.'

'I don't know that story,' said Pat, although there was this nagging doubt at the back of his mind that he had heard of it before but he couldn't bring it into his mind. He often had the feeling that part of his mind remained somehow shut off and not available to him. It was a strange feeling to have, that behind locked doors in his head another person lived and was ready to spring out at any minute. He had discussed this problem with Marie and she had joked, 'Get over yourself - you must have multiple personalities like in the films.'

Teresa was talking. 'A real Gothic tale. Marie Monk or a ghost writer created a sensational false story about her sexual abuse in a Montreal Convent in 1816. The "Black Nuns" as she called them were virtual prisoners in the convent. The priests from the seminary next door entered the convent through a secret underground passage and had their way with them. Nuns who didn't comply disappeared. The nuns first baptised the babies born from such liaisons and then threw them into a lime pit in the basement. It's all made up of course; following a brain injury she suffered as a child, Marie Monk couldn't tell fact from fantasy. She had a tragic life. She was a tumbled woman and her only contact with the nuns was when they rescued her from the streets and took care of her.'

'What's a tumbled woman?'

'Teresa smiled; an expression my mother used to describe a prostitute.'

'It's terrible to pretend that it's a true story. What kind of people would do that?'

'There was a lot of anti-religious stuff about at the time and even later. There was another infamous story around in 1834 about the Ursuline convent school in Charlestown, Massachusetts. Allegedly the Reverend Mother was holding a nun in the convent against her will. Rabble rousers incited a mob and they marched on the convent and burned it to the ground. This incident was the result of a nun leaving the convent and her superior, Mother Mary St. George, going after her and persuading her to return to the religious life.'

'What was so awful about that?' said Pat, touching the brake pedal to slow down for another sharp corner. The County Council probably wouldn't get around to straightening these bends in his lifetime.

'I didn't know any of these stories,' he said, checking the time on his watch. The office traffic would be long gone when they reached Dublin.

'There's no reason you should. I probably wouldn't have heard of it either, but we had a good library in the convent and I had time to read. You could say I was trying to educate myself.' Teresa laughed at her own joke. Pat didn't understand what was funny about it, but he smiled anyway. He didn't want to ask her for an explanation or she would think he was a dodo.

They were on the outskirts of Castlebar and usually on these trips he stopped at the 'Travellers Friend' for lunch. It had an advantage in that he could park the hearse outside the dining room window and keep an eye on it. Maybe, he was being overcautious, most yobs probably wouldn't vandalise a hearse, but he couldn't be sure about that, considering that they were capable of worse; breaking into a cemetery and desecrating the graves, for instance. He selected a seat by the window where the hearse was in full view.

'The fish here is good. We're not that far from the sea and they get it fresh every day,' he said, pushing his chair back a bit from the table.

'I like fish,' she said and pulled her chair in closer. He hadn't noticed before, maybe that was another difference between men and woman. He didn't have a clue what it meant and he wasn't about to discuss it with her. They both ordered salmon. A long silence developed between them. Pat didn't like long silences when he was with people but there wasn't a choice on this trip; normally he preferred and mostly travelled alone. Indeed they thought of him on the island as a bit of a loner. That was OK, he could live with it. He broke the silence, 'What was the convent like?' Teresa froze for a second with the fork half way to her mouth. She put it down and looked at him. She was about to say something and then seemed to change her mind and develop another train of thought.

'When I got out of rehab in Paris, I was in a delicate state, a bit lost and depressed. My aunt and uncle arrived over from Belfast and persuaded me to return home. At the time, I wasn't capable of deciding on anything and when they suggested that I join a convent, I went along with it. I really wasn't in my own head and while I didn't have a vocation the Reverend Mother thought it might come to me over time. That was it, one fine day in May, with a few others, I became a Dominican postulant. Of course I didn't have a clue what I was letting myself in for.

'Was it that bad?'

'No not at all, but it wasn't the Folies Bergère.' She smiled.

'The Reverend Mother had programmed our day from getting up in the morning at twenty past five, to bedtime.'

'What time was that?'

'Nine O'clock. Throughout the day, we had prayers, Mass, meditation, reading and Novitiate lectures. That was our day.'

'That would drive me mad as I like making things with my hands,' said Pat, aware that some of the other diners were casting furtive glances at the hearse. People don't like thinking about their own mortality, but regardless of how it was upsetting them, he had to eat.

'It was strange at first but I eventually settled into the convent regime. With regular hours, I got my health and strength back and eventually the big day arrived when the postulants became nuns; professed. My aunt and uncle were there and they were so proud of their niece. Little did they know what was going on inside my head. I felt a cheat and that I shouldn't be there, but the Reverend Mother assured me that I would become more spiritual from that day on. I think she was right; many people grow spiritually over their lifetime both in religion and in the outside world. So that was it, almost before I knew it, I was a fully professed nun. The Reverend Mother expected me to act the part to the outside world and I wasn't sure that I could. Thank God the dreaded uniform of the veil and all the trimmings had gone or I don't think I could have worn it in public.'

They had finished the meal and Pat signalled to the waitress to come over.

'Do you take sterling?' Teresa asked the waitress, as she searched in her bag for a cheque card.

'No, no, it's my treat. I can claim it as expenses,' said Pat taking the bill. With the meal paid for and a tip left, they were back on the road again, heading for Dublin. Pat still had many questions about Teresa's life but he wasn't about to ask her. It was up to her to elaborate or not and anyway he had more serious business to think about. He turned on the CD player and lowered the sound as 'Lady in Satin' drifted out from the speakers.

12

With Castlebar no longer large in the rear-view mirror and the sound of jazz from the CD player mixed with the familiar diesel engine knock in the background, Pat was able to relax, but not for long. The urgent ringing of his phone disturbed his tranquillity. He pulled over to the side and when he answered he heard the same bad-tempered voice as before,

'Why the hell did you stop back there?'

How did he know that? Pat turned and looked behind him but there was no other vehicle in view. There was no one following them as far as he could tell so the drug dealers must have some other way of keeping track on the hearse.

'We stopped at 'The Travellers Friend' for something to eat.'

'Who are we – have you somebody with you?

'No, just me and the hearse,' Pat said, gesturing to Teresa to remain silent.

'You're a weird bastard. It wouldn't surprise me if you slept in one of your bloody coffins. Don't stop again.' The phone went dead.

'They know our every move,' said Teresa looking at him with fear in her eyes.

'They don't know you are with me.'

He started the engine, checked the mirror, and slowly moved back on to the Dublin road. He had a problem, the drug dealers were outsmarting him, and he would have to change that quickly. It was possible that they had foot soldiers stationed in the bigger towns keeping track on the progress of the hearse, but they couldn't have that many men available. It was more likely that they had attached a simple electronic device, similar to the ones used by transport companies to keep track on the movements of their fleets.

'What do we do now,' asked Teresa nervously, 'We must be carrying millions of pounds worth of heroin in the back.'

'We'll stop at the next garage and examine the underside of the hearse. There must have stuck something to it.'

In French Park, the next town, they got directions to the local garage. It was down a narrow lane with the forecourt littered with bits of agricultural machinery. Pat navigated around the debris and drove into the garage. It was dark and dingy. Breathless, the owner, a fat elderly man came rushing out to see what was wrong. A hearse had that effect on people and this was more than likely the first one to come to his premises.

'Hello, have you a problem?' he asked with concern in his voice. He was probably making up horror stories in his head about having to work on a hearse with a rotting corpse in the back.

'Can you put the hearse on the ramp and check the tank for leaks?'

'Do we have to take out the coffin?'

'No. I'll drive it up the ramp for you.' The owner seemed relieved and Pat sensed he wanted to get them out of his garage as fast as possible. Even if they had a leak it was unlikely that he would have wanted to fix it. With the hearse up on the ramp the garage owner started to examine the fuel tank and the feeder pipes. Pat was carrying out his own inspection, and he found what he was looking for, a small transmitter taped to the chassis. He removed the transmitter and when the garage owner wasn't looking he squashed it underfoot.

'Everything seems dry enough. You have no leaks that I can see.' He lowered the ramp.

'What do I owe you for that?' said Pat pulling out his wallet.

'Nothing at all.' He looked at Pat for a minute, 'There's no way I could do your job.'

'Somebody has to do it,' said Pat handing him a twenty note.

Back on the road, Teresa said, 'Did you find anything?'

'Yes, a small transmitter, I smashed it. I wonder when they stuck it on there.'

'Maybe in Birmingham or on the ferry,' said Teresa taking a quick look behind her but the road as far back as she could see was clear of traffic.

'Could have been in either place,' said Pat, looking out the side window.

The sea and the rugged mountains of the west had given way to sprawling meadows of the midlands, where cattle grazed peacefully. Even the cattle herds were different, no more of the small black Kerry breed, but a larger animal the French Charolais in the fields. Dry stonewalls that defined the farming landscape of the west had gone and neatly trimmed hedgerows had replaced them. Here farming was a business in contrast to the west where it was it more of a hobby. He remembered a story told in the island pubs about Charolais. A farmer in the south of England imported a herd of Charolais, free from mad cow disease, from France, but frustratingly they didn't understand his commands. He had to hire a Frenchman to teach him enough French to communicate with them. Teresa interrupted his musings with a question.

'Can you trust Detective O'Neill to stand by if you're caught with those drugs?'

'He's a sound man. I have no worries about him,' said Pat, glancing towards her.

'I hope not, you could go away for a long time if they find you with that stuff.'

'O'Neill is with me all the way on this one.'

'Prison is not nice, I can tell you that you wouldn't like it,' she said, folding her arms across her chest.

Taken aback by what she said, Pat slowed the hearse. He hesitated for a second but felt he should ask, 'Did you do time?'

'Not in that way but I might as well have. As a nun I worked in the Crumlin Road Prison chaplaincy for a few years. Believe me, it wasn't exactly the Ritz Carlton.'

'You don't look like a criminal, but I worried about you there for a minute.'

'Did you ever hear it said; "There is no art can show the mind's construction in the face"?'

'No, but then I'm not as well-read as some of them.'

'That's what they like to think. I didn't want to go back to a school when a teaching job came up, but luckily they advertised a chaplaincy vacancy at the same time.'

'Was it in the papers?'

'I don't know. The notice of the job came from our Mother Superior. It annoyed her that I wasn't going back to teaching.'

'More money for the convent if you were teaching,' said Pat. The odour of the anti-perspirant he had sprayed under his armpits before they started out was chocking him. The joke that undertakers smelled of death bothered him and just in case in was true he had bought the spray - Congo in the Pound Shop. It was cheap to buy and had a cheap smell, and as his father often said, "You get what you pay for." He had a wise saying for every eventuality. Pat wished he could talk to his father; there was so much he would like to discuss with him.

'Anyway I applied for the job and got it. Then they sent me to England on a three-months training course in prison ministry.'

'Where did you go in England?'

'Wakefield Prison in West Yorkshire. It's well-known; that is where they held Harold Shipman, the doctor who murdered 15 women. The mulberry bush growing in the prisons yard is famous. It's the one in the nursery rhyme "Mulberry Bush". They wrote it during the time it was a women's prison.' Teresa recited all the verses. He liked the clear sharpness of her voice.

> *"Here we go round the mulberry bush...*
> *Here we go round the mulberry bush,*
> *So early in the morning.'"*

Considering his recent history with Birmingham, Pat was glad she hadn't trained there. He wouldn't have liked her to have had any contact with the place.

'One bright morning, fully qualified and rearing to go, I presented myself at the gates of the Crumlin Road Jail. It was a strange feeling to hear the doors clanging shut and locked behind me as an officer escorted me through the prison to meet the warden.'

'Never met a prison warden, what was he like?'

'He was like every other civil servant I ever met; the rules from the circulars on the prison service were his bible. He filed and bound them in volumes on the shelves behind him. He was such a pompous ass sitting there behind an enormous antique desk.'

'There's a lot like that,' said Pat, changing his grip on the steering to hold it at the bottom. His father had told him it was the most relaxed way to drive but he wasn't sure.

'With me sitting in front of him, he reached up to the shelves and took down several volumes. He selected some circulars from the ring-binders and handed them to his secretary for photocopying.'

'I would say a prison is a rough enough place to work, maybe the job got to him,' said Pat, switching on cruise control for the straight road ahead. He didn't have much driving to do on this road apart from adjusting the steering wheel now and again if they hit a bump. It was one of the features of the hearse that it had all the modern innovation like cruise control and air-conditioning.

'I think he came into the world like that, but why did they have to put him in charge of a prison? I have to say that I didn't like the man. He was a cold fish all right and the prisoners thought the same of him. I got his do's and don'ts lecture that morning.'

Pat swerved to avoid a dog that rushed out barking from the side of the road. The dog gave up chasing the hearse after a few hundred yards. Any other cars on the road and he might have hit it. Teresa stopped talking during the swerve and then continued,

'I left his office clutching a sheaf of photocopies and I was so mad that I threw them into the first rubbish bin I came across. It was clear that he didn't want me in his prison. I was lowest on the food chain and if I broke his rules; goodbye prison.'

'Did he have the power to do that?'

'I think he could, if he said I wasn't suitable for the work and demanded a replacement. It was a great start to a new job.'

'Right enough, it was no way to start.'

'A prison officer took me down to meet the other in the chaplaincy. They were a great bunch and I got on with most of them. We must have looked a strange lot from the dishevelled pony-tailed humanist to Jewish Rabbi who as an orthodox Jew didn't shake hands with women outside his own family.'

'All religions have their own way of looking at things,' said Pat.

'I think an overused expression at the time fitted my situation exactly: "Welcome to the real world."'

'If anything is real,' said Pat. He didn't elaborate as he might be the only one who thought that he was never fully inside his body. He sometimes felt that part of him was away living somewhere else. He hadn't discussed how he felt with anyone, and he wasn't about to tell this girl, a stranger he had met recently under bizarre circumstances.

'You name it, we had all of them in the prison - murderers, rapists, robbers and everything else in between.

'A scary place?'

'I was afraid at the start but the longer I stayed the easier it got.'

'That's the way with a lot of things,' said Pat, rubbing his eyes.

He needed to stop soon to give his eyes a rest for a few minutes as they felt dry and itchy as if filled with sand. An optician would probably recommend spectacles but in his line of work it would be easy to mislay them. It wasn't beyond the bounds of possibility that the spectacles would disappear inside one of the corpses. Then there was the cost of replacing them as it wasn't an option to exhume a corpse to retrieve lost spectacles.

'Myself and the humanist became close friends and in time we were meeting secretly outside the prison.'

'You were still a nun at the time,' asked Pat.

'I dressed like a nun, but I'm not sure that I ever gave myself over fully to being a nun.' Pat didn't understand that, with his way of thinking she was either a nun or she wasn't.

'I was getting along fine with my humanist friend until one day he took me to an open-air concert. Later in the evening, the music had people high and some of them started to jump from the stage into the crowd. Some fellow landed hard on my friend and injured him. He spent a long time in the City Hospital with back and neck problems. He never got over it and he went back to drug using again. I didn't know he was a former drug addict, he didn't tell me. Anyway he couldn't take it anymore and one night he booked into a centre city hotel in Belfast and jumped from a fifth floor window.'

A long silence developed between them. Pat was first to speak.

'We'll stop for a break. There's a great view of Lake Derravaragh.' He followed the arrow sign into the deserted car park and switched off the engine. The lake stretched out below them as if they were sitting on the rim of a bowl looking down into it. The surface of the water was flat and placid; disturbed now and again by ripples caused by fish jumping. And in the distance, fishermen in rowing boats were like dots on the horizon. Pat closed his tired eyes.

'O, this is Lough Derravaragh of the Children of Lir fable. I loved the story as a child, do you know it?' She didn't wait for a reply.

'King Lir married Aoibh and they had four children - daughter Fionnuala, and three sons, twins, Fiachra and Conn and their brother Aodh. Then an awful thing happened to the children, Aoibh their mother died and they missed her terribly. Time passed and Lir married their aunt Aoife. She was jealous of the love Lir had for his children and she decided to get rid of them. She cast a spell on them that turned them into swans and they had to spend three hundred years on Lough Derravaragh, and three hundred years on the Sea of Moyle, and three hundred years in Broadhaven bay near Erris. Meantime Saint Patrick converted Ireland to Christianity and when the swans heard the church bells, the sound released them from the spell and they took human form again. However, they were no longer young children but nine hundred years old. Once baptised, they died on the spot.'

'The old stories are the best,' said Pat as he closed his eyes again. Then the phone rang. He let it ring a few times before he picked it up and said sharply, 'What now?'

'You bloody little waster where are you?' It was the drug dealer again.

'Near Longford.' The phone went dead.

'I'm trying to confuse them, we came through Longford a long time ago and we are almost in Mullingar,' said Pat. A red van belching plumes of exhaust gas pulled in beside them. Before Teresa could answer, a dirty unshaven individual reeking of sweat and alcohol yanked open her door and hauled her out on to the tarmac by the hair. He pushed her up against the side of the hearse.

'What have we got here, a nice young filly,' he said, as he tried to kiss her. She struggled but he had her pinned against the hearse. She looked to Pat for help but the second traveller had manhandled him out of the hearse and was throwing a punch at him. Pat easily dodged the blow and countered with an elbow in the face. It broke his attacker's nose and a stream of blood shot into the air. He tumbled to the ground when Pat kicked him in the calf. Still holding on to his attacker's arm, he swung it around until the shoulder dislocated and fractured. Teresa recognised the crunch of breaking bone from her prison days.

Her attacker let her go and rushed at Pat but he didn't fare any better than his friend and he was soon lying on the tarmac writhing in agony. Pat pulled them on their backs across to the van and left them lying behind the rear wheels. He jumped into the driving seat and there was a noisy whirring from the starter motor and back firing from the engine before the van started. They screamed as he reversed the van slowly over their legs. Teresa was crying, shocked by the display of violence she had witnessed. She could see the broken bones sticking through the traveller's trouser legs and she knew compound fractures didn't heal easily. Without a word, he lifted her bodily into the hearse and closed the door with a bang. To her amazement, he had metamorphosed from a mild mannered individual into an aggressive cage fighter. She was looking at Pat's other persona; one that she didn't know existed.

She was afraid to say anything. He shouted to a woman who had driven into the car park, to call for an ambulance. He drove back on to the main road and continued towards Mullingar. A few miles down the road, he pulled into a lay-by and slumped over the steering wheel. A few minutes later he straightened up; the old Pat had returned.

He yawned. 'I must have been in a heavy sleep. I feel so tired,' he said, rubbing his eyes.

'You don't remember anything that happened?' Teresa looked at him with astonishment.

'What happened?' He looked puzzled by her question. An ambulance, with blue lights flashing and siren wailing, went past at speed going in the opposite direction.

'You almost killed two men back there.'

'Me, I have never hit anyone in my life.'

What was this girl talking about? Maybe the trauma she had been through had affected her mind or possibly none of what she had told him was real. That's what you get for striking up with strangers; you don't know what baggage they're carrying.

'I can't take this, another man with big problems. Leave me at the train station in Mullingar.' Teresa sat rigid in her seat and stared straight ahead.

'OK.'

His father would say it was like the teapot calling the kettle black. Somebody had a problem and he was sure it wasn't him. They were silent all the way to Mullingar train station. She got out of the hearse at the station.

'Do you need money to get to Dublin and Belfast?'

'No thanks, I have a credit card.'

They heard the noise of a train coming and she rushed off to catch it. She didn't look back. On the train she rested her head against the back of the seat and closed her eyes and listened to the clanking rhythm of wheels. She felt exhausted but her mind was too active for sleep. It was all too much and when she reached Dublin her first duty was to report Pat's violent behaviour to the Gardaí. It was only luck that he hadn't killed those men.

She opened her eyes and tried to focus on the green fields and hedgerows that flew past the window but she was too upset for that. Another disturbing thought entered her mind, if she made a statement to the Gardaí, their run in with the loyalist murderers would have to be part of it and then what?

The assassination of the Major might unleash a terrible retribution of murder and mayhem in Northern Ireland. She wasn't going to be responsible for that. What was done was done and she would let it rest.

Then she started to cry. There was something else she would have to consider, her deep feelings for Pat, she was in love with him and it would break her heart to part from him.

13

Pat turned the hearse around at the Mullingar station and drove back the route they had came to the Dublin road. There was more traffic than in the West of Ireland and it took him a few minutes to adjust to driving in convoy. He became aware that out of respect for the dead the cars behind were reluctant to pass and were forming into a funeral cortege; he pulled in to the slow lane to let them pass. If they knew what he was carrying in the coffin, they wouldn't have given that much respect.

Was the Teresa incident real or did he imagine it? Recently, he was having a problem working out what was real and what wasn't. The phone rang and he let it ring until he could pull into a lay-by. What did the gang want now? He put the phone to his ear,

'Hello.'

'Hello, John O'Neill here.'

'O, hello John. I thought you were one of the gang, they're keeping tabs on me.' Pat turned off the engine.

'They're not far behind you, in a black 4/4 off-roader with tinted windows and two our lads are following them in a yellow transit van. Is the girl with you? The reception on Pat's mobile wasn't good and amid the crackle of static he could only just about make out what O'Neill was saying.

'No, she's not.' There was no sense in telling him Teresa's cock and bull story about him battering two men back there.

'That might be a problem, she knows a lot about our operation.'

'She's OK,' Pat lied. He wasn't sure about that at all after his experience with her.

'We are going to set up a roadblock ahead; checking tax and insurance as it were, to see who is in the 4x4.'

O' Neill started to cough.

'I can't get rid of this bloody summer cold.'

'It's going around,' said Pat, more concerned about the occupants of the 4x4 than O'Neill's coughing.

'I'll be in touch after the roadblock.'

Pat didn't know O'Neill's mobile phone number. He hadn't given it to him. He couldn't call him back even if he wanted to. Blocked in some way, O'Neill's number didn't come up on Pat's phone. He pulled back into the traffic and sure enough 4x4 was there travelling in the fast lane. It moved lanes to get in behind him. He couldn't see anything through their darkened windows. Minutes later the ubiquitous Ford transit came into view. It was good choice for a surveillance vehicle; it could stay behind the 4x4 for as long as needed without raising suspicions. The Garda 'Slow' and 'Prepare to Stop' signs appeared further down the road and two officers were standing out in the roadway, halting traffic and directing it into the lay-by. They waved on those they didn't want to examine in more detail. It was an elaborate guise just to stop one 4x4 but it was worth it if it helped to catch Mr. Big. Two officers signalled to him to drive the hearse into the lay-by. In his rear mirror he could see other Garda pointing to the 4x4 to do the same. All the officers were wearing side-arms; that was unusual considering the country had an unarmed police force. They were probably the Garda rapid response unit trained to deal with armed criminals. Were the occupants of the off-roader armed? Pat wasn't exactly in the safest place if a shoot out started. He considered his choices and his best course of action, if a ruction started was to dive under the hearse. He could position himself at the exact spot which would allow him to roll under the hearse without getting tangled with the wheels. The transit pulled up close to the drug dealers. They were now like meat in a sandwich, with Gardaí in front and behind them.

'Step out,' said the taller Garda, Pat got out. He positioned himself at the point he had worked out in his head and he looked behind in time to see the drug men emerge from the 4x4. He didn't recall meeting this particular pair in any of his dealings with the gang. The

Garda did a cursory search of the hearse but their main focus was on what was happening on the roadway behind them. On high alert they were ready to fly into action to support their colleagues at the slightest provocation. They donned gloves before opening the tailgate of the hearse. The uninitiated with the usual fear, that they might catch a terrible disease from the coffin. The Garda at the front of the drug dealers 4x4 held up his thumb behind his back, a signal that they had the situation under control.

'OK, drive on,' said the smaller Garda as he closed down the tailgate of the hearse. Pat got behind the wheel and eased his way back into the traffic. The 4x4 soon followed and he suspected the transit van wouldn't be far behind. The convoy had resumed and he was the lead vehicle. His phone rang and he turned on the loud speaker.

'Hello, John O'Neill here.' The voice faded for a few seconds.

'Hello John, what happened back there?' Pat pulled on to the hard shoulder and switched on his hazard lights.

'They are only a couple minions, cannon fodder for the big boys. There are no drugs in the 4x4 and they're unarmed. Don't worry about them.'

'That's good to hear.'

'The transit is going to leave at the next junction, but some more of our people are joining the convoy to keep an eye on things. You might not recognise them so easily this time. Bye.'

'Bye,' said Pat and drove out into the traffic again. The 4x4, parked in a lay-by further down the carriageway was waiting for him. He would have liked to have asked O'Neill a few more questions; for example why were the drug dealers following him? He looked in the rear-view mirror to try to pick out his new undercover Garda escort. They weren't the old couple driving behind him in the ten-year-old ford and they were unlikely to be the honeymoon couple in front with white bunting streaming out behind them. It didn't matter whether he recognised them or not as long as they were there if he needed them. It was a bizarre situation: followed across Ireland by drug dealers and Garda. In his wildest dreams he couldn't have envisaged such a scenario.

"You never know where life will land you," was another of his father's wise saying. It was coming true.

On his left-hand side he was driving past a sign post and plaque He stopped for a short break and read the inscription.

The poem 'The Old Bog Road,' written by a local girl Teresa Brayton made this road famous. Born in Kilcock in 1868, she emigrated to America 1895. She returned permanently to her home village of Kilbrook in 1932 and she died there in 1943. Her three published books of poems are, "Songs of the Dawn," (1913), "The Flame of Ireland," (1926), and "Christmas Verses," (1934). In exile, her poems capture the sense of nostalgic loss of homeland.' He got back into the hearse.

The steady knock of the diesel engine was always reassuring company to Pat on his long journeys. It was like a willing draught horse that never grumbled under load. That reminded him of his trip to Áras an Uachtaráin, with the Victims of Crime organisation. An interesting part of the visit was to the Áras stables to see the horses of the Garda mounted unit. The handlers were happy to discuss the animals.

'That fellow always wants you to go over to his head, rub it and talk to him – he's a right cod,' said his Garda handler pointing to the huge grey horse in the corner stall. So human, it seemed.

'The Irish Draught horses make the best police horses anywhere,' said the handler as he fed each of them ryegrass. Ordinary grass, because of the dust, gives them breathing problems. The North Yorkshire Police bought as young animals in Ireland the eleven horses now in use with the Gardaí. They trained them for police work and when they disbanded their mounted unit the Gardaí bought their horses and equipment. Huge and docile, these horses relished human company and turned their heads around to follow the group with their eyes as they left.

Pat was keeping a close eye on the mirror trying to spot the undercover Gardaí. He started to wonder if they were there at all. Maybe O'Neill just said that to reassure him. His mind drifted back to the Garda horses and their treatment. During the summer they spend their holidays in County Meath where they are free to roam in open fields and where, at the end of their working life they spend their retirement. A warm fuzzy story, it's a pity all life isn't like that but from experience Pat knew it was far from it.

The cars ahead had reduced speed and a tailback was developing. At first he thought it might be a crash ahead, and then he saw 'Slow, Road Works Ahead.' There was other writing on the sigh but he didn't bother reading it apart from noticing that EU funding supported the project. Cars were all around him and one particular car, a green Renault caught his eye. There was something unusual about it and it didn't hit him for a moment. He had never seen anything like it, a nun driving a priest. He slowed and as they came up closer in the outside lane he saw the tell-tale sign, a communication antenna in the centre of the booth cover. They were his Garda escort. What would they think of next?

Past the road works, Pat drove a steady pace to the outskirts of Dublin. He had a plan to give his escorts the slip and make the rest of the journey on his own. He caught them off-guard in the outside lane when he took the feeder road to Palmerstown. They couldn't cut across two lanes of traffic to follow him.

His phone rang.

'O'Neill here – you have cut off?'

'I'm tired of them behind me.'

'Where are you now?'

'I'm going up Knockmaroon Hill to Castleknock and then on to the Phoenix Park.'

'The drug men will know where you're going. Do you want our lot to meet you at the main gates of the Park?'

'No I'll be OK.'

'Ye sure?'

'Yes.'

'Right – I'll be in touch.'

O'Neill didn't sound impressed that Pat had slipped away from his escort. His detour probably wouldn't make sense to anyone else but he just wanted to feel free from having them follow him. When he hit the Quays there was no one following him and it was a relief when he stopped outside his funeral parlour in Irishtown. He sat there behind the wheel for a few minutes and closed his eyes. His father would describe it as studying himself.

Pat's life was so stressful that it was almost unbearable. When he opened his eyes he saw through the gloom of late evening Teresa emerge from the side of the funeral parlour. She was walking towards him.

14

Pat rolled down the window as Teresa came over to the hearse.

'I didn't expect to see you.'

'I said I'd help you. You over-reacted back there and I still think you have two very different personalities inside that head of yours.' She was looking at the ground as she said it.

The same old tune. He was tired of hearing it and he didn't have the energy or the inclination to fight back. She was a bit crazy all right.

'I don't feel like emptying out the hearse tonight. I'll lock it up in the garage and it should be safe enough until morning.'

'Give me the keys and I'll open the door,' she said, stretching out her hand.

'No need – I have a gizmo here that does it.' He removed the keys from the ignition and pressed the button on the electronic door opener. The horizontal steel slats started to roll on to a cylinder at the top of the door jamb.

'It works like an old fashioned roll top desks with a motor,' he said, looking into her face as he explained how the garage door functioned.

'I love those old roll top desks. I always wanted one.'

'There's one inside in the office. It's oak and it's ancient. I keep the accounts in there, but they're in a mess. I'm not good at paper work.'

'Office work is not everyone's cup of tea but it's a necessary evil.'

'You can say that again. Step back there for a second.'

With her clear away from the hearse, he drove into the garage. There was little else, apart from coffin lids stored inside. He was half way out of the hearse when the black 4x4 pulled into the driveway behind them. There was no mistaking it.

'Here comes trouble but don't worry they're not armed. They have followed me half way across the country.'

He ducked back into the hearse, snatched the Glock pistol from under the dash and hid it in his trouser pocket. Teresa had dropped to her hunkers in the corner of the garage and had her hand clasped tightly in front of her. She had gone deadly pale. The pursuers jumped out and strode belligerently towards the garage. The stockier of the two deliberately bumped into a coffin lid, knocked it to the floor and trampled it into matchwood. An aggressive warning. Teresa saw the danger signals when Pat's face changed and for a fraction of a second he was his other self, ready for violence. He looked in her direction and everything changed, his face relaxed and the old Pat returned. The drug dealers had a lucky escape and they would never know how near they were to getting beaten to pulp. Pat pulled the Glock from his pocket and pointed it at the one who'd destroyed the coffin lid.

'Pick up the pieces and put them into the waste skip or I'll put a bullet up your backside,' he said, holding the gun in both hands and gesturing towards the skip at the rear of the garage. He held him in his stare until the job was completed.

'Right first things first, why are you following me?'

'Sullen and angry, the second criminal answered, 'We need to check to see that the gear is all there for the big fella.'

'Get your knees and put your hands in front of you.' They moved slowly and reluctantly and did what they were told.

'Teresa, bring over the cable ties. They're hung on the wall beside you.'

She came over with the ties.

'Don't get in my line of fire. Go around behind me and tie their tie wrists together.'

With their hands tied, Pat opened the coffin and unzipped the bags.

'See It's all there, go back and tell your boss.'

'I can't drive with my hands tied like this,' said the taller of the two as he struggled to free them.

'You'll manage all right,' said Pat hauling him to his feet.

'I'll crash into something.'

'Cut the ties, Teresa. If I see either of you around here again you'll get a bullet. It's what you deserve.'

He held the gun on them until they were in the 4/4 and speeding away.

Pat closed the coffin lid and locked the hearse.

Teresa, was in shock, staring ahead, and her body was rigid as if bolted to the floor. Then she started weeping hysterically. Pat took her in his arms and her wailing subsided and an uneasy silence descended on the garage. The evil that had entered it was somehow still there and visiting it again would never be the same for Pat. They remained locked in embrace for a few minutes.

'I'm sorry about the hysterics but I had to release nervous energy.' Still in his arms, she looked up into his eyes. He wiped away her tears with his finger and bent down and kissed her. They lingered for a while before she pulled away from him.

'Let's get out of here,' she said.

He tapped the security number into the burglar alarm and waited for her to step outside before he closed down the roller door with a button click.

'Do you think they'll come back?' she said, looking at him anxiously.

'Not tonight and I'm ready for them. Anyway if they harm me that'll cut off their drug supply.'

He let them in by the side door and climbed the stairs to the apartment.

'This is amazing. I didn't expect anything like it,' said Teresa gazing around the apartment.

'Marie got an architect to design it. I suppose over a funeral parlour, it needed to be unique.'

It was special all right. It had cost a small fortune to refurbish but in those days he would have spent any amount of money at Marie behest. It wasn't as if she was careless with money; no, she knew the value of every cent. Maybe they went a bit over the top with the carrera marble sink top, the all stainless steel fitments, the centre floor island, and the mood illumination but overall it was probably worth it.

'The lighting is something else. This kitchen could feature in one of the glossily interior design magazines,' said Teresa.

'Sit down and I'll make some coffee,' said Pat going to one of the units and taking out a percolator.

'My goodness you have everything here. That percolator must be catering standard.'

'No rubbish here,' said Pat laughing. 'How did you manage to find this place?'

'I lived in Dun Laoghaire with a relative, Joan for a few years after leaving the convent. She was an amazing character.'

'Why do you say that?

'Well as everyone knows there is always some trouble or other in Northern Ireland and in the 1920s her family had to flee from Belfast. They settled in Dunlaoghaire where her father set up a business. She was a bit of a tomboy and in her early years rebuilt bicycles with her brothers by cannibalising bits from discarded ones.'

'Very few girls would have done that in her day,' said Pat, keeping an eye on the coffee maker. He was always fascinated by the way the liquid dripped down into the cups.

'That was the way she developed mechanical skills and when she emigrated to England during the Second World War she put her training to good use. She passed the mechanical aptitude test with ease and was recruited for the new Spitfire factory in Castle Bromwich outside Birmingham.'

'I heard some old fellow from the Island had worked in that factory in his young days.' He couldn't remember his name except that he came from the upper part of the Island.

'Loads of Irish people were involved in one way or another in the Second World War, but they don't get mentioned much. They taught Joan new skills, fitting/turning, grinding and welding and how to read technical drawings. She was one of the few in the factory who could dismantle and rebuild the Jaguar Merlin Spitfire engine all on her own and she got promoted to a supervisor. That's was how she spent the war years.'

'It must have been rough over there with the bombs and everything,' said Pat, passing her a cup of coffee.

'Thank you. This looks good,' she said as she took a sip form the cup.

'She talked about sitting out on the roof of the building where they lived drinking wine and watching the bombers coming in. They had little to eat but for some unknown reason had plenty of wine.'

'That would shorten the war all right,' said Pat with only half his mind on the story. He was thinking she was an added complication at this difficult stage in his life. It would have better if she had stayed away altogether. Perhaps the easiest way to deal with her was either to send her packing or else offer her a job in the office. He couldn't deny that he needed someone to keep that part of the business right.

'Joan was married four times and divorced three times all to service men. Her first three husbands were killed in the War. Her last husband certainly earned the moniker of desert rat, he lost a leg fighting against Rommel.'

'That's some history. Is she still alive?'

'No, she was old even when I knew her first.'

'One of the Spitfires you talk about ran out of fuel and crash landed on Sandymount Strand during World War 2. No one was hurt and the plane wasn't damaged. The story goes that an Esso petrol tanker drove on to the strand and refuelled the plane and it took off again,' said Pat, feeling drowsy. Stretched out in his favourite Parker Knoll recliner, he'd have been asleep long ago if she wasn't here.

'I didn't know about that, but during the worst night of bombing in Belfast, the Dublin and Dundalk firemen came up with their fire engines and helped to put the fires out,' said Teresa, sipping her coffee.

'Loads of things happened at that time. Part of Dublin was wrecked in May 1941 when German bombs fell on the North Strand. Twenty people were killed and about ninety injured. A US Air Force B-17 bomber crash landed in Athenry in Galway on its way to Saint Anglo air strip in Fermanagh. There were no casualties of any kind,' said Pat, trying to stay awake.

'The Athenry one I didn't know about but what the Dublin firemen did is well known. Did any German planes land in Ireland?' said Teresa looking in his direction. She must have detected by now that he wasn't full alert.

'A few Luftwaffe planes crash landed around the country and the crews were interned in the Curragh camp for the length of the war. Not all of them made it alive. They're buried in the German cemetery in Wicklow.' To stay awake, Pat adjusted the back of his chair into an upright position.

'How do you know all this? I though you told me you don't read very much,' said Teresa.

'I spent too much time in pubs and that's where I heard all kinds of stories. No all of them true I would have to say.'

His breathing had slowed and it was an effort to keep his eyes open. It had been a long tiring day filled with difficulties. His one man battle against the drug lords was taking its toll. Teresa was saying something about the job she did when she lived in Dublin and that was the last thing he heard before becoming engulfed in a deep sleep.

15

The screech of brakes and the roar of a high-powered engine woke Pat from his slumber.

'What the hell is that?'

Teresa, sleeping on the couch jumped up,

'Oh my God.'

He rushed to the window and outside on the forecourt the drug men were about to drive the black Jeep through the window of the funeral home. The bull bars fitted on the front were an effective battering ram for smashing the floor to ceiling pane of glass. The Jeep started its run, and the building vibrated when it hit the window. It shattered but didn't break. They reversed and with the second run, the window broke into smithereens, and they drove in among the display coffins. Pat was on his way down the stairs when they reversed again, did a handbrake turn and drove off.

The place was a shambles, with broken window glass and bits of coffins everywhere. This mess would cost him more than he cared to think about unless the insurance policy covered it. It might even put him out of business. Teresa was at his side.

'They are not going to give up,' she said, stepping carefully over shards of glass.

'Neither will I until there is an end to their gallop.' He said it with a bravado he didn't feel. He was fighting this battle alone against a criminal gang that would stop at nothing, even murder, to achieve their aim. Where were the Gardaí when he needed them? Those on the night shift were probably drinking coffee in a café somewhere. Nice life if you can get it.

'Will I clean up?' she said, bending down to pick up an advertising card praising the virtues of his priciest coffin. She placed the card against the wall.

'No leave it as it is. I'll ring the Gardaí; the insurance assessors will need a report from them.'

He dialled 999 and a girl with a Galway accent answered, 'Pearse Street Garda Station, how can I help?'

'Ringsend Funeral Home, we have had an off-roader driven through the showroom window. Can you send someone out here?

'Sorry to hear that, are you hurt?'

'No we're Ok. We're in the upstairs apartment.'

'Just damage to property,' she said. He could imagine her painstakingly writing it down in a big ledger, although she was more likely typing it into a computer. The days of record books were long gone, or were they?

'We'll have a patrol car with you as soon as possible.' She hung up keen, he thought, to get on the radio and notify the nearest Garda car; another case logged, job done.

The double glazing salesman had convinced him to get argon gas pumped into the cavity between the glass panes. He described it as, "as a safe inert gas that makes double glazing as good as triple glazing," but salesmen would tell you anything.

He thought he could smell gas, and he didn't know if it was explosive or not. To be on the safe side he called the fire service, 'Fire service. What is your emergency?'

'A showroom filled with argon gas.'

'Is there a fire?

'No just the gas.'

'Argon gas is an inert gas, and it can't make you ill or hurt you in any way. Stop worrying about it. Do you need us to come out?'

'No, that's fine. Thanks, bye.'

One less worry.

A Garda car screeched to a halt, and two female Gardaí got out and walked towards the wrecked showroom.

'Did someone escape from a coffin and jump through the window?' said the younger one smiling. She looked young enough to be a school girl and Pat guessed she was a trainee. The older woman with Sergeant's stripes on her shoulder looked aghast at her flippant attitude, but she ignored it.

'You've had trouble here.' She took out her notebook and stopped for a second to consider something before turning to the younger woman,

'You have opinions on everything. Take a history of the incident and get it right.' Anger showed in her face as she shut the notebook and pulled down the narrow elastic band to keep it closed. The younger woman took a list of interview questions from her pocket, a handout from the Garda training college in Templemore, no doubt.

'My God did you learn anything in training? You should know that list by heart before you start interviewing anyone.'

'It's just an aide-memoire. Everyone uses them.'

'Aide-memoire my arse. Get on with it.'

The younger girl's hands were shaking and to break the tension, Teresa moved up beside her and said, 'They drove through the window of the showroom in a Jeep with darkened windows.'

'Did you get the number plate?' she asked without looking up from writing.

'No, I was in shock with all that was going on.'

'What about you?' she said to Pat.

'No I didn't get it either. It happened so quickly. One minute they came through the window and the next minute they were gone.'

That was a lie. He knew the number of the Jeep. It was the same one that had followed him halfway across Ireland. It wouldn't help his mission to discover the identity of the big man if he was responsible for getting some of his foot soldiers arrested.

'Right, I'm leaving now and you stay on until morning. I'll be back later to check on you,' said the sergeant as she strode to the Garda car with its flashing strobe lights. Pat was wondering if he could legally fit such lights to the hearse. Other vehicles would get out of his way and allow him a clear passage. It would save him hours of time on a journey.

'That woman is one hell of a bitch. She has it in for me. She would kick me off the force if she could,' said the young Garda looking after the departing car.

'You goad her a bit. Why don't you try to get on with her?' said Teresa, 'She might send in a bad report about you.''

'Mother Theresa couldn't get on with that one. The report doesn't matter that much, except they could send me to the worst Garda station in the country.'

'Something like – "the pint or the transfer," said Pat laughing.

'I think that doesn't exist any more. What that woman needs is a man. Watch yourself; she still thinks she has a chance.'

'I will,' said Pat, 'would you like to come up for a cup of coffee?'

'I would love a coffee,' she said as she followed them up the stairs to the sitting room.

'O my God this is palatial. I would kill for an apartment like this. It must have cost a bomb.'

'Not when we did it. Prices have gone up since then,' said Pat, making the coffee.

'That sounds like a country accent. Where are you from? asked Teresa.' She sat down beside her on the settee.

'Kildysart, County Clare. I was in the bank for a while, but I just couldn't stand being inside all the time. That's why I joined the Garda.'

'Do you like it?'

'It was OK until I ended up with this old biddy of a sergeant.'

'You're only going to be with her for a short time,' said Teresa.

'That's true unless I marry her.' They all laughed.

'I'm lucky to be in the Garda at all; I'm so small. It wouldn't have happened years ago when they had a height requirement. We had a mix of nationalities in the training college; it was great, "Representing a multicultural Ireland" they told us.'

Pat badly needed sleep. When he looked across at Teresa her eyes were heavy and about to close.

'Why don't you stretch out on the settee for the rest of the night and don't spare the coffee,' he said.

'I will and if that old biddy calls, I can say I was inspecting the inside of the building.' She smiled at the thought of getting one over on the Sergeant. She took off her belt, opened her tunic and lay out on the settee and closed her eyes.

Teresa went up the next flight of stairs to the bedrooms ahead of Pat and she turned around on the landing,

'Which is your bedroom?' she asked.

'The front one to the left.'

Teresa walked into the room and stood in the centre taking stock before jumping on to the bed and bouncing up and down.

'I'm sorry; I couldn't resist it. I always did that as a child.'

Pat was a bit confused about what to do next. If she was going to take over the main bedroom then he should move out to another one.

It was unusual behaviour for a guest, but then again, she was more than that. He had never met anyone like her and truth to tell he was developing strong feelings, or maybe it was passion for her. He was missing his wife. She had left a void in his life, the presence of a loving woman. He was vulnerable and did not know how to talk to women. He didn't understand them and he hadn't a clue what this one was thinking. He should say 'good night' and go now before he made a fool of himself.

Teresa came out of the bathroom wearing one of Marie's nightgowns,

'Were you thinking about making your escape,' she said, laughing, 'I'm going to sleep here tonight, undressed.'

'Ok.' He knew it was a weak response, but his head was in turmoil. None of his father's sayings fitted this situation. He turned off the light, put on his pyjamas and got into bed beside Teresa. He lay on his back leaving a space between them until she turned over and clasped her hands around his neck and kissed him. He remembered little else until after they had made love, and he fell asleep with her arms wrapped around him.

Loud snoring woke Teresa and for a moment she was disorientated as she tried to work out where she was and who was causing a racket. It came back to her in a rush; the snoring was coming from the ban Garda sleeping downstairs on the couch. Until she did something about that noise coming from her adenoids, she would never get a man to share her bed, unless he was an insomniac. It sounded as if nothing short of an operation would get rid of that blast although she had heard of a plastic nose clip that helped with the problem. In the morning, she should tell the Garda about her loud snoring or, maybe, she should leave it to a close friend.

Pat was already up and moving silently around the room and for a second a shaft of moonlight lit up his face and to Teresa's surprise it was the face of his terrible twin. She pretended to sleep and through half closed eyes followed his every move. He rolled back a corner of the carpet, lifted a piece of floor board and took out a machine pistol which he tucked into the waist band of his jeans. Teresa felt amazed that she had no fear as she watched him prepare for some armed mission. Somehow she knew the other Pat would take over and save her from harm.

He moved like a shadow out of the room and down the stairs past the sleeping Gardaí. Teresa quickly pulled on her trousers and top, and from the window saw him cross the yard to a wooden shed, unlock the door and step inside.

She started down the stairs, hesitantly feeling for each step and easing her weight on to it to test for a creak. No sound came from the treads until she reached the last step. She was feeling confident at that stage and trod on it with her full weight. The creak it made was as loud as a pistol shot and the Garda stopped snoring and shifted on the settee. She mumbled, 'That cow is a right bitch.'

It wasn't difficult to know who she was talking about, and she started snoring again. Teresa waited for a few seconds and then tiptoed past. Her Sergeant would not find her dereliction of duty amusing although she would probably never find out. Teresa stood behind the kitchen door and through the glass panel she could view the backyard. Pat had already opened the big gates leading to the street. Minutes passed before he emerged from the shed dressed in biker leathers, pushing a Harley Davidson. Good Lord, this man was full of surprises.

16

She had every intention of following him; she had experience in covert surveillance. When he had gone she headed across the yard to the discarded Volkswagen beetle. It had seen better days and the way the headlamps looked at her reminded her of an obedient collie dog. She almost patted its long bonnet. The keys were in the ignition and the engine roared to life after the second turn of the starter. She drove on to the street in time to see the taillights of the Harley disappear around the corner to the left.

He was driving slowly, probably not wanting to attract attention and she had no difficulty following him. He turned left into a narrow street so she moved closer. She didn't know this part of the city and could easily lose him. From that point on she had no idea of their destination as she blindly followed the Harley's taillights. She was driving for what seemed an age until he pulled the motor bicycle into the parking lot of a pub.

Car number plates had fascinated her since she was a child. Her father had used the number on the car ahead to teach her sums by adding them up. As she grew older he taught her to split the number into halves and to subtract the totals. She still did it and managed in the VW headlamps to add two of the parked number plates. There was something familiar about one total, as if she had added it before.

The building and the parking lot were in darkness apart from an occasional flash of light as a customer entered or exited the pub. It was well past closing time and she didn't think this illegal drinking went on any more; it was difficult to understand how they were getting away with it. He entered the building and she considered the wisdom of followed him as there was no telling what danger was waiting inside. Briefly she thought about turning the VW around and heading back to the funeral parlour. It was undoubtedly the wisest course of action but she didn't always follow her own good advice. She cautiously followed him into the pub. The burly doorman treated her with suspicion,

'You haven't been here before?'

'No.'

'Are you on your own?'

'Yes.'

'Are you a working girl?'

'No.'

'Are you a plain-clothes Garda?'

'No, I'm coming to meet a friend.'

'No one has any friends in here. In you go. I'll be keeping an eye on you to see what your game is.' She couldn't blame him. She should have told him that she was a working girl. He moved sideways and opened the door to let her in.

It took a few seconds to adjust to the dim interior and it was not like what she had expected. It was spacious, recently refurbished. The glass column bathed in soft blue light in the centre of the room, surrounded by a circular bar made from dark mahogany. Drinkers occupied most of the high stools around the bar, and tables and chairs, with passages between filled the rest of the floor. Snugs like the private boxes of the Showtime and Vaudeville era draped with velvet curtains provided a backdrop along the wall of the pub; an ideal setting for clandestine meetings. She searched for a dark corner where, secreted away, prying eyes would not see her. She found one between two snugs. One small table and chair, darkened by the shadows of the curtains. Minutes later she heard a drunken voice,

'What about a bit of company, what are you drinking?'

'No thanks, I'm waiting for a friend.'

'Stuck-up bitch,' he mumbled and staggered back to his table. There were loud guffaws from the others at the table. A barman came to her table,

'Would you like to order? Your man over there wants to pay for it.'

A man sitting at the bar raised his hand in greeting and shouted, 'Hi.'

She didn't respond but looked away. That should be enough of a signal to let him know that he didn't interest her.

'I'll pay for my own drinks,' She took out a few notes and placed them on the table.

'Have it your way. What do you want?'

'Gin and tonic.'

She felt more like a glass of water, but it felt prudent to ask for an alcoholic drink. Good Lord, she was getting paranoid thinking everyone was watching her.

Pat appeared from somewhere at the back of the room and swaggered to the most prominent table in the room. He placed his helmet in the centre of the table, and took off his leather jacket and hung it on the back of the chair. He pulled the machine pistol from his waistband and laid it down carefully beside the helmet. The tables around him quickly emptied. He seemed unconcerned and sat down, relaxed and ready, like a tiger waiting to pounce on its prey. She could almost taste the tension in the room. One of the waiters approached him cautiously and hesitantly asked, 'Would you like something to drink, Sir?'

'Water.'

His choice of drink increased the tension; this was a man who didn't want to dull his senses with alcohol. He just sat there watchful and alert.

Teresa surveyed the room trying to work out who he was going to attack but couldn't find any clues. The types in the pub were similar to those she had seen in prison. Huge neck and biceps muscles developed by weights and covered in grotesque tattoos. Criminals were not the only people to have tattoos nowadays. They are fashionable and it wasn't usual to find the girl next door returning from a holiday with tattooed images in discreet places but they didn't appeal to Teresa.

In the casino corner of the bar the seats around the two gambling tables for roulette and Texas Hold Em were full. The croupiers in tuxedos and bow-ties looked ridiculous in the bar.

'Here's your drink,' said the waiter and then added, 'We need a female croupier, it's a pity you can't do something useful like that.'

Teresa's temper flared and getting up she said, 'Oh but I can.'

Before she had fully realised what was happening, she was standing beside the card dealing croupier. It was a stupid thing to do just to get even with a waiter. It was all coming back to her. The long hours she had stood behind the gambling tables in the Lido, trying to make ends meet for herself and that no good boyfriend, dealing cards for Blackjack, Pontoon, and Texas Hold Em. The croupier stood aside nodded to her and said, 'Take over.'

'What are the percentages?' she asked as she broke open a new deck of cards.

'Ten per cent of everything on the table goes to the dealer.'

In a one-handed move she spread the cards out in a half circle face up on the table and gathered them back into the pack.

'The other girls wear baby doll uniforms, it brings me luck,' said one of the gamblers grumbling.

'You make your own luck.'

What he wanted to see was more bare flesh which had nothing to do with luck. If the girl croupiers in this place were anything like their Paris counterparts they probably wore fully body stockings which covered them from head to toe. On top of that fishnet and whatever was the flavour of the day; skimpy, nurses, policewoman or nuns outfits. He was still looking at her, probably undressing her in his mind. Sometimes she just hated men.

She held the cards out for one of the gamblers to cut the pack and then she shuffled them. She pulled a card at random, the four of diamonds and destroyed it. If anyone played a similar card in this round she would know they were cheating. She dealt the cards and it was game on.

'You haven't brought me any luck; this is my worst night yet.'

'It'll change before the night is out,' she said without much conviction.

In the Lido, croupiers didn't speak to clients but this was Ireland and maybe it was different. She had enough of gambling talk after about an hour and she signalled to the male croupier to take over.

Her percentage chips had mounted into a sizeable pile and she guessed she had a least a thousand Euros. They were high rollers all right. A man in a suit wearing glasses standing near the gambling table came forward to talk to her,

'I'm the owner, there's a full-time job going here for you if you want it.'

'No, but thanks for offering,' she said.

'Well it's here for you anytime. It's difficult getting trained croupiers in Ireland.'

Teresa cashed in her chips and returned to her seat. Pat was motionless and hadn't even taken a sip from his glass of water. He didn't seem aware that she was in the pub.

In front and over to her left, two individuals with hells angels emblazoned on their fleece jackets were making noise, banging their empty glasses on the table, demanding attention.

'We need a drink; a man could die of thirst in here.'

'We'll get it ourselves, no good waiting for these losers,' said his companion, getting up and knocking over the table and littering the floor with broken glasses. They pushed others out of their way to get to the bar and no one retaliated. Strange, for such a tough place, thought Teresa. The barman filled and placed the glasses of Guinness in front of them. Pat got up and slowly walked up the bar. Much smaller but broader than the two toughs at the bar he pushed them aside,

'You're the comedians that burst up my showroom, I didn't like it at all,' he said as he picked up their glasses, one in each hand. Teresa remembered where she had seen the number plates on the Jeep in the car park.

They looked down at Pat and the smaller one, with a loud laugh, shouted,

'What are you going to do about it?'

'Plenty,' said Pat as he poured the Guinness over their heads. Then he brought both elbows up simultaneously. The taller one took the blow on his Adams apple. He was gasping for breath when Pat hit him again, this time a knee in the groin. He roared with pain and collapsed to the floor. Pat grabbed his arm and twisted it backwards across his knee until it broke, with a sickening cracking sound. The other thug's broken nose was bleeding, a pool gathered at his feet. Pat stepped to the side to avoid the blood and in one movement caught his arm, and forced it up and around, dislocating his shoulder and fracturing it. He moaned as he fell to the floor into his own blood.

'Call an ambulance,' Pat said to the barman before walking slowly back to his seat. He checked the pistol in his waistband, put on his leather jacket and slowly looked around the room as if searching for something. A third thug broke cover from his hiding place at the back of the room and rushed for the door. Teresa hadn't known there was a third man in the Jeep, he must have been in the rear seat. Pat strolled out of the pub after him and Teresa followed. Once clear of the pub he ran for the Harley; jumped into the saddle, started it and drove out of the car park with Teresa not far behind in the VW. His quarry was running down the footpath a few hundred yards ahead. The Harley drew level and slowed to stay with the runner. Exhausted, the thug had to stop, with blood flowing from his nose he bent over gasping for breath. He was easy prey for his pursuer who didn't delay in catching his arm, twisting it until his shoulder dislocated and fractured. He passed out. Pat hauled him like a sack of potatoes across the rear seat of the Harley and drove back to the pub where he dropped him at the door. The violence sickened Teresa but it was unlikely to stop until the two different people inside Pat's head became one whole person that he had control over; if that were possible. Mother of Divine, she was becoming the new patron for hopeless cases. She seemed like a magnet for attracting men with baggage. She would save herself heartache if she took the morning train to Belfast and forget about this whole episode, but she knew she wouldn't do that. As long as there was another hopeless case looking for tender loving care, she would be there.

Back at the funeral parlour, Pat parked the Harley, removed his leathers and went in through the back door to the apartment. With the VW back in place in the yard, Teresa waited for about half an hour before followed him up the stairs to the bedroom. He was back in bed, and from the sound of his breathing sleeping heavily. She changed into her pyjamas and, making an effort not to disturb him, slid in under the covers. He grunted and asked, 'did you find the bathroom,' before drifting off again. Teresa didn't sleep well, dozing, tossing and turning for the rest of the night. It was just so strange having two different men in one man's body sleeping beside her.

Teresa was awake with her eyes closed when Pat got out of bed carefully so as not to wake her. This was the old Pat, thoughtful and considerate. He went down the stairs and the Ban Garda said a cheerful, 'Good morning.'

'Good morning. I'm going to cook a full English breakfast for all of us even though it's Ireland. The full deal, bacon, egg, sausages, with black-and-white pudding and pan toasted bread,' said Pat getting the pan from a kitchen cabinet.

'I'd kill for full English. The only time I have that is when I'm in a hotel on holidays.'

'You don't have to kill anyone this morning,' said Pat, turning on the cooker.

'I'm imposing a lot but can I take a shower?'

'No problem, turn left on the landing and take the second door.'

Teresa heard her climbing the stairs and then the shower came on. She dosed and woke when Pat came in with her breakfast on a tray.

'Wake up and shine to another sunny day,' said Pat waiting for her to sit up and make a place to put the tray.

'You're spoiling me; I could have gone down to the kitchen to eat. It's enough to cook it.'

'You're worth it and more,' said Pat gingerly balancing the tray on the outline of her thighs under the covers.

'You're kind Pat, go down and have your breakfast.'

'Enjoy,' Pat said as he turned around and left the bedroom. He apparently had no knowledge of the mayhem he had caused last night and it was difficult to imagine that he was capable of such violence. She had finished her breakfast when the Ban Garda came in wrapped in a bath towel.

'It's so refreshing. My head was bursting yesterday, the night before I was out with the girls and we got wasted. You should come out with us.'

'Maybe sometime,' said Teresa, knowing that she meant never. That's all she needed, getting wasted with a bunch of giggling girls.

'That man is a treasure. Is there anywhere I could get one like him?,' she said, sitting on the end of the bed. She seemed to have the ability to fit in and make herself at home wherever she was.

'Hope and pray,' said Teresa with a laugh.

'What about a ménage à trois, then. It's the next-best.'

'Don't know about that, but I lived in Paris before joining the convent. It's the land of the ménage à trois and it didn't work there.'

'You were a nun, wicked.'

'On the contrary, it was anything but,' she said haughtily.

'I went to a convent school. As pubescence girls with hormones raging we had a terrible name for nuns,' said the Ban Garda.

'What was it? I probably heard it before.'

'It's the worst, "Mickey dodgers."'

'Haven't heard that one?'

'I better dress and ring for a car to take me back to the barracks. Then I have to report to her - Attila the Hun in uniform,' said the Ban Garda with a smile as she got up off the bed and made for the bedroom door.

Up and dressed, Teresa got downstairs in time to meet the insurance assessor and the double glazing contractor.

'There is no extension to the policy to cover furniture and coffins but we will cover everything else,' said the insurance agent, looking to Pat for a response.

'That's OK,' said Pat, the company will have to cope with the loss of the coffins. He felt relieved that they hadn't a clause excluding damage caused by wilful destruction.

'If you like, I can work out a price with the assessor and when you come back this evening the windows will be all fixed up. It would be as if nothing had happened,' said the contractor starting to work out prices on his scribble pad.

'OK,' said Pat.

'I accidentally picked up two copies of the Irish Times at the newsagents, would you like one?' said the assessor to Teresa.

'To see what's going on in the world,' she said, taking the paper from him.

Turning to her, Pat said, 'We are not needed here, would you like to go for a walk along the sea front?'

'That would be great,' said Teresa, she had a lot on her mind to work out and a long walk might provide the opportunity.

17

Pat and Teresa went upstairs to the apartment, and left the contractor with the assessor to work out a price for replacing the window.

'I'll put something together for a picnic' said Teresa, opening the fridge and examining his stock of food.

'I think there is avocado and kiwi fruit in there, and I like to put them in a sandwich,' he said. Marie had introduced them into their diet and while they were an acquired taste, he had grown fond of them. He got a flask out of a cabinet and searched for his backpack under the stairs. He hadn't used it for a long time. Teresa filled the kettle at the sink, replaced it on its base and pressed the switch to turn it on. While waiting for it to boil, she browsed the Irish Times, and one headline caught her attention.

'Oh my God, listen to this.'

'What is it?'

"BODY FOUND NEAR THE BORDER IN BELLEEK COUNTY FERMANAGH."

"A Co Fermanagh woman walking her dog last night near Belleek found a man's body on the roadside believed to be that of Mr. Billy Saunders, a widower from Belfast. The body is due for a post-mortem later today in the Erne Hospital, Enniskillen.
"One resident, I talked to was in tears when she told me,"
'"We are in shock. This is a peaceful town where we get on with one another, and we have never had anything like this before.'"
"Mr. Marshall known as major was an active loyalist and paramilitary. Both nationalists and loyalist feared him.

While working as a prison officer in Long Kesh, he became a born-again Christian. Following his conversion he renounced all violence; particularly paramilitary violence. He became somewhat of an ambassador for peace in Belfast, which was in stark contrast to his earlier life. His former loyalist colleague had accused him of being an informer; passed on information to the security forces. The PSNI strongly denied this rumour. For his own safety, the authorities advised to leave the country, but he chose to ignore that advice.

A white tent covers the spot at the roadside where the body lay and the PSNI have cordoned off a wider area with yellow crime scene tape. Forensic officers in protective clothing are constantly coming and going, and they are the only people allowed inside the tape.

The PSNI arrested three men near the border last night,

shortly after they found the body. All three, well-known loyalist paramilitaries, have addresses in Belfast.

The three suspects went under armed escort to Belfast this morning, and they are in holding cells in different police stations throughout the city. The PSNI is not looking for any other suspects in connection with this murder.

Belleek is a sleepy border town best known for its fine Parian china pottery that's sold worldwide. Belleek China from the pottery is collectable and dealers pay high prices for older examples.

The pottery has a long history going back to its establishment in 1884 by two men, a mineralogist named John Caldwell and business man David McBirney.

At the editor's request, I took a tour of the pottery, and a feature will appear in next Saturday's Irish Times Supplement."

'We were unlucky to find ourselves in the middle of a loyalist's feud. Sometimes I feel it didn't happen,' said Pat as he turned the rucksack upside down and gave it a shake. A scatter of dust, like a small cloud, drifted onto the kitchen floor.

'Aha, I didn't expect that, where does all this dust come from?'

'We didn't have a choice with the loyalists. Unfortunately, they came to us. I shiver every time I think about them. At least they are going to pay for the murder of that evil Major,' said Teresa, laying out the picnic ingredients on the kitchen counter.

'Well, I hope that's the end of it, but I won't forget it in a hurry,' said Pat, turning the backpack inside out and brushing the residue of dust and fluff from the seams.

'Neither will I, it's the stuff of nightmares. The only good that came out of it was to bring us together,' said Teresa, making the sandwiches.

They were silent, coming to terms with the murder they had witnessed. Pat felt he would never be the same again after seeing that terrible slaughter. It disturbed him in every fibre of his being. Maybe the educated had fancy words for the way he was feeling, but he couldn't describe it. It was a terrible emotion, and he couldn't make it go away. He didn't know how to explain to Teresa the turmoil that was going on in his head.

The sound like a steam engine coming from the kettle changed to a click as it reached the boiling-point and triggered the off switch. Pat made the tea in a teapot which was something he hadn't done for a while; nowadays it was usually a bag in a teacup. Living on his own, eating wasn't that important to him and his evening meals came mostly from the chipper down the road. Somewhere he had heard that in a lot of situations joy is enhanced when it's shared and loners don't often experience this. He didn't know if that was true or not. He filled the flask to near the top and added milk.

When the sandwiches were ready, Teresa covered them in a plastic film and passed them to him. He stacked them in the front of the pack to prevent them from getting squashed. To stop the flask from popping open and showering him with warm tea, he carefully swung it on to his shoulders. They were ready for the off.

'Where are we going?' asked Teresa, stood there in a pair of Marie's flat shoes she found in the bottom of the wardrobe.

'A mystery tour, we leave here and walk to Irishtown through the Sean Moore Park, on to the Nature Trail and along the pier to Poolbeg Lighthouse,' said Pat from halfway down the stairs.

'The lighthouse sounds great. Who was Sean Moore?' she said, catching up with him on the stairs.

'I think he was a Lord Mayor of Dublin sometime in the 1960s, but that's all I know about him.'

They walked side by side in silence through the park, now and again stepping aside to let others pass. He could feel tension in Teresa, and he would have liked to know what was going on in her head.

The rustle of the grass under foot, dogs barking and songs of the birds in the trees reminded him of the island. How he wished he had never left it. He could have made a decent living had he restricted his business to the island and kept away from Dublin where his life had turned into a fiasco. Maybe he was too ambitious in those days, wanting to make something of himself. Now there was no certainty on how it would all end.

There were many features ahead on Sandymount strand that he could have shown Teresa, like the monument presented by the Mexican government, but he decided not to disturb her mood.

She was first to speak, 'What is that square thing on the strand?'

'Cranfield baths, in the old days that was a swimming pool but since the 1950s it hasn't been used.'

'It looks big,' said Teresa, linking her arm into his.

'I have been out to see it. It's about thirty metres square.'

'How did it work?'

'What I heard in the pub's all I know, that's when I was drinking. The incoming tide filled the baths.'

There was a lot more he could have told her, but somehow he was reluctant to let her know that he had an excellent memory; he could retain most of what he heard. After a few minutes he decided to go on talking.

'The fellas in the pub said that in 1883 a man called Richard Cranfield left no stone unturned to get work on the baths started. He died here in Irishtown in 1859.'

'That's very funny, they actually had to turn a lot of stones to build the baths,' she said squeezing his arm and laughing.

'Not that much. It's built from concrete. Cement was invented a bit before that over in England in 1724 by John Smeaton, a civil engineer.

'And not many people know that,' she said jokingly.

'In those days Sandymount was a great place for people from the city to come to on a Sunday afternoon. If the tide was in, they had a swim in the baths. If it was out they picked cockles and shrimp on the strand. There's some cockles there now but the shrimp has gone.'

'Oh there's a sandpiper,' said Teresa, pointing to a small bird feeding on the sand, 'at this time of the year, we might also see heron, cormorant and, of course, gulls.'

'I don't know much about birds,' said Pat, adjusting the straps of his rucksack to a more comfortable position.

'I bet that along this stretch of strand, they get a lot of other birds like the lark, kestrel, kingfisher, snipe and brent goose,' said Teresa walking a bit ahead of him, excited by the prospect of seeing more birds. Her knowledge impressed him, apart from the common varieties like crows, larks, sparrows, magpies and gulls the rest were a mystery to him. He wouldn't recognise those exotic birds she was talking about even if they were under his nose.

Pat's phone rang and he searched around in the pockets of his waterproofs for it.

'It's in the pocket of your backpack. I'll get it,' she said, pulling open the Velcro held flap and handing him the phone. It was from Pearse Street Garda station, he stopped walking.

'Hello.'

'Pat O'Neill here, are you OK? I heard they rammed your showroom window and made bits of it. By the way, you put two men in hospital last night.'

What the heck was he talking about? He hadn't put anyone in a hospital last night or any other night. He would let that go.

'I'm fine. The contractor is working on the broken window, and the other damage is a few smashed coffins. The insurance will take care of most of it.'

'Have you still got the goods in the coffin?'

'Yes, let me know when they call you.'

'OK.'

The phone went dead.

'You heard all that,' he said to Teresa.

'Yes,' she said as she started walking again. The last time they had a conversation about what he did and didn't remember it didn't go well, and she would leave it for the moment. Soon she hoped he would become aware of the problem and at that point she would source whatever help was available. She decided to steer away from the topic.

'Tell me more about the sights around here,' she said waving her hand in a half circle and taking in all of Poolbeg peninsula.

'Over there the tall chimneys are the ESB generating station. The Dublin waste to energy thermal treatment plant is across the road from it,' he said, pointing to them.

'The chimneys are a Dublin icon, and it caused some furore when there was talk of knocking them down. It was in all the papers,' she said, shifting her gaze to a man digging on the strand.

'They're not in use anymore, and I suppose as long as the structure is sound they'll stay up. That man out there on the strand is digging for bait - lugworm,' he said without breaking stride.

'It's barbarous pushing those poor live worms, on to a hook,' he said, pulling a disgusted face. 'What do they expect to catch?'

'Those casting their lines from the pier beside the lighthouse could catch a load of different kinds of fish like pollock, bass, mackerel, mullet and conger eel.'

'I didn't expect that much variety of fish,' she said, trying to keep up with him.

'Don't forget they are at the end of the pier, and that's 2 kilometres out to sea. The other kind of fishing around here is casting from the shore and without having to go anywhere near the pier they can catch flounder and bass,,' he said, slowing down for her to catch up.

His phone rang and this time, there was no caller ID. That's the way the drug men operated. Get a new sim card for each call and that made it difficult to trace them.

'Hello.'

'I'll deal with the men you put in a hospital when they get out. What's the damage?'

'The insurance is taking care of it,' said Pat. They were half way down the pier, and he continued walking. Here it went again. This thug was speaking about the people he put in a hospital. They must have mistaken him for somebody else.

'We need to collect the goods from you. Drive to Dundalk tomorrow and somebody will meet you in the Ballymascanlon Hotel car park.'

'That was not the deal,' said Pat aware that it could be a set-up to take him out of the game permanently.

'I'm looking after you. There's an envelope in your letter box to cover all the costs. Can you drive an articulated truck?'

'Maybe,' said Pat, not wanting to commit himself to anything until he discussed with O'Neill.

'In a few weeks I want you to take a container lorry from the docks to Dundalk.'

'That wasn't part of any deal either. Let me think about it. Can I get you at that number?' The phone went dead.

He thought the container would probably contain contraband cigarettes. He had seen a TV programme on smuggling cigarettes into Ireland. They were made in China or the Philippines and taken to the Free Trade Zone in China for packing into containers destined for an English port and labelled as toys. From there it was a short hop to get them to Ireland. For her own safety, he didn't tell Teresa about the plan. The less she knew about what was going on the better.

106

'You heard that, I'll call O'Neil,' he said, starting to type in ι number.

'It's strange that he doesn't give you his mobile phone number,' she said, suffering a bit from painful heels. She probably would have blisters when they got back. That was a difficulty with wearing somebody else's shoes - they rarely fitted comfortably.

'I'm too committed now. I have to trust him,' said Pat, as the station switchboard put him through to O'Neill.

'John, I'm delivering the stuff to Dundalk tomorrow.'

'That's fine; we'll be close behind in unmarked cars to make sure the cargo never gets to the markets.'

'He wants me to drive an articulated lorry to Dundalk from the docks in a few weeks. What do you think?'

'Go with it; cigarettes most likely and we'll follow to keep an eye on things, and we will take the consignment away from them after you have gone.' He put down the receiver with a click.

'Put it all out of your head for now. We'll sit here and have our picnic, and you can tell me a bit more about the history of the place,' she said. She put her hand on his arm and guided him to spot on the pier where they sat with their legs dangling out over the sea.

'These sandwiches are good,' he said taking his second big bite.

'Flattery will get you everywhere. I haven't had this mix of kiwi and avocado before, and I like it,'

They finished the picnic and sat in silence, watching the twin hulled Liverpool ferry going out of Dublin port. It passed the outer channel markers, and the pilot climbed down a rope ladder from the ferry and into a tender to get him back to his base in the inner harbour. A thank you blast on the ship's horn and the ferry in open waters increased speed.

'When I see something like that I feel I'd love to go somewhere, anywhere would do,' she said putting her arm into his and pulling him closer before kissing him on the cheek.

'My father used to say "Wherever you go to you bring yourself with you"'

'Wise man. Come on start talking and tell me more about this place.'

'Right, I give too much detail but here goes. This pier we are sitting on is made from granite blocks, which replaced the old wooden piles in 1735. The way they did it was to build outer and inner walls about twenty feet apart and fill in the centre with sand and stones.'

'You just love talking about building and engineering stuff. Maybe it's a man thing,' she said with a smile and gave him a nudge.

'I do. I would like to have been involved in building it,' he said examining a settlement crack in the pier. When he was talking like this it distracted him from his worries.

It's amazing when you think about it that the granite blocks weighed nearly a ton, and they were lifted into place without the aid of modern lifting gear. At 2k the pier is the longest of its type in Europe.' He stopped for a breath.

'Let's walk to the lighthouse and tell me all about it as we go.'

'Well, it was built in 1767, and it replaced a lightship anchored in the bay. It took six years to build, and it was the first lighthouse in the world to use candles instead of coal.'

'A first, isn't that something,' she said, holding onto him for support over the rough stone surface of the pier.

'The foundations are made from granite blocks held together with iron bands and laid on the seabed.'

They stood at the base looking at the alternate strips of red and white painted around the circumference of the tower from the bottom to the top. It reminded him of his school football socks.

'There's something majestic about the way it stands,' she said, her eyes fixed on the glass reflectors housed at the top.

'Aye, it met the purpose for which it was built, saving lives in the days of sailing ships. You can't expect more than that from anything. We had better start walking back,' he said, turning and bringing her around with him still clinging to his arm.

He was going into himself again, brooding, and she wanted to get him out of it. 'You must have more stories about this place?'

'There are loads of them, but I think this next one is one of the best. The Pigeonhouse was originally called Pigeon's house. He was the caretaker and his job was looking after the wooden building used by the Port Authority for storing tools and equipment. He and his family also lived in the building.'

'It must have been shocking cold in the winter time,' she said, putting her weight on his arm.

'People wore heavier clothes in those days and put up with a lot less heat in their houses,' he said, losing her grip on his arm.

He continued on with Pigeon's story.

'In the summer time the river was a popular place for boat trippers. Pigeon saw a business opportunity and with his family started to provide refreshments to the boaters. Eventually, he purchased a boat and leased it out to the well to do trippers. The business flourished and before long he owned a fleet of boats for leasing. Over time, he became a rich man. His prices were high and his overcharging became known as 'Plucking the Pigeons.'

'Has Poolbeg any connection at all with your island?' she said, tightening her grip on his arm.

'Funnily enough it has. The music composer, C.S.L. Parker, I think he's from New Zealand, originally retired to the island and has celebrated Poolbeg with his composition The walk to Poolbeg Lighthouse.'

'Isn't that a coincidence, I never imagined that there could be any kind of association between the island and this place except the sea,' she said, playfully hauling him along by their linked arms.

'Oliver Cromwell, came ashore here with his army in 1649 and as you know, caused death and destruction before he departed,' said Pat, wriggling out of her grasp and keeping her at arm's length to get walking on her own.

'You're good at remembering dates. I couldn't recall any of those, and I didn't know Cromwell landed here. I did know about the bad things he did from school.'

'Some things are better not remembered,' he said thoughtfully. They returned along the pier, through the park and into the village.

'Come on, let's go for a cup of coffee in Browns Café,' she said with her hand on his arm directing him across Sandymount Green towards it.

'OK, I haven't been in there before.'

'You'll enjoy it. A quiet moment before we get back to the rough and tumble of our lives,' she said, as she bent down to see her reflection in the café window.

'My hair is a sight after getting blown to bits on the pier,' she said running her hands through her hair to tidy it up before going into the café.

'You look fine,' he said, pushing open the door. A bell attached to the door jamb gave a tinny jingle, a piece of nostalgia from former days.

They sat down at an empty table and a waiter came over, took their order and came back quickly with a black coffee and a latte.

Hesitantly and not looking at her Pat blurted out 'I have a problem I've tried to deny it and it's time to face up to it. Another part of me that I know nothing about is wreaking havoc all over the place,' he said with elbows on the table and his head in his hands. She gently prised his hands away from his head and held them in her own.

'Pat I'm going to get help for your multiple personality disorder and also for the dyslexia. Loads of people have these difficulties and they get over them,' she said, still holding his hands in hers and she lifted them up and kissed them. They sat silently for a while till she said, 'Finish the coffee and we'll go back to see if the window is finished.'

Coffee finished, they started back. He felt so fortunate to have found her willing to support him through what was going to be a difficult time. As they came near the parlour they could see that the window was replaced and Johnnie was loading a coffin into the hearse surrounded by mourners; women wearing black mantillas and men in dark suits. A priest blessed the coffin, shook holy water and recited the rosary before the rear door of the hearse was closed. Pat and Teresa stood aside as the mourners trooped out past them to their cars.

'It's such a sad sight, it reminds me of all the deaths in my family,' she said with tears in her eyes.

'I should be immune to it, but I'm not. I find it hard every time when I'm called on to bury a child or a young person,' he said, nodding to the people passing. It was a Ringsend person in the coffin and most of them knew him as the local undertaker. They might not be so friendly if they knew what he was carrying in the other hearse parked beside the morgue. He would garage it as soon as the place was clear.

'I know it's one of the beatitudes, a corporal work of mercy, to bury the dead but I wouldn't make a good undertaker,' she said, drying her tears with the back of her hand.

'I suppose, as my father used to say, "Death is part of Living." That saying has kept me going for a long time especially when I'm confused and trying to make sense of it all,' he said.

She slipped off her shoe and exposed a huge blister on her heel.

'It looks sore, I have plaster in a drawer somewhere,' he said, bending down to examine the blister.

'I'll sterilise a needle in boiling water and burst the blister before I put on the plaster,' she said, hopping along on one foot to the hall door and up the stairs to the apartment.

18

Pat's phone rang the following morning and with no caller ID he knew who it was.

'What now?'

'Get to Dundalk pronto.' The phone went dead.

'Dundalk here we come,' he said, taking the hearse's keys from the bowl. The system worked well as long as he remembered to return the keys to the bowl.

'I'm coming with you and I'm not taking no for an answer,' she said, getting a brush from her bag and tidying up her hair. Then she checked her face in the hall mirror, first the view from the front, and then from the back, half turning and looking over her shoulder.

'My other self has put two of their men in hospital and they may be out for revenge. It's no place for you,' he said, twisting the keys around in his hand. This trip wasn't going to be a proverbial walk in the park or anything like it. He liked her too much to put her in that kind of danger.

'Look, I'm going and you won't talk me out of it.'

He sighed. 'OK.'

He was starting to realise there wasn't much point in arguing with Teresa.

They were soon under way, driving across the toll bridge and heading for the M50. A flat bed builder's lorry pulled in behind them and stayed close.

'Poolbeg is such a gem of place. I knew nothing about it when I worked in Dublin,' she said, unclipping her seat belt to take a twist out of it.

He assumed that she had no knowledge of Dublin and it surprised him to hear that she had worked in the city.

'Where did you work?' he asked.

'It's a long story. When I left the convent, I saw an advert in the Irish Independent; UCD offering an evening course in Private Detective training, and I applied.'

'That's an unusual job for a woman,' he said, taken aback.

'Well I always fancied myself as a PI similar to the glamorous ones on the TV with a top of the range sports car and all that goes with it. The realities of the job are nothing like that. They don't show real PIs lying in ditches on cold winter nights keeping surveillance on, say, a farmyard. It's no job for the faint-hearted. I got a place on the course, and it was a strange mixture of saints and sinners from various backgrounds.'

'I suppose there's always a mixture of the good the bad and the ugly.'

'Law enforcement has a strange fascination for criminals and there were a few on the course. That didn't mean they wouldn't be good PIs. I didn't stay in contact, and I don't know whether they got on, but is there not something about the poacher turned gamekeeper?'

'A gamekeeper on the island would be a rare sight,' he said, keeping a watchful eye on other traffic.

'The course covered a range of topics and they are imprinted forever on my mind. I can still reel them off by rote. Here goes. Law and how it affects the work of the PI, understanding documents, surveillance, observations, digital photography, fingerprinting, handwriting analysis, fire and fraud investigation. How is that for a good memory?'

'I couldn't do that much study,' he said, driving faster.

'You have loads of ability. Just wait until we get your dyslexia sorted out.'

'If it's ever sorted out,' he said, checking his mirror. Sure enough the builder's truck was still there as if attached to them with an invisible rope. They were his Garda escort.

'I passed the final exam, and my first job was a store detective in Geraghty's ladies fashion shop in Grafton Street.

'They are not there any more, and I'm not surprised with the pilfering that went on - and that was only the staff. My responsibility was watching out for shoplifters posing as customers.'

'Nice work if you can get it,' he said, slowing to let a passing car cut in ahead.

'It wasn't. My first day on the job, and these two women came in pushing a go-cart minus a child. I suspected they were up to no good from the start, and I followed them around the shop without attracting their attention.

They had a gadget for neutralising the magnetic security strip attached to the garments and they filled up the go-cart with some of the most expensive stuff in the store. Of course they left without paying and I followed them out into Grafton Street.'

'Why did you not challenge them in the shop?'

'That's not legal; technically they haven't stolen anything until they hit the street. They gave me a tongue-lashing and then one of them jumped on my back, and when I fell over she dragged me by the hair down Grafton Street while the other one kept kicking me. Someone shouted Garda and they split, leaving the goods behind.'

'I'd say you took a fair battering,' he said as the truck behind flashed its lights, as they left the motorway. This was where their jurisdiction ended and they were handed over to Drogheda Garda division. Trying to figure out which vehicle was his next Garda escort was like playing a game of cat and mouse in his head.

'I had bald spots for weeks where she pulled out lumps of my hair and I was black and blue everywhere. That evening I resigned from the job. It was the first time a store detective had recovered stolen stock for the owners and they didn't want to let me go. I think the other detectives turned a blind eye to much of the pilfering.'

'Or two blind eyes, they probably wanted an easy life,' he said as the motorway sign for Drogheda came up. The Church authorities have on display a saint's relic in the RC church in Drogheda but he couldn't remember which saint. It might be the skull of St. Oliver Plunkett. He would ask her about it when she stopped talking.

'I then decided to set up my own detective agency. It was a grandiose title for a pokey office on the second floor over a shop in Dun Laoghaire. I had a sign out on the street directing potential clients up the back stairs to my office. It was one of those signs with a solid base, a long pole and on the top a circular sign – Private Female Detective. Confidentiality guaranteed. Reasonable Rates.

'It was the female bit that did it. I had all kinds of weirdoes coming in asking me out; for a coffee, to the pub, a night on the town, a swinger's session and heaven knows what else. They must have thought I was running an escort agency. When I deleted the female from the sign it got a bit better.'

'Miss or Ms in the telephone directory can bring a lot of nuisance calls as well,' he said.

Teresa was looking out over the roofs of Drogheda as they passed the town.

'The roofs in this town are a boring black, either slated or tiled, and pitched at the same angle. In other countries they use the roof space for living in and they have lovely windows and balconies. It's always interesting looking at them; the angular way they connect with each other and the different colours they use,' she said.

Pat's phone rang and he glanced at it. Same as before no ID, and there weren't any prizes for guessing who was on the line. He motioned to Teresa to answer it. She put it on speaker.

'Hello.'

There was long silence.

'Get that Biddy off the line,' said the voice. She handed the phone to him.

'What?' Pat said angrily.

'Where are you?'

'Near Dublin Airport.'

The phone went dead.

'Looking for us near the airport when we are twenty miles away will keep them busy for a while,' said Pat, looking over at Teresa. She'd gone ashen.

'They're a bad lot, I'm afraid for you,' she said briefly, placing her hand over his on the steering wheel.

'We should be OK, with our Garda escort.' He wanted to change the subject,

'What's the name of the Saint whose relic is on display in Drogheda?'

'Saint Oliver Plunkett's mummified head is in St. Peters Church. I went to see it one time on a pilgrimage with my mother. It's terrible to think about it, they found him guilty of treason and his life ended in London, hanged, drawn and quartered.'

A loud bang came from the hearse, and startled them. He braked hard, and the hearse went out of control.

'A blowout damn and blast it,' he said as they veered across the road to the centre division and scarped along the metal barrier. He swung the steering in the opposite direction but over corrected and they careered across the road and bounced off the bank on the other side. As he fought for control they zigzagged down the motorway for about thirty yards before stopping. The white van tailing them came alongside and took a look and drove on. Obviously they were his new Garda escort and they didn't want to blow their cover by stopping.

'Are you OK?' he said to Teresa.

'I'm fine. That could have happened to anyone.'

'We have done some panel damage but it could be worse. They are fairly new tyres and I'll be back for a replacement. I better change the wheel.'

'I'll help.'

He went around to the back of the hearse and the rear inner tyre was in shreds on the rim. No need to look further for the problem. He lifted the tailgate and took out the tools from under the coffin platform to get down to the floor where a metal plate covered the spare wheel. Four nuts secured the plate to the floor. He unscrewed the plate, and lifted out the jack, wheel brace, and spare wheel.

'Let me take off the wheel,' said Teresa keen to help. She attached the brace to a wheel nut and tried to unscrew it. The nut wouldn't budge and jumping up and down on the handle of the wheel brace made no difference.

'While I accept this equality business, I think some jobs are more suitable for men than women,' he said, taking the brace from her and loosening the wheel nuts.

'Men design wheel braces for men,' she said ready to do battle.

'You have a point but, I'm not putting women down by saying that.'

'I know. If women had a lever long enough and a fulcrum big enough they could move the world,' she said, carrying the jack and wheel brace to the rear of the hearse.

'That's an old one,' he said and they both laughed, light relief after the drama they had been through. With the wheel changed and all the tools packed away they were ready to continue.

She took a packet of wet wipes out of her handbag.

'My hands are a mess. Here take some of these to get the dirt off your hands,' she said, holding out the packet of wipes to him.

'Nothing less than swarfega would make any impression on my hands,' he said, looking down at the ingrained grease on his fingers. He took the packet of wipes from her anyway. Apart from cleaning skin they were great for shining up the leatherette on the dash board.

He drove cautiously for a few miles to find out how the hearse was driving. It was driving well and hadn't suffered any serious damage. A dented fender wasn't conducive to good business. Apart from that and out of respect for the dead and their families he had never gone to a funeral with a bashed or dirty hearse. He would have to get it repaired before its next outing.

Teresa looked a bit shattered and to get her mind off their situation he said,

'Tell more about your PI work.'

She hesitated as if it was an effort to bring her mind back to another place and time and then she started to speak.

'Even though I had my famous sign out on the street in Dunlaoghaire, most of my work came by way of telephone calls. One evening after lunch I got such a call from a man who asked my help and I made an appointment to meet him for a consultation in the Royal Marine Hotel. I told him to give his name to one of the receptionists and I would make contact. Have you been to the Royal Marine Hotel?'

'No.' He'd spotted the white van ahead parked on the hard shoulder with its hazard lights flashing. His Garda escort was waiting.

'It's a lovely hotel with a real oldie world feeling. As you probably know they called Dunlaoghaire, Kingstown in the old days, and the hotel makes me feel like I'm in a time warp transported back to another era.

'Older ladies sitting and sipping afternoon tea out of china cups with servings of scones with jam and clotted cream and real linen napkins. I half expected a carriage and four to pull up outside the front door. That's my view of the place – my imaginary one.

'Maybe even a hearse from the old days: a carriage and four,' he said as the white van moved out from the hard shoulder and took up station behind them.

'I went to the reception desk and they pointed him out to me. He was about forty and dressed in a dark business suit, white shirt and tie. The dark theme continued even to his spectacle rims. Serious and dull is how I would describe him.'

'Many of them are like that,' said Pat, becoming aware of a scraping sound, smoke and a smell of burning rubber coming from the front of the hearse when he braked or turned the steering wheel to the left. He had an idea of what was happening; in the aftermath of the crash against the barrier the wheel arch was rubbing against the tyre. Made from plastic, it wouldn't cause a tyre burst, but he would need to fix it when they stopped again.

'He stood up when I introduced myself and he respectfully stayed standing until I sat down. He had ordered afternoon tea for me and only a coffee for himself. I guessed he was trying to reduce his paunch by eating less. Without any preliminaries, straight away he got down to business.

'He was a solicitor working locally and he had for some time suspected his wife was being unfaithful. Mentally I filed this case away in the domestic category in my head. His wife went to play bridge every Thursday in the parochial hall while he stayed at home minding their two children. On her return she often smelled of drink. He wanted me to follow her and find out what was going on. He came prepared with photographs of his wife and of her car. Before leaving he insisted on paying me for one evening's surveillance. After he left I sat there for ages enjoying the afternoon tea and the ambience.'

'The perks of the job,' he said, changing down instead of braking and trying not to turn the steering wheel to the left.

'There weren't many perks.'

'Parked nearby the following Thursday, I watched his wife's car emerge from the tree-lined driveway. I followed her to the parochial hall and took a few photos of her playing cards at a table with other women. No one was drinking, but as if set up for the photo, an empty wine bottle sat in the centre of their table. There were few men in the place.'

'A parochial hall, I don't know how the churches would survive without the support of women,' he said, slowing slightly to lessen the screeching from the tyre.

'I was about to go and report to the husband that he had nothing to worry about when she got up and left the hall. She wrapped her scarf tightly around her neck against the chill of the night air and started walked towards a large house across the road so I followed. Imagine my surprise when I discovered it was the parochial house. She rang the doorbell and disappeared inside. A light came on in the front room and I figured that's where the drama was going to play out if there was one. To get up to the window I stood on the kerb surrounding the flower bed and got a good view into the room. The parish priest had laid the table for two with loads of food and wine.'

'The husband was on to something all right,' Pat said. A plan was forming in his head of how to deal with the handover of the cargo he was carrying. That was the most dangerous part.

'That was only the start. The two of them came into the room. The parish priest had dressed up in her clothes, the lot, frilly pink knickers with stockings, suspenders and bra and she was wearing his collar and nothing else. The black bib attached to the front of the collar did little to protect her modesty. The cross-dressing duo surprised me so much I lost my grip on the windowsill and landed on my backside in the flower bed. It cushioned my fall but destroyed my suit. I should have billed him for a new one. Anyway I got back up and took a few photos.'

'Did they not see the flash?'

'I had an infrared camera - all the right gear. When they finished the meal they changed back into their own clothes, and without any physical contact, carried on.'

'I never hear of anything like that. What did you tell her husband?' he said.

'I had a dilemma on my hands. On our course they taught us, "Report what you discover, nothing more or nothing less."

'That's OK in theory but if I reported to the husband that his wife was cross-dressing with a parish priest, that could have a devastating effect on their marriage and children. I would argue that they were harming no one with their carry-on.'

'What did you decide to do?'

'I met the husband again in the Royal Marine. As he walked across the foyer he looked pale and drawn with clenched jaws and stress lines on his forehead. He sat down at the table and without looking at me said, "I was right, wasn't I?"'

'At that point it came to me exactly what I should say to him. "I followed your wife to the Parochial Hall and these are the photographs of her playing bridge at a table with other women. Note the empty wine bottle."

I placed the photographs on the table in front of him. He examined them for a few seconds and then he smiled and his face relaxed, the lines disappeared as his anxiety lessened and his colour came back. "That's her all right. I'm indebted to you for that. I think you deserve a bonus," he said as he pulled out a chequebook from his inside jacket pocket.

'No, no, I did nothing. It was so easy that I have decided to return your original cheque, I said, taking the cheque from my bag. He wouldn't hear of it and insisted that I take the bonus cheque as well. Before he left he ordered afternoon tea for me and, with a friendly wave from the doorway, he was gone. It was tremendous to see such a transformation in a person from glum to happy in a matter of minutes. I felt good about altering the truth although purists would say a lie is always a lie regardless of the consequences. To my way of thinking it was outrageous to destroy a marriage and separate a father from his children over her peccadillo for dressing as a priest.'

'Bugger the purists, you did the right thing,' said Pat, slowing down to save the front tyre from unnecessary wear, brushing against the wheel trim. He intended to pull in at the next filling station and try to fix the problem.

'It was a bit like Judas Iscariot and the thirty pieces of silver, what should I do with the cheques? I didn't agonise for long before I tore them into small pieces and deposited them into the silver ashtray. Nowadays with the smoking ban the ashtray is of little use except as an ornament. I enjoyed the afternoon tea.'

'You shouldn't have given it back. You earned it. After all you saved a marriage.'

'I suppose...'

His phone rang.

'Hello John.'

'You must be near Dundalk?'

'We have a bit to go yet, we had a blow out.'

'Who are the we?'

'Teresa is with me on this trip.' There was silence on the other end of the line registering O'Neill's disapproval of having taken Teresa with him.

'I'll be up there myself when we arrest them somewhere near the border. We'll take the stuff for evidence. Mind your driving.'

'I will.'

'Does he normally go out on drug bursts?' said Teresa, taking the wipes out of her bag again and trying to clean the remaining grease stains from her fingers.

'I don't think so. He spends most of his time in the office, but this is a big haul.' The sooner they got to a filling station the better; as well as an increase in smoke the scraping sound was louder.

'I don't trust that O'Neill. There's something about him I don't like,' she said, vigorously rubbing her fingers.

'He hasn't crossed me yet. Tell me more about your PI days.' It would shorten the journey.

'Most of my time, I dealt with domestic problems but now and again an insurance fraud case came my way. One of the big insurance companies contacted me to investigate a builder who had made a claim for injury. He lived out the country in County Wicklow, near Avondale.'

'A lovely part of the country, I had a few burials out there. They were Wicklow people who lived most of their lives in the city, and wanted back home for their final resting-place.'

'This particular builder had contacted his insurance company about an injury to his back. Supposedly it happened when he fell over a ladder he was carrying on a site. He was in a wheelchair when he went for the insurer's medical assessment, but the doctors couldn't find anything wrong with him.

'It was such a long drive that I thought I would never get to the place. Anyway by 8.00 a.m., I had set myself up crouched behind a ditch keeping surveillance on his bungalow. I focused my camera on the front of the building where he had his pickup and Jeep parked. I hadn't long to wait before he came out, walking normally. He jumped into the pickup and drove out the gate.

'I moved fast to get to my little car and follow him. He drove kilometres into the countryside before he stopped at a building site somewhere near Tinahely. All on his own he was building this house for some client. It was no surprise to me to see him climbing on to the roof and laying tiles, that was hardly the place for someone with a bad back. I got all the photographs I needed and, since I was in the vicinity, decided to visit Avondale house.'

'What happened to the builder?'

'I don't know, I just sent in the photographs to the insurance company but I imagine he didn't get any compensation. I didn't really like that type of work, it was spying on people.'

'It's not the kind of job that would suit me,' he said, noting the sign for an Esso filling station ahead. It was a welcome sight as he couldn't have gone much further without repairing the front of the hearse.

'What's Avondale like?'

'It's great, a period house, a coffee shop and a selection of exotic trees growing in the grounds. The main attraction is that Charles Stewart Parnell used to be the owner.'

'I believe he was something else?'

'He had a good political brain. He stared a party and held the balance of power in the British Parliament with his Irish MPs.'

'A woman brought him down.'

'Many forces were acting against him at the end and none greater than the RC church. Divorce wasn't popular in those days. I like to think he lost it all for the love of Kitty O'Shea.'

'Romantics will always be with us,' he said, turning off the motorway, on to the slip road and into the filling station. He stopped beside the diesel pump and an attendant came up to his window.

'You need to straighten out that mudguard, it's tearing hell out of the tyre,' he said, bending down to have a look at it.

'I will after you fill her up,' said Pat, searching his pockets for a credit card. He paid for a full tank of diesel and then parked in a vacant lot and got out the crowbar from under the coffin platform. He had to pull out the empty coffin before he could get to it and there were curious glances in his direction. The petrol pump attendant came over to help him. Pat wedged the crowbar in behind the bent fender and they both pulled it, nothing happened. Another man came over and with their combined weight the fender slowly pulled away from the tyre.

'You're going to need a new tyre when you get home and some expensive bodywork,' said the attendant.

'I will. The coffin is empty. Can I leave the hearse here for about an hour? I want to take a taxi into Dundalk.'

'No problem. I'll ring for a taxi and I won't let anyone go near the hearse while you're away,' said the attendant, going back to the filling station to phone.

'The taxi will take us to the Ballymascanlon hotel car park and we can have a look around. They may set a trap for us,' he said to Teresa, sitting back into the hearse to wait for the taxi.

'It's a good idea. I hope they don't recognise us in the taxi. I'm so scared I could cry,' she said, nervously lifting her handbag from the floor onto her knees.

'Don't forget we have a Garda escort,' he said, though aware that in any dealings with thugs bad things can happen in an instant. He should have been tougher with this girl and insisted that she stayed at home well away from those brutes.

To say the taxi driver was suspicious of them was an understatement. Who could blame him, picking up two passengers who were leaving behind them a coffin in a battered hearse on the forecourt? Pat felt sure the taxi driver was trying to figure out what scam they were up to. He didn't say a word throughout the journey.

The Garda escort sitting in the pickup, parked on the hard shoulder of the motorway, didn't even look up when the taxi passed.

Almost filled with Northern Ireland registered vehicles, only one van in the car park with two men sitting in it caught his attention. He had no doubt but they were waiting for the hearse. It was what he expected, and he could cope with that. He felt it was safe enough to drive in with the goods.

Back on the forecourt he paid the taxi driver and thanked the forecourt attendant. As the hearse passed the Garda escort they left the hard shoulder and drove in behind it.

'Am I glad to see the Garda. It's such a relief,' she said, sighing as some of the tension left her.

'They spotted us this time all right,' he said, 'but if we were real crooks we could have escaped in the taxi.'

The rest of the drive back to the Ballymascanlon hotel car park was uneventful. Pat stopped the hearse near the thugs' van and waited for them to come to him. After a few minutes one of them jumped out of the van and came over and handed him a large brown envelope.

'What's this?'

'The big man wants to talk to you,' he said, giving Pat a mobile phone.

'What now?' said Pat into the phone pretending he felt irritated and angry. He though it was the best way to deal with this gangster.

'Your money is in the envelope, is the seal broken?'

'They haven't touched it,' said Pat examining the wax seal on the envelope.

'Not if they value their lives.'

The phone went dead and Pat handed it back. He opened the tailgate and lifted the lid of the coffin. The newly designed lids were light and flat whereas the older ones were more ornate, and heavier with built up steps on the top. He lifted out the six bags of dope and gave them to the crooks. They loaded them into the van. Job completed, the bigger man challenged Pat,

'Tough guy did you think you'd get away with beating up two of our mates?' Aggressively he started to advance and Pat backed away from him.

Teresa saw Pat's face change. 'No, No,' she said,

'He stepped forward. Startled, the thug tried to run away but it was too late. Pat caught his wrists and, like a hammer thrower preparing to launch, he spun him round faster and faster until he built up enough momentum for the thug's feet to leave the ground. Then he let him go like the hammer thrower releases the weight. He flew through the air and crashed into the side of a parked van. Unconscious, he fell to the ground.

'Oh, my God,' said Teresa, crying. 'If this doesn't end soon he will kill someone.' The other crook held up his hands before Pat turned on him.

'I have no issues with you - I'm only the driver,' he said. Pat walked over to the unconscious crook, caught him by the collar and hauled him to the back of the van. His heels left a trail along the ground as if a monster snail had crawled along it. With a mighty heave he hoisted him into the passenger seat beside the van driver.

'Get going before I change my mind.'

The engine started with a deafening roar and they were off leaving behind a trail of black exhaust gas.

The change occurred instantly and the old Pat returned. He looked perplexed. 'Did it happen again?'

'Yes, but not much mayhem this time. It wasn't your fault they attacked you,' she said, getting out of the hearse and putting her arms around him to comfort him. One Garda came over.

'O' Neill wants to talk to you,' he said, holding out a phone to Pat.

'John O' Neill here, another crook bites the dust. You're carving out a reputation for yourself. Give the Garda the envelope, and I'll look after it.'

'OK, Pat said, wondering what damage he had inflicted on the thug.

'There's O'Neill at the far end of the car park,' said the Garda as he took the envelope and gave it to his colleague. They drove over to O'Neill and gave it to him and he left the car park.

'Strange how he didn't come over to talk to us. It's almost as if he doesn't want to involve himself,' Teresa said, putting away her phone.

'He'll have some good legal reason. We'd better get out of here,' he said getting back into the hearse and starting the engine.

Teresa planned it all in her head on the journey back to Dublin before falling into a tired sleep. She intended to go to Pearse Street Library the following morning and source out names of local therapists that could help him. She would make an appointment for him.

She expected a typical male reaction that it was a sign of weakness to have a mental health problem. He would not want to attend the session but she would get him there even if she had to drag him shouting and screaming.

The RTE evening news gave coverage to the Garda drug bust near the border led by Detective Inspector John O'Neill. It was probably an oversight when the newsreader stated the Gardaí had confiscated only two bags of drugs when Pat had handed over six bags to the crooks.

19

Teresa thought that Pat was driving along Merrion Road to his first therapy session in the basement flat of house Number 2002. She had arranged it by telephone.

That was the plan, but he wasn't following it. He didn't fancy the idea of therapy, so he decided to attend a hypnotherapist instead. She'd throw a fit if she knew what he was up to.

He was sitting in the VW outside a hypnotherapist's apartment in Sandymount, psyching himself up to making the short walk to the front door. He was sweating and his breathing was shallow. He could hear his heart pounding in his chest, and if he didn't keep control he would faint. Were there any diagnosed mental health cases in his family? He didn't know the answer to that as he never knew any of his relatives. He felt annoyed the news might get back to the island that he was a head banger attending a hypnotherapist.

Teresa had been sympathetic. She said the attacks were no big deal - a feeling of panic and anxiety worsened by his multiple personalities. She was in no doubt that therapy would get rid of all that, but she didn't even consider hypnosis. It troubled him that he didn't know what to expect in the hypnotic session.

He rang the doorbell, and a young woman came to answer it. Somehow he thought all hypnotherapists were men. If Teresa heard that she would ask, "Did he not know that women are doing it for themselves nowadays?"

'Hello, you're Pat. Come on in.'

From the hallway, she led him into a sparsely furnished room to his left, with an easy chair, chaise lounge, and an abstract picture hanging on the wall. The room was warm. Before the hypnotherapist sat down, she signalled to him to stretch out on the chaise lounge. He felt defenceless lying there, and he immediately sat up again.

'It's OK. No one is going to harm you. Please lie back down,' she said, putting her hand on his shoulder.

'Is this your first time seeing a hypnotherapist?'

'Yes.' He felt trapped. If he was out in the VW he would get as far away from this place as he could.

'Try to relax. People on their first visit to me are always a bit nervous, but there's no need to be. I think it's fear of the unknown.'

'Can you hypnotise everyone?' he asked, lying back down.

'Almost everyone, but I haven't met anyone yet I couldn't hypnotise. All that happens here is that I will put you into a deep relaxation. Then I will take you back to your childhood, and you can tell me all about it. It's called regression.'

'I can't remember anything about my childhood,' he said, beginning to feel sleepy from the heat of room. He should have told Teresa about the hypnotherapist, and she probably would have advised him against it.

'That's OK you must have suppressed memories in there. People in a hypnotic trance will not do or say anything they wouldn't normally do. We can stop the session any time you want. Now apart from trying to recover lost memories, what are the other reasons for coming to see me?'

'Anxiety, panic attacks and a multiple personality disorder,' he said. A few weeks ago and he wouldn't have known that, but Teresa had put words to his symptoms. He wondered if he should tell the hypnotherapist about Teresa but decided against it.

'It will amaze you how easy this is. Let's start.' Her voice lowered to a soothing purr.

'Close your eyes, the lids are feeling heavy and relaxed…Your head is a dead weight pushing back against the chaise lounge…It's the same for your neck, chest, arms, stomach, legs and right down to your toes…Your whole body is feeling so heavy that you can't even lift your arms…You are going deeper and deeper…You must always listen to my voice. Don't go to sleep now.'

He was feeling drowsy, but he would do his best to stay awake for her. The relaxing technique she was teaching him, he felt he could use

128

again. It would help him getting over to sleep on those nights he tossed and turned, grieving over the loss of his wife. That was another thing he should talk to her about. She was speaking again.

'I want you to imagine it's a lovely summer day, and you're on holiday at the seaside. You're strolling along a wooden deck and with each step you take you are getting more and more relaxed…

'A stair with ten steps leads down to a sandy beach, and you want to go down there. Stand on the first step and, as you start climbing down to the beach, count each step as you go. With each step you take, you are getting more and more relaxed…Tell me when you get to the last step. Again, you are going deeper and deeper into relaxation…'

'I'm on the last step.'

'Stand there for a few seconds and look around you…there's no hurry…You can see the sea ahead, and you can hear the sound of the waves gently lapping on the shore…Now step onto the sand. It's soft and warm on the soles of your feet, and feel it running down between your toes like powder. You are going down deeper and deeper, but you will always hear my voice. Stretch out on the sand, feel its heat all over your body. Rest on the sand for a while and relax…You see a small wispy cloudy drifting lazily across the sky. Go deeper and feel more and more relaxed, all your worries are drifting…*drifting away.* You're going deeper and deeper…"

She waited a few minutes and said, 'Starting with today, I want you to go back year by year not stopping at any particular incident to your childhood. Talk to me in an adult voice and tell me what you see and hear.'

Pat hesitated for a second and then spoke, more eloquently than usual.

'I'm walking along the corridor to the sitting room of the orphanage, holding the hand of my favourite nun. I'm dressed up for a special occasion to meet prospective foster parents. Lads that returned from fostering told us about how good it is, sweets and everything. Nevertheless, I'm feeling apprehensive. I don't want to leave the security of the only home I have ever known.

'In the sitting room two couples are waiting for our arrival, they are all smiles, and drinking tea from china cups. We never get this kind of crockery in the refectory. Three of the other orphans are there before us, and each couple will select the child they want to foster. I'm so scared now that I hope they don't want me. Maybe I should throw a tantrum fit. When the nun introduces me, I'm holding on to her long black skirt and peeking out from behind it.

'"This is Pat. He has the best memory of any child we have ever had in the orphanage, almost total recall. He scares us at times. He's no trouble at all. He gets on well with the other children, but prefers his own company. I would love to know what is going on inside that head of his. He came here to us as a baby, and he's my favourite child. While I hate to see him go, I think he would benefit most from living with a family, it might get him out of himself," she said, giving me a reassuring hug.

'The elderly couple looked at me smiling and said without any hesitation, "We'd love if you would come and live with us Pat." They put down their cups and saucers on the coffee table in front of them signalling a done deal.

'That was my introduction to Mr. and Mrs. Doherty from Galway City.'

The voice of the hypnotherapist cut in.

'You are going deeper and deeper getting more and…more relaxed. You will not feel disturbed by anything you see or say. You will always hear my voice. Continue.'

'They were the first parents I ever knew, and they were so kind to me. He was a banker in the Galway city and Mrs. D was a stay-at-home housewife. They sent me to a private fee paying school, and I enjoyed it. They spoilt me and life was good. Every Saturday and Sunday we drove up to the Great Southern Hotel in Eyre Square where we had lunch, and afterwards we always walked for a kilometre or two on the banks of the Corrib. As we strolled along dressed in our Sunday best he always talked to me. A heart-to-heart if you like, or maybe it was a father talking to the son he never had. He often repeated the message.

"Clothing defines the person. First impressions are important."

'Then he'd walk in silence for a few minutes before saying,

"When you meet someone for the first time they decide within thirty seconds whether they like you or not, and it's mostly based on what you're wearing. Don't ever forget that Pat."

'He'd straighten his tie when he said that. He could be a bit pompous at times, but his heart was in the right place, and I would have liked to have stayed with them forever, but that's not the way my life worked out.

'I'm a bit unclear about what happened next, but I think some rule or other decreed that foster children only stayed with their foster family for a specified time. Then if they were young enough they returned to the orphanage, and if not to some other form of institutional care. I think that was the reason I had to leave the Dohertys. They were inconsolable when the social worker came to take me away, and I can still hear them crying as I got into her car. They were good people.'

The hypnotherapist's voice cut in, 'Stay relaxed you are going deeper and deeper…'

'The social worker was kind to me. She took me home with her for a week. She probably broke all the rules of her profession by doing so.

'When I was with her, she was on the phone for hours trying to find a residential home in the Galway or Mayo area that would take me. They were all full and she finally had to admit defeat and accept a place in an industrial school for me. I was only seven or eight years old at the time, and I'm not sure about its location. It could have been in County Mayo or in County Galway.

'One morning she drove me there, and she cried all the way. She was muttering to herself, "I can't do this anymore. This is a sham. I'm going to quit and go to England. I have a sister in London."

'I saw the industrial school from a long way off, a large grey building sitting on top of a hill that looked like a prison. It was a landlord's house in former times, a vantage point to see out over the countryside. It had a row of thirty to forty large windows on the ground floor, slightly smaller ones on the second floor and tiny ones under the roof on the top floor.

'There was something foreboding about that building even from that faraway. The road followed the perimeter wall for about half a kilometre before we came to the entrance to the school. An iron gate decorated with scrolls and circles kept the inmates in, and I don't think the monks cared about keeping anyone out. From the gate lodge a monk appeared and unlocked the gates to let us in.

'The driveway, flanked by trees and arable land, curved for half a kilometre up to the house. Lads were working in the fields dressed in what I now know were their standard industrial school gear - blue shirts, corduroy trousers, and hobnailed boots. The tractor drivers and supervisors were in the main brothers supported by a few lay people.'

Pats phone rang. He jumped up from the couch confused and startled. For a few seconds, he couldn't work out where he was. It all came back to him. To see who was calling, he took his mobile phone from his pocket. There was no caller ID and that told him a lot. He didn't want to appear curt to the hypnotherapist, and he said a respectful, 'Hello.'

'Get down to the dock tomorrow morning and someone will meet you at the gate. Deliver to the same place in Dundalk and leave the keys in the artic's ignition.'

The phone went dead but Pat pretended he was still talking to the other person on the end of the line.

'Thanks for that, bye.'

'That was my fault. I should have told you to switch off the phone before the session started,' she said, leaving her chair and coming over to stand beside him. Suddenly, she tapped him hard on the arm, and said, 'Sleep'

He went back into a deep trance.

'You are letting go going down deeper and deeper and feeling more and more relaxed...Tell me more about the industrial school, continue from where you left off.'

'A prefect was waiting at the reception desk to take us to the Brother Superior's office, up a flight of stairs to the first floor. As you would expect it was a large corner office. That's always where the most powerful person in any organisation sits. Are we not tribal or what?

'He greeted us warmly with a handshake. A bent old man racked with arthritis with a long mane of grey hair. He exchanged pleasantries and then turned to me, although he was really talking to the Social Worker. It was all designed to impress her as I don't think anyone would talk to a child that way.'

"Welcome to our school, Pat, and I hope you will have a successful time here. The primary object of the school is to rehabilitate boys who, one way or another, are out of control. Many have indeed broken the law, and because they are children, they avoided a prison sentence. We are their prisons."

"Our regime is strict and maybe a bit harsh. I think there must be better ways of dealing with these lads, but we haven't discovered it yet. It's not a suitable place for an orphan who hasn't broken any laws but then that's what we have ended up with.

"If I had the power, I would change it in a heartbeat. We will do our best to make you feel at home Pat and come and talk to me any time. My door is always open."

'In saying his goodbyes to the social worker he said, "I'm retiring in a few weeks. This job has got too much for me, and I'm destined for a retirement home with other crocked out brothers. What a prospect." Then he smiled and said, "There's always the good Lord. I probably won't see you again so the best of luck."

'With tears in her eyes, the social worker hugged and kissed me, and then she was gone. They were all gone - everyone I knew in the whole world, and I was alone and deserted. I felt so small and defenceless. I could have cried and cried, but they didn't give me time to do that.'

The hypnotherapist's voice cut in again. 'You are going down deeper and deeper, more and more relaxed...'

She waited for a few minutes and said, 'Go back in your memory to the industrial school, and again talk to me in an adult voice and not as you were at time, just a child.'

'I was now part of a well-rehearsed system and this was the first day's induction. They didn't take me back to the Superior's office but to a dorm where I would live with thirty other orphans, and they allocated a bunk to me. They took away my case filled with treats from the Dohertys, and it felt like I was losing part of myself. The only reminders of my past life were memories, which were shaky at the best of times.

'Years later I wondered if being with the Dohertys had been real or imagined I had nothing tangible that connected me back to them; and if they were real why did they not come and visit me?

'Next was the tailoring workshop where rows of lads were sitting crossed legged on tables making suits and shirts. The younger lads were sewing the buttons on garments. The brother in charge looked at me over his glasses, perched precariously on the tip of his nose.

"What have we got here - a new lad? He's small for his age unless I have guessed his age wrong. We'd better kit him out," he said, taking a tape from around his neck and measuring me. He then selected a suit, short trousers, jacket and two shirts from a rack.

"That's what you wear from this day forward. Good luck in here," he said, ushering us out the door. So many people were wishing me good luck that I felt I couldn't possibly go wrong. Outside the prefect was giving me advice.

"Keep your fecking nose clean and watch your back in here. Don't join any bloody gangs or you could get the daylights knocked out of you." he said, leading me to the next workshop, the shoemakers. The chief as the lads called him was a middle-aged lay man with a big smile on his face.

"How are you doing young fella, we'll soon get you kitted out with shoes and socks in here. You don't know what size you are? OK then, try these on and make sure there is plenty room at the toes."

'I pulled on the long socks and they came to my knees and then the boots. The leather was rough but there was plenty of room to wriggle my feet inside. The shoemaker pressed his fingers around the boot until he found my toes.

"They should be OK, there's enough space for your feet to grow but if you get any blister come back to me young fella."

'The prefect took me on a tour of all the other workshops, the engineering shop for training the lads in fabrication, fitting, turning and welding. The next visit was to the construction workshops for teaching electrical work, carpentry, joinery, bricklaying, plumbing and plastering. The list of trades they offered seemed endless. For additional space they had built Nissen huts in the yard for miscellaneous crafts like silversmithing, jewellery, printing, coffin making, laundry and bakery. Much later I got my first introduction to coffin making. The prefect was talking again.

"I'm in this hell hole for seven years for taking a bag of crisps from a shop. I don't think it would be any fecking worst if I robbed a bank or killed some auld fella.'

"Toe the line and, don't answer back or they'll flay you alive. Those bloody canes would cut strips of you. If you raise your hand or show that your mad at them you're a dead man. Some lads have died in here and no one gives a damn about them. Always look down at the fecking ground when they talk to you. Don't tell them I told you all this or I'm a marked man."

'He was scaring me witless and I resolved never to show any anger. For the many years I was in the reform school, I forced myself to look as docile as a newborn lamb on the outside. Inside I was like a raging bull at all the injustices I was suffering at the hands of the brothers.'

"In here, I've finished my electrical training, and they're looking for a contractor to take me on as an apprentice. After that, I want to get out of this fecking country as fast as I can. It never did anything for me and I'll never come back"

'Will they give me the training I want?'

"Fat chance of that, they'll shove you in anywhere they need someone."

'There was bitterness in his voice. We had reached the football fields by this time, and they seemed to stretch for miles with goal posts facing in different directions. I was tired and overwhelmed by it all, and I wanted to shut it out of mind and curl up in a ball somewhere safe, but I didn't have that option. I was getting more instructions from the prefect.'

"Here's what happens. You're up at seven in the morning, rush bare arsed for the lavatory where you do your business. Then it's a cold shower. It's first come first served in the showers. The last man in and the last man out gets a lash from the cane on his bare backside from the brother in charge. After that running along the cold concrete floors and stairs will soon fecking wake you up."

"You won't have much time to nurse the bumps on your arse until you're on your way for eight o'clock Mass and prayers in the Chapel. Then, hail rain or shine we march to the front square. The brother in charge must think he's an American drill sergeant like in the films with the way he bawls at us. It's fecking murder, and everyone gets blisters on their feet."

"Your class, the high infants, starts school at half past nine, and lunch for everyone is at half past twelve in the refectory. Believe me you won't get fat with the little they give you. At half past one the senior lads return to the workshops and for your crowd it's back to the classroom.

"After school you'll have an hour's sport - football, and hurling in the playing fields - and then prayers in the chapel before you get your dinner. The day is not over yet, there's another two hours of study and more prayers before you get to your bed. It's fecking hard at the start but you'll get used to it. Your best bet is to follow what the others are doing and you'll be O.K. Right, I'm going to take you to your classroom."

Pat's phone rang again. He didn't jump up this time but sleepily took it out of his pocket. It was Teresa calling.

'Hello, I expected you home. Where are you?'

'I'm still with the therapist.'

'Sorry about annoying you. I was worried that something had happened.'

'No I'm OK. I'll go straight home after the session.'

'Bye.'

The hypnotherapist stood up, 'Switch off the phone, Pat, we don't want to be disturbed again.'

He did as she asked, and she touched him lightly on the arm with her fingers, and said sharply, 'Sleep...take me back to the industrial school.'

'The classroom was old with green distemper peeling from the walls. The heating was a pot-bellied wood-burning stove in the corner of the room just behind the teacher's desk, and he got the most heat from it. The pupils sat two by two in the desks. The cast iron frames had seats and tops of pitch pine covered in ink stains.

'One of us, not considered the sharpest knife in the drawer had the job of keeping the stove filled with wood and coal from the stacks at the back of the school. We envied his freedom to move about the room and outside at will.

'Half way through that first afternoon I was feeling so tired that I nodded off to sleep. The brother walking up and down between the rows of desks saw what had happened. He came up behind me and hit me across the face with his open palm.

''Stay awake sleeping beauty,'' he said and caught me by the hair and banged my head off the desk a few times. A fistful of hair came away in his fingers.

'The pain was awful, my ear went deaf for the rest of the evening and I had a headache as well. I didn't cry, I was determined not to show weakness. After our evening meal we were back in the classroom for another two hours of reading and study. It was all too much for me, or indeed, for any child on their first day in such a place. I fell asleep at my desk again, and the boy beside me shook me by the shoulder and whispered, ''Wake up before he sees you.'' Too late, the brother came up behind me and, whacked me on the knuckles and across the shoulders with his cane.

''I have met your sort before, but I'll keep you awake,'' he said, giving me another lash on the arm. I cried and from then on I was terrified of the brothers. If one came near me I trembled.

'There were other shocking things going on.' After he said that his mind went blank and he couldn't remember what the terrible stuff was.

'You must stay relaxed, go deeper...deeper and deeper...you will always hear my voice. Tell me about those shocking things.'

'It's all out in the open now about how the brothers abused, and raped the children in their care. I was one of those children.'

Pat started to cry like a child and the hypnotherapist did not intervene. Minutes passed before he started talking again.

'We had dim lights in the dorms. Every night I curled up with fear as a dark figure of a brother moved silently between our beds selecting an unfortunate child for mistreatment. I can still hear the nightly whimpering of those abused and abandoned children. At other times a brother would take one of us to his room and abuse us there. Not all of the brothers were like that but a lot of them were. For me the industrial school was the nearest thing to hell upon earth.

'The years went by and I learned to stay out of trouble, and comply in every way with the brother's harsh regime, but there was no way to escape their sexual advances.

'A vacancy came up in the coffin making and, while it wasn't the type of training I wanted, I had no choice but to take it. Strange the way things turn out, coffin making turned out to be my salvation and it's now the way I earn a living.'

He had a strong compulsion to tell her everything, including importing drugs, but he didn't. Even hypnotised he had some control over what he said.

'The state paid for our cheap coffins to bury people who didn't have next of kin to look after their funeral arrangements. The undertakers who specialised in this side of the business bought the coffins directly from the brothers, and I'm sure it benefited both parties money wise. I think I don't want to say anything more about the sexual abuse.

'My days in the institution stretched into weeks and months and finally into years but the abuse didn't stop. Why should it. Forgiveness for the brothers was no farther away than the confession box. They told their sins to the priests and, given absolution and were free to abuse again and yet again. "Whose sins you shall forgive they are forgiven and whose sins you shall retain they are retained."

'I became institutionalised, and had developed a pathological fear of leaving the industrial school. The brothers reinforced my fear of abandonment and isolation. They told me that I was on my own from the day I walked out through the front gates for the last time to take up a job. There was no coming back to the school. Maybe they were trying to instil in us the idea of being independent but I don't know. It had the direct opposite effect on me. I felt it was a terrifying prospect, with no parents, brothers, sisters, uncles or aunts or anybody else to fall back on.

'I'm sure I wasn't alone in my thinking. I expect all the orphans were probably frightened of what they thought the outside world had in store for us. Anyway, because of my age, I knew I would have to soon leave the place.

'Finally it was the day for my departure. The coffin shop supervisor came to talk to me as I was fitting the lid moulding to a coffin. It was apt, as it was the final act before the coffin went to the polishing shop. He was a likeable lay man with little respect for the brothers. He said to me, "Pat, we have an elderly husband and his wife with us from Achill Island. They have no family. They are looking for a lad to adopt and train into their undertaking business and later hand it over to him. It's a great opportunity and I've recommended you for the job. Come with me until you meet them."

'Will I change out of my overalls?'

"No, you're grand. It will let them see you're not afraid of a bit of work."

'We went along to the lounge where the elderly couple were drinking tea and waiting for us. I warmed to them immediately, they were the parents I never had, and I could see that they liked me as well. The supervisor introduced me.

"This is Pat. He's a bit small for his age, but he's the best worker I have."

"It's good to meet you, Pat. I'm not that tall myself and it never made any difference to my life. We hope you will come with us to the island and that you'll be happy there."

'I would like to go with you, sir,' I said and that was the first conversation I had with the man I'm proud to call father.

'The supervisor was talking again.

"Pat is slow with reading and writing but he is OK with numbers. He has an extraordinarily good memory, just about remembers everything. We have never seen anything like it."

"That's all right. I'm not that brilliant at paperwork myself. We have a girl who runs our small office and we don't have to worry about it."

"Do you want Pat to go with you today or maybe you would rather call back for him another day?'"

"If it's OK with Pat we would like to take him with us today. It's a long drive from the island to Galway and we would prefer to do this in one trip. Aha! I must be getting old. We definitely need you Pat."

'Much to my astonishment I heard myself saying, 'I'll come with you today.' That was the start of my new life or perhaps I should say the start of my real life although my head was never fully in the right place.

'After I settled in on the island, my adoptive dad arranged for me to return to school, this time to the Franciscan monks. With their sincerity and religious commitment they didn't ill-treat anyone. When my adoptive parents died, I inherited the business and I am now the only undertaker on the island.

Years later I heard on the radio that the brother that abused me most had died. Death suits some people. They buried him with full church honours; I almost said full military honours. They had a concelebrated mass before his funeral and a number of bishops attended. Now that I'm on a military theme I think of the bishops as Church Generals in full military dress uniforms, down to their ceremonial sword, the crosier. With a crooked handle it's symbolic of the shepherd staff for looking after his sheep and the bishop for caring for his flock.'

'Stay relaxed Pat, you are going deeper and deeper…into relaxation…lying there on the powdery sand watching the lazy waves come in and go out, and bothering no one…Down deeper….*Deeper and deeper.*

'To survive in the industrial school you repressed all those feelings of anger and resentment, but they emerged as a multiple personality disorder. We are going to get rid of that here and now. First, you must understand that it is OK for you to have feelings of anger and aggression. They are part of you and everyone else for that matter.

'You must recognise and accept the other part of your personality and take ownership of the harmful feelings and destructive actions that come with it. I want to teach you to take control over your vicious impulses. From now you will be in control of your total personality and whenever you clench your fist all your negative thoughts and actions will evaporate and not cause any more trouble. Do it now for practice.'

Pat closed his fist and for the first time became aware of his other combative personality, but now he had control of it.

The hypnotherapist was talking, 'Get up off the sand and walk to the bottom step of the stairs leading up from the beach. Climb the stairs slowly and with each step you are becoming more and more awake. Your worries have melted away and you feel happy and relaxed. Keep on climbing. When you reach the top step open your eyes. You are fully awake and ready to get on with your life. To reinforce the work we did today I want you to come back for a few more visits. What about the same time next week?'

'Yes that fine,' he said and paid the hypnotherapist. He left her house but he wasn't fully back to himself. He felt fuzzy like someone was squeezing his head in a vice. It was no wonder he felt out of sorts after that session. It reminded him of going to confession but instead of telling your sins you talked about the bad things that happened in your life. On the way out the flowers and trees in the garden were brighter than before and flashing like strobe lights. He was staggering without realising it and almost walked into the gate post. He fumbled with the keys before getting the car door open, and sat into the driver's seat but couldn't figure out how to start the car, he was still in a bit of a dream. Now an aura of shimmering light had formed around everything he looked at. None of it was right, he was either in a parallel universe or losing his mind. He tried to call Teresa but couldn't use the phone: it slipped out of his hand when he fell into a deep sleep. An hour later he woke and as far as he could tell he was back to normal. He drove back to the funeral parlour.

20

Teresa heard Pat's footsteps on the stairs and she switched on the high-tech coffee-maker with its plethora of controls and dials. There might even be a gizmo on it that recognised footsteps on the stairs that turned it on automatically. She had given up trying to understand the coffee-maker's many functions and had simply resorted to switch it on and off at the wall.

'Hi,' Pat said from the doorway.

'Hi yourself, how did the therapy go?'

'It didn't, I chickened out and went to see a hypnotherapist instead.'

She looked at him quizzically, from her seat at the island in the middle of the kitchen.

'Sit down and I'll pour you a cup, and then you can tell me all about it,' she said, filling his cup and adding milk. He sat on one of the designer stools chosen by his wife when they refurbished the apartment. He took a sip before answering.

'I bet you're furious, and I can't blame you. Finding a therapist for me was difficult enough, and I've thrown it back in your face.'

'No nothing like that. I'm pleased that you made your own choices. It's taking control of your life, and that's a positive. The effects aren't permanent. You'll need the other therapist as well but it's a start and I want to hear about what happened.'

'The hypnotherapist relaxed me down into a trance and all my childhood memories came flooding back. I'm still reeling from the shock of some of it.'

He told her about the industrial school, and the daily sexual abuse by the brothers, and how the hypnotherapist had shown him a method of dealing with his other personality.

'I think I would like to find out more about my real parents,' he said.

Teresa looked shocked, and in tears at what he had told her.

'Pat, I'm sorry that you had to suffer so much. When I think of myself, all I went through was just discomfort in comparison to your torment. I will help you to find out who your parents are.'

She got up from the table came over to him. Hugging him, she put her arms around him, and held his head tight to her chest. They were like that for some time until he gently pushed her away and said, 'Right, back to the present, it's time to move on. The drug dealers want me to take an artic to Dundalk tomorrow. I'm to collect it down in the port. To get me back here again, I need you to follow in the VW. It's going to be an early start.'

It took Teresa a while to respond. She was coming to terms with what he told her, and she was full of sympathy for him. While she tried to understand his suffering, he was the only one who knew the tortures he had been through. From her experience of life, he would need years of help to get his head right. Even with that, he probably would never banish from memory the ill-treatment he received at the hands of the brothers. She forced herself back to the present.

'Yes that's OK. What's in the truck?'

'I talked to O'Neill and he thinks it's a container of cigarettes. Illegal imports of course.'

The next day they were on the road early. With Teresa driving, they crossed the toll bridge before seven in the morning, and they took the right fork from the roundabout past the Point Theatre.

'Have you ever been in that place?' he asked, pointing to the building that still looked more like a warehouse than a theatre.

'Yes, I have. Hasn't everyone seen Riverdance?' she said, braking hard to allow a car with four teenagers to cut in ahead of them.

'I bet they're rushing home after a night on the town. They'll get an earful from the parents for being out all night,' she said, braking again to stay well back from them.

'If they don't kill themselves before they get home with the way they're driving. Marie took me to Riverdance. I enjoyed it but the thunderous noise of so many feet thumping down onto the stage together almost blotted out the music.'

'The heavy Irish dancing shoes they wear caused that. We had special light ones, pumps we called them in the Lido, and they never made a sound.'

'So that's what the noise was about. You learn something every day. Good Lord, I'm sounding like my father. That's exactly what he would have said.'

'Where do I go from here?' said Teresa, slowing to prepare for a change in direction. As if on cue in a TV drama, the cars behind started to hoot their horns.

'When did the Irish start to get so impatient? Can they not see that I don't know where I'm going?'

'The Vikings gave us that,' said Pat with a grin. 'Slow at the next set of traffic lights and take the right turn and that's the entrance to the port and docks.'

She was in the wrong traffic lane and a cacophony of sound greeted her as she cut across the traffic. One angry driver was shouting at her through his open window, and he wasn't saying prayers. Pat clenched his fist as the hypnotherapist had told him, and to his surprise remained calm. The implanted hypnotic suggestions were working. He was in control of his anger and his other destructive self. For now, at least.

'They wouldn't do anything like that in the USA or somebody might pull a gun and blow their head off, although at the minute Dublin is bad enough.'

'And other places as well but there is one city, Rome, where the drivers shout and roar at one another all the time,' she said.

'With all the tripping you are doing around Dublin you are ready for a job as a tour guide,' he said jokingly.

'I wish. I'd have a better chance of showing people around Belfast,' she said as a security guard jumped out of a Jeep. He stepped out in front of them, and signalled them to stop. He was the only sign of life about the place.

'Another criminal in a 4X4 using a respectable job as a cover up. What is it about 4X4s and gangsters?' said Pat.

'They think it makes them look tougher, and the jury is still out on security guards. They are not all altar boys,' she said, pulling up alongside him.

She rolled down the window expecting him to come over to talk to them. He didn't, but walked suspiciously around the VW inspecting it from every angle before coming to the window. He unhooked his radio, switched it on and tested it before bending down to look into the car.

'What's your business in the port?

'I'm here to collect an artic truck, and they told me you know all about it,' said Pat, leaning across Teresa to talk to him.

'What's your name?'

'I'm known as the Coffin Maker.'

'Wait a minute.' He walked a bit away from them, dialled a number on his mobile and put it to his ear. The conversation was a short one, and he closed down the phone and put it into his pocket.

'I was expecting a hearse and there was no mention of a woman. She'll have to stay here in the car. Come on.'

'Will you be OK on your own?' Pat asked as he opened the VW door.

'Yes I'll be fine but be careful out there. It might be a set-up. You can't trust this lot,' she said, placing her hand on his arm.

'Don't worry, I'll be careful,' he said, pulling on his gloves, not intending to leave fingerprints on anything he handled. There shouldn't be a problem with O'Neill backing him, but he felt safer doing it. He got out of the VW and climbing up into the front passenger seat of the Jeep. Before he had time to fasten the safety belt, the Jeep jerked forward as the driver released the clutch too quickly. They were off with wheel spin, burning rubber and skid marks on the road. It was a show of machismo which didn't impress Pat. He had seen it all before.

When the Jeep drove away, Teresa felt vulnerable sitting there on her own in the car. She locked the doors and wound down the passenger window a tiny bit to let air in. Most people would describe her as an independent and resourceful person, well able to take care of herself but that didn't apply any more. She needed Pat, and she was missing his reassuring presence already. She had only known him for a short time, but she would now find it impossible to live without him. His absence was like having part of herself missing.

From all her many experiences in life, and some of them were strange, she had always taken away something positive. Her time in the convent as a nun was no exception. In the mornings the nuns, although not compelled to do so, spent fifteen to twenty minutes in their rooms contemplating on a recommended passage from the bible. It was such a relaxing exercise that after a few minutes she invariably fell fast asleep.

She had changed the practice over the years and had progressed to a form of Christian meditation using a mantra, 'Mar-an-athâ'. Almost any word would do, and one of her other choices was 'Peace.' The technique was to repeat it over and again without effort silently in her head for twenty minutes night and morning. If another thought intruded, she would gently shoo it away and return to the mantra.

She was so concerned for Pat's safety that anxiety was getting the better of her. She was hyperventilating and her forehead was damp with sweat while the rest of her body was freezing. Her hands were shaking and she was sobbing quietly, if there was ever a time she needed to relax this was it. In her present state, she was no good to Pat or anyone else. She couldn't settle into traditional meditation but decided to try a waking mantra. The only one she knew of was the Buddhist, 'om mani padme hum' which is a holy prayer for compassion and enlightenment. She repeated it over and again and within minutes, she was fast asleep.

Sitting rigid in the driver's seat, the criminal security guard stared straight ahead and ignored Pat. On this trip, he was certain there wouldn't be much conversation. He was watching out for any tricks, and at the first sign of trouble he would make a run for it. He regretted not bringing the pistol with him. Not that he wanted to shoot anyone but, its presence was often enough of a deterrent, but he was not buying into the notion that guns were peacemakers.

The docks were much bigger than he thought, and it surprised him to find it set out into streets with nameplates. They were going further into the dockland and he was committing to memory every twist and turn, in case he had to get out in a hurry. It was a perfect spot for a murder. A weighted body dumped in one of the deep water harbours would disappear forever, and there was plenty of scrap iron lying around fit for the purpose. It was not a comforting thought.

Until a security gate blocked their path, he hadn't realised that up to now they were only driving on the fringe of the dockland. They hadn't entered the port proper yet. The security guard used his identity card to gain admittance, and they drove on through the gates. They automatically closed behind them. From the names on the warehouses, this was an area rented by some of the biggest retailers in the country. Here they stored their imports unloaded from cargo ships, and there must be millions of Euros worth of goods in those warehouses, ready for the taking. In that context strict security made sense except they were not getting that. If the other security guards were anything like this one, everything was at risk. He wouldn't be surprised if a lot of stock vanished.

The large cylindrical tanks of the major oil companies stood at the end of the docks. From a distance, they looked like gasometers of yesteryear. They were a landmark from where Pat had built a plan in his head of the rest of the dockland area. He didn't feel so nervous now he knew exactly where he was.

With a handbrake turn the security guard brought the Jeep to a screeching halt outside the compound of parked artic tractor units. The business end of the truck you might say; the cab that housed the engine and gearbox to which they could attach all kinds of trailers to carry container.

He unlocked the gate and gestured towards a North of Ireland registered artic with two containers attached. They hadn't told Pat about the extra container and with the little experience he had of driving artics this was going to be a difficult job for him.

'That's the load, get it out of here.'

Pat didn't answer and didn't look at the crook when he talked to him. It was like a game of chicken. Neither of them was going to show the first signs of weakness.

Pat climbed into the cab of what was likely a stolen truck and turned the ignition key. The starter motor turned and whined, but the engine didn't start. He tried it a few more times without success. This engine wasn't going to fire up, and he started to look for the problem.

The obvious was an empty fuel tank but the gauge was showing three-quarters full. The battery seemed OK. It was turning the starter motor but maybe not fast enough. He could ask the security guard to attach jump leads if he had them, to give the battery a boost. Failing that it could be a problem with the fuel pump or an airlock in the supply line. Anything more serious than that like a diesel pump or injector failure, he couldn't do anything about out here. He opened the cab door and shouted to the security guard,

'We have a buggered engine. Have you jump leads?'

He wasn't expecting a reply, and he didn't get one. He climbed down from the cab and walked a short distance away to phone Teresa and to let her know about the delay.

'Who the hell are you calling?

Pat didn't reply but felt concerned when Teresa didn't answer her phone. It probably was in the bottom of her handbag, and she didn't hear it ringing, or she might be asleep. He didn't want to think about the other alternative that some harm had come to her.

The security guard connected the Jeep and truck batteries with the jump leads. The truck still didn't start.

'Check the fuel line for an air lock,' said Pat, turning his back to the security guard. He decided to call O'Neill to get the Gardaí to check on Teresa. He shouldn't have taken orders from this mobster and insisted on bringing her along with them. He wouldn't make that mistake again. He dialled the Pearse Street Garda station and a female voice answered.

'Can I speak to Detective O'Neill?'

'Who's' calling?'

'The Coffin Maker.'

'Hold on a minute and I'll put you through.'

'O'Neill.'

'Hi John, Pat here.'

'Where are you?'

'In the Port, the artic isn't starting. I left Teresa in the VW near the way into the port. She's not answering her mobile. Can you send someone to check on her?'

'Hold on a sec.' Pat could hear him talking on the radio.

'A squad car will be with her in about ten minutes. I'll call you back.'

The security guard disconnected the fuel line from the filter and bent down into the engine bay to suck diesel from the tank. Within seconds his mouth was full of diesel. He spat it out and rubbed his sleeve across his mouth to clean it away. He was sucking diesel all right, as the Americans say and that was proof there was no blockage in fuel line. They had a big problem, and this artic wasn't going anywhere in a hurry.

The security guard dialled a number on his mobile, and talked for a few minutes. He snapped the jump leads from the batteries and banged down the bonnets. He searched among the parked trucks until he found what he was looking for, a left-hand drive, foreign registered artic used for hauling containers around the yard. It had Latvian stickers on the windscreen.

Pat felt dismayed by the state of it. Definitely not a Mack truck - more like something rescued from a scrap yard. With a grinding sound and a belch of black exhaust smoke the engine fired and, despite sounding rough, continued to turn over. If this artic managed to get him to Dundalk it would be as big a miracle as the apparition at Knock. Pat's phone rang.

'O' Neill here, the squad car is with her now. She's OK. She just fell asleep. Did the artic start?'

'Thanks for doing that, John. We had to change to a left-hand drive, foreign banger. It's not running well.'

'We'll have someone close behind you.'

'OK, John.'

Pat's phone went dead.

The security guard set about connecting the Latvian tractor unit to the containers bound for Dundalk. Pat wondered if he had done the job correctly or not, as he didn't seem to know much about connecting the towing linkage. He felt anxious in case one of the containers came adrift on the motorway, and that would cause a hell of an accident.

'Get in and follow me,' he said with urgency in his voice. He wasn't as confident now. The possibility of getting caught increased the longer they stayed in the port. The drug dealers must have something big on this fella to justify the risk he was taking, or perhaps it was just that he was greedy for money. Pat ignored him; the link between tractor and trailers was still worrying him. Even though, he didn't know how it worked, he decided to inspect the connection, and as far as he could tell it looked all right.

Pat climbed into the cab and was almost sick with the smell of, vomit, urine, stale beer, and rotting food. It would take a power washer to clean this lot out. He went to open the window but the winder didn't work. The truck manufacturers might have made the window from safety glass. If that was the case it would break into small granular pieces that wouldn't cause him harm when he smashed it. He hit the glass a sharp blow with his elbow, and as expected it shattered and sprayed glass particles out on the roadway. The fresh gust of air was a welcome relief, and a deep breath took away some of his nausea.

He engaged first gear of the semi-automatic gearbox, and an unmerciful whine came from it. They used this truck for more than taking an old Mormon lady to church on Sundays. With the accelerator pedal fully to the floor the unit lurched forward ungainly as he followed the Jeep towards the exit of the port.

Teresa got a fright, when the Ban Garda tapped on the VW window. Startled, she woke from a deep meditation sleep, and she felt confused for a few minutes, and couldn't figure out where she was. Good Lord something awful had happened. The drug dealers must have shot Pat. The Ban Garda reassured her.

'He's OK there's a delay. They can't start the truck, but he'll be along shortly,' she said. Teresa recognised her as one of the Gardaí that had previously escorted them.

'Thanks for letting me know.'

The Ban Garda smiled and within minutes the squad car disappeared. She turned the VW around, facing out of the port. She didn't have long to wait before she heard the truck coming. It appeared around the corner of a warehouse swaying all over the place and belching black smoke from the vertical exhaust pipe sticking up behind the cab. The containers looked in danger of toppling over at any minute.

Pat intended turning on the headlights, and dipping them to let her know he was driving through without stopping. When he rotated the switch for the lights nothing happened - no horn, wipers or indicators either. Had this bloody heap of garbage any electrics at all?

He tried to halt next to the VW, but when he pressed on the brake pedal the rig started to drift sideways. One or more of the brakes were grabbing, it was likely the security guard hadn't connected the brake lines from the truck to the trailer. It was a death trap, and he should park it and get as far away from it as he could, but he wasn't going to do that. He would see this through to the end.

Through the smashed window, he gestured to Teresa to follow him. He took the slip road from the port to the motorway and on to the roundabout. He carved up a few car drivers, forcing them out of his way. That didn't impress them, and they shouted obscenities, blew their horns and waved their fists at him. There was no choice driving this rig. On the motorway he relaxed a bit, and it was all straight ahead to Dundalk. He wouldn't be sorry to see the back or this rig.

Thankfully, it had a rear-view mirror, and he could see the VW following close behind and in the distance the flat bed truck, his Garda escort. Writing a snag list for this truck would fill a book or two as another problem emerged. The engine was misfiring on one or more cylinders, and it sounding rough, even with the accelerator pedal pushed to floor, he moved at a crawling pace. It was going to be a slow trip to Dundalk.

On the first steep incline on the motorway, the gear lever jumped out of forward drive, and the rig started to roll back. Pat acted quickly and, using both hands, he forced the lever back into gear producing a horrendous rasping sound from the gearbox. Great; for the rest of the journey to Dundalk he would have to hold the lever in gear with his left-hand while steering with his right.

He noticed a white van driving erratically, about to join the motorway ahead of him. He reckoned it would get to the junction before he did, and that would prevent it getting entangled with the truck.

That was the theory, but unfortunately it didn't work out that way. Without warning as he came up the junction the van came at him from the slip road. He tried to avoid a collision by jumping on the brakes and spinning the steering wheel. The brakes pulled the rig sideways. It jack-knifed and the white van crashed into it head on.

He heard the shearing noise of crumbing metal as the van hit the front bumper. The seat belt didn't hold him and, flung forward, his forehead hit the windscreen. The impact threw him back against the headrest, and he hit it hard. His neck and shoulders took the brunt of the blow, and he felt a searing pain in the back of his head. The last he saw before passing out was a large blood spatter on the shattered windscreen.

'Pat are you OK, answer me?' Teresa was shouting up at him from the roadway.

'I'm fine.' He didn't feel fine at all. His head was sore and spinning, and the broken windscreen was emitting shimmering circles of blue and gold. He closed his eyes and gradually he began to feel better as his head settled. He might have whiplash or something, but he decided he was well enough to carry on.

'I'll get down in a minute,' he said to Teresa. Their escorting Ban Garda joined her, looking up at him. He put his feet together and kicked out the windscreen. He climbed down and felt dizzy when he stepped on to the road; he staggered a bit. They were both looking at him with concern.

'Are you sure you're OK?' asked Teresa, she needed reassurance.

'Yes, I'm just a bit dizzy, but it'll go in a minute.' He should have added, I hope.

'You might need a check-up in hospital,' said Teresa, who didn't seem convinced that he was OK. The Gardaí were giving the van driver a breath test. He was sitting in the back seat of the squad car with his legs hanging out.

'You're in the clear. It wasn't your fault. The van driver looks blind drunk,' said the Ban Garda, unclipping her phone from her shoulder lapel. She listened and said, 'All right I'll tell him.'

'The local Garda have taken over. They are charging the van with drunken driving, and since there aren't any injuries, they'll be nothing more about it. O'Neill wants you to finish your journey and make the delivery.'

She left them and walked back to the flat bed truck, waiting for him to get underway again.

'Are you ready for this Pat?' asked Teresa, holding his arm, and looking at him.

'We'll finish what we started,' he said, that was if he could. He was feeling ropey and if only he could lie down he would.

The fire brigade had pulled the van away to the side of the motorway, and he went to the front of the truck to inspect the damage. It had lots of bent and torn panels, but there was nothing that would stop it driving. Reluctantly, he climbed into the cab and started the engine. Manoeuvring forward and back a few times he got the rig straightened out and headed down the motorway towards Dundalk. He left behind him a line of flashing vehicles, Garda cars, an ambulance and a fire engine. He was lucky that one of the containers hadn't burst open and covered the roadway with cigarettes. Funny, with the excitement of the crash that was something he hadn't thought about.

It wouldn't take a motor mechanic to know there was something seriously wrong with the steering. In the crash, the left-hand side of the rig had taken the brunt of the smash and that was where the problem was. Probably, a bent track rod and that wouldn't fix itself. He hoped to God it didn't drop off and leave him without control, a spectator as the rig ploughed into one of the fields by the roadside. After that he would need some luck if he didn't end up fitted with celestial wings. The rig was crawling along at no more than ten kilometres an hour, and Pat had a pain in his back from leaning over to keep the gear lever in drive, and a sore shoulder from struggling with the steering.

Regardless of what O'Neill wanted this was the last time he was going to drive a wreck like this. It was all getting a bit out of hand, and he was no nearer finding out the identity of the 'big fella.' Sometimes he felt O'Neill, in furthering his career, was happy to let this go on forever without a resolution. For the future Pat would take more control over what was happening and become less of a pawn, and more a player in solving this.

It was a close shave, but he managed to drive the rig into the car park without hitting the gateposts. He sat for a minute with his eyes closed to orientate himself and then climbed down from the cab. Teresa was waiting for him on the tarmac.

'Pat you look strained and exhausted.'

'That was a hard shift all right,' he said, rubbing his lower back to get rid of the pain and stiffness.

'Let me do that,' she said, going to massage his back.

'No that's OK – give my right shoulder a pummelling.'

With both hands, she started to knead his shoulders, as if she was mixing dough for a cake.

'That feels good,' he said, moving his shoulder as she worked on it.

One of the occupants got out of the van he had spotted earlier when they reconnoitred the car park. He came over to the rig and walked around it.

'You have made some bloody mess of this truck. You are one right arse hole.'

For a second Teresa saw Pat's face and posture change as his other personality appeared, but when he clenched his fist it vanished. The hypnosis had worked.   He turned, walked away and got in the passenger side of the VW; she sat in the driving seat.

'Pat did you black out when you hit your head off the windscreen?'

'I think so but only for a second.'

'I'm going to take you to a hospital, and I don't want a discussion about it. It's about your health and that's important.'

'OK, that's fine,' he said. With a sore neck and a splitting headache, he felt too tired to argue. He rested his head on the back of the seat and fell asleep.

He woke as Teresa parked in an ambulance space outside the casualty at St. Vincent's Hospital.

'You're awake, I thought you had died on me,' she said jokingly.

'No, I'm still here but only just.' He moved his head 'Ouch!' his neck was sore and stiff. A porter came rushing over.

'You can't park that car here. It's for ambulances only.'

'I'll only be a minute. This man was in a road accident.'

'Don't be long then.' The porter left them.

Pat regularly visited hospitals to collect corpses but this was the first time he was coming as a patient. The casualty receptionist was businesslike; she took his details and told them to take a seat in the waiting area until called. There were many people waiting.

'Mother of Divine we are going to be here all day with all those before us,' he said to Teresa, reading a copy of Woman's Own she had selected from a pile of magazines.

'They might get through them fast,' she said, knowing that it wasn't unusual to have to wait for anything up to six hours in a casualty. They called his name unexpectedly soon, and he and Teresa entered an office with a nurse sitting behind a desk.

'Hello, I'm the triage nurse, and I decide who gets attention first. The priority is head injury, chest pain and haemorrhage. You fit the profile.'

She examined him thoroughly and then everything moved fast. They asked Teresa to stay outside in the waiting room, and before he knew it, he was lying flat strapped to a trolley with a neck brace and polystyrene wedges jammed against his head. Immobilised he could hardly move a muscle; it was the most uncomfortable position he had ever experienced.

'I know it's unpleasant but this gives us time to set up a scan for your head and neck,' said a nurse before she hurried away to deal with another patient. It was an odd spot to be in. He could only look straight up at the ceiling and nothing to the left or right, or not even down at his toes. Anyone talking to him was just a voice, unless they bent right over him.

Time was beginning to drag, there was plenty of movement going on around him, but he was not part of it, just lying there. He was about to doze off when he sensed someone near him.

'Are you a' right?' asked an elderly man bending over him.

'I'm OK.' Trussed up like a turkey he must have looked anything but all right.

'I had an accident myself with a circular saw.' He held up his hand where Pat could see it and unrolled the bandage from his thumb. He had cut off half his thumb, and the rest was a ragged edge of flesh and bone. The sight made Pat nauseous. Prone on his back, he shouldn't allow himself to get sick, or he could easily choke on his own vomit.

'Bandage it up again. You need to keep it covered to stop infection,' said Pat, relieved when the thumb went out of sight.

'What age do you think I am?' said the voice. This usually came from someone who felt he looked younger than his chronological age. Pat couldn't see him very well, but he deducted twenty years from the age the voice sounded like.

'I'd say about sixty?'

'I'm eighty-six next birthday,' he said, and there was no mistaking the proud tone in his voice.

'When I retired, I turned my garage into a workshop. This is the second time the power saw caught me. A few years ago I cut of the tip of that thumb, and today I lost half of it. I was cutting up pieces for firewood, and I didn't know anything had happened until I say all the blood on the ceiling. It was flying off the saw blade. My son came into the garage and he fainted when he saw the blood. Young people nowadays are soft. He's fifty years old, but he's young enough to toughen up as he gets older. Do you think the blood will rust the saw blade before I get out of here?'

Pat didn't have time to answer before his trolley was on the move. 'You're going to x-ray for an MRI scan. It's like having a picture taken of the inside your head. Don't forget to smile,' said a voice with a laugh from behind him.

'I won't.'

It was a short journey from casualty to x-ray, and he was there in minutes. From what he could see of it, the MRI scanner looked like a two-metre long stainless steel cigar wide enough to hold a person. That's where he was going. Four people in masks were looking down at him and then on the count of three, eight pairs of hands moved him from the trolley to the scanner bed.

'Are you claustrophobic?' one of the techs asked.

'No.' Perhaps he should have said 'Yes.' The more he looked at where he was going to the more apprehensive he got. He heard the Japanese provide beds something like this in hotels. The unstated motto was to pack as many people as possible into a small space.

'What happens here is that you will be in the scanner for about twenty minutes and after ten minutes, we pull you out for a contrast injection. It's going to be noisy but that's normal. If you want out anytime let me know. Have you chromed cobalt dentures?'

'No dentures.'

They pushed him into the tunnel that was the MRI scanner, just broad enough for his shoulders. Brightly lit on the inside and the curved roof was inches away from his face. Piped music was feeding into the capsule, and he recognised Beethoven's fifth. That was something else that people didn't know about him - that he had a good ear for music, and almost perfect pitch.

'Are you OK in there?' The tech's voice came from somewhere above his head.

'I'm fine.' That was a lie, he felt like screaming, 'let me out of here,' but men didn't do that. You had to play the macho game, even if it killed you.

'Ok, prepare for the noise.'

The sound when it started blocked out the music and was like someone battering the outside of the scanner with a sledgehammer. He tried to distract himself by counting, one, two, three... The noise finally stopped and the tech said, 'We are going to pull you out and the nurse is going to give you the contrast injection.'

'It's going to feel warm going up your arm, but that's normal,' said the businesslike nurse.

'Right, it'll soon be all over,' said the tech, pushing him back into the machine where he had to endure another ten minutes. It seemed longer until the tech finally said, 'We are all done here,' pulling him out of the scanner. He was certain of something, the next time he had a scan, he would willingly accept the offer of tranquillisers. Eight hands moved him from the scanner bed back on to the trolley. 'We are going to take you to casualty to wait for the results,' said a voice from behind him.

Casualty was still bustling like Waterloo station with staff rushing around taking care of patients.

A nurse came to tell him the news, 'No permanent damage. You will need to keep wearing that neck brace for awhile. You have badly torn muscles.' She removed all the strapping and helped him to sit up.

'You're going to feel dizzy for a few minutes. I'll help you out to your wife or is she your girlfriend?'

'Girlfriend.'

She was right about the dizziness, and he was glad for her support. Teresa looked so worried, 'Are you OK, Pat?

'He'll live,' said the nurse, smiling and letting go of Pat's shoulder.

'Thanks for everything, nurse,' he said, and he meant it.

'No problem, that's what we are here for. Good luck.'

'Goodbye' they both said to the nurse.

'I'm so glad to have you back,' said Teresa, putting her arms around him.

'Me too,' he said.

21

Pat woke with a start. There was something wrong. He sat up in bed and listened for a few seconds, but there was no sound apart from Teresa breathing. It was likely the after-effects of hypnosis were making him jumpy. He was about to lie down again when he smelt burning rubber. He gently shook Teresa's arm to wake her, before rushing to the window. The VW beetle was blazing in the yard, and the flames were spreading to the wooden shed housing the Harley. He was just in time to see two hoodies scrambling over the back fence. He knew who they were, the same men who had driven through the show room window. Before hypnosis, his Hyde persona would have given chase, and put those crooks in the hospital. Thank God he had changed.

'Teresa, call the fire brigade.'

'What's wrong?'

'The VW is on fire, and it's spreading to the Harley shed.'

She grabbed the mobile phone from the bedside locker and dialling 112.

The fire officer had insisted on putting a large fire extinguisher in the morgue, and if Pat could get to it, he might prevent the fire from spreading until the fire-fighters arrived. While struggling to pull on his trousers, he tried to take the stairs two at a time but that wasn't a good idea. He stumbled, lost his balance, and fell headlong down the stairs landing heavily on his back. Winded, he lay there for a few minutes taking stock. He was alive and as far as he could tell everything was still in working order. This time he was lucky, he had heard of people breaking their neck from falling downstairs.

'I heard a bang, are you all right?'

Teresa was standing on top step looking down at him.

'I'm fine. I just tripped.'

It was technically true, but he didn't mention that he had fallen from the step she was standing on. With difficulty, he pulled on his trousers. With the way he was hurting, he probably had bruises all over.

'The fire brigade is on its way.'

'I'll let them in the back gate.'

He opened the door from the kitchen into the backyard. Too late, in the glow of the flames he saw a wire attached from the door handle to a petrol can sitting in the centre of the yard. The flash and bang were almost instantaneous, and the massive explosion sent flames high into the sky spreading debris across the yard. He though he heard the rushing sound of air before it lifted him off his feet and propelled him along the hallway. It was no soft landing. He thumped into a wall and ended spread-eagled on the concrete floor. Someone was praying for him; apart from a twisted ankle and cuts from flying glass, he was OK. That was the nearest he had come to his demise since entering the cloak-and-dagger world of the drug barons. He felt strange. His eyes were misting over, and then it was darkness.

Teresa was kneeling beside him, holding his hand when he regained consciousness. He was lying on a stretcher in the kitchen with a drip in his arm and a paramedic in a green uniform holding a resuscitation kit.

'Thank God you're back. I thought you were dead,' she said crying, and kissing him lightly on the cheek.

'I'm Ok. It's just a fainting fit.'

Out of the corner of his eye, he saw the now familiar figure of the Ban Garda that escorted them to Dundalk, leaving the yard without speaking to anyone.

'Did you hit your head?' the paramedic asked.

'No, just my back, and I think I have sprained my ankle.'

'Have you pain anywhere else?'

'No, just bandage the ankle.'

'The ambulance is outside. I would like to get you to the hospital for a scan on your head and neck,' said the paramedic as he cut open Pat's trouser leg with scissors. It was fortunate that he had on a matching pair of socks without holes, but it annoyed him the paramedic was destroying a good pair of trousers. He couldn't see the need for that; for goodness sake it was only his ankle hurting.

'I have a lot to do today. I don't need a scan, and I'll be as right as rain when you fix up my ankle.'

'I think you should go to the hospital, just for a check-up,' said Teresa, looking concerned.

'I'll go tomorrow if I'm not feeling well.'

The paramedic bandaged Pat's ankle, and gave him a walking stick for support from the ambulance.

'If you feel unwell, don't hesitate to come in. That's what the hospital is for.'

'I will, and thanks for the help.'

The ambulance moved off and the paramedic on his motorcycle followed them.

'Are you sure that you are OK?' asked Teresa.

'I'm fine. Give me a hand to get up.'

Back on his feet the stick was a Godsend. Without it, he wouldn't have managed to walk at all, but his ankle hurt like hell. He hobbled over to the fire chief who was holding his helmet in his hand.

'An atomic bomb must have gone off here with the state of the place,' he said, gesturing with his helmet.

'Thanks for putting out the fire and tidying up. I was lucky not to lose more. I can rebuild the car and the Harley.'

'I'll sign the insurance forms, and we'll be on our way. You need to fill in that crater in the yard before someone falls into it,' said the fire chief.

'I have a man working with me, and he'll do it when he gets in. I can hardly imagine that a can of petrol could do so much damage,' said Pat, holding the signed insurance forms in his hand.

'We see it all the time, even a match is enough to cause havoc, but there was more than petrol in that can,' said the fire chief. He shook hands with Pat, got into the front cab of the fire engine next to the driver, and they drove off.

Teresa was tiding up already, and he marvelled at her instinct to clear up. Perhaps women had this innate tendency, and depending on their childhood training, they developed it to a greater or lesser extent. He would keep that theory to himself, unless he wanted to start another battle of the sexes.

His phone rang, and it was pure luck it still worked. With a search, he found it in the pocket of his torn trousers. With no caller ID, he knew who was calling, and would prefer not to hear from him at this time. He toyed with the idea of and letting it ring out, but the urgent sound of a phone ringing always compelled him to answer.

'What have you to say?'

'I have a run to Birmingham lined up for you for Friday week, everything the same, place and time. The men who tried to torch your place are with me now. They will pay the price for acting on their own. I have asked them if they have any last requests like seeing a priest or saying goodbye to somebody special. They haven't much time left in this world.'

He laughed and the evil of it startled Pat. He heard whimpering in the background and the dull thud of blows striking flesh. He switched off his phone, and immediately turned it back on to call O'Neill at Pearse Street Garda station. He would try to prevent these men from being murdered.

'Hello, could I speak to Detective O'Neill?'

'Who's calling?'

'The coffin maker.'

A few seconds later O'Neill answered, 'Hello Pat. I hear there's not too much damage?'

'Just a burned-out car and motorcycle. The kingpins called me, and the two who did the torching were acting on their own. As we speak, he is torturing them before he kills them. Is there anything you can do?'

'I have an idea where he might be holding them. I'll get some men over there right away.'

'They want me for another run to Birmingham on Friday week.'

'Go ahead with that.'

O'Neil hung up.

Teresa took the next call in the office, and she put her hand over the receiver, 'It's from our hairdresser in Irishtown. She's giving up the business. She wants to thank you for all the work you gave her, with the corpses.'

'Why is she closing down? It's such a going concern.'

'She's pregnant and wants to get away from all the chemicals; sprays, shampoos, hair dyes, setting lotions, and I'm sure there's loads more of them. There are probably not good for an unborn child.'

'Well we need a hairdresser.'

'You go and lie down for a while, and I'll go and talk to her, maybe we can sort something out.'

That was the best suggestion he had heard all day. Teresa went out, and he lay down on the bed. In a few minutes, he was in that dreamy space between awake and asleep where he experienced some of his worst nightmares. A feeling of abandonment came at such times. How could his parents, if they loved him, give him away to strangers to use or abuse? They mustn't even have liked him; what did that say about him, and what type of people where they? He didn't know but in his dreams ghoul like faces often came floating out of the ether screaming at him. They represented the parents he never knew, he'd decided, and their black holes for eyes remained with him long after he woke.

Awake, he took a more reasoned view. Perhaps he was the product of a passionate affair between a couple already married to other people. They hid him away in institutions far from scandal and gossip; out of sight, out of mind. He was a mistake, their momentary ramble from the path of righteousness as his confessor might say, if he had one. Love the sinner and hate the sin, but it was unlikely that he would ever meet those sinners, the parents who had disowned him, whoever they were. They probably never gave him a second thought.

This was rubbish, his mother was probably no more than a child when taken advantage of by a predatory male. Ireland at the time of his birth was a land of hypocrisy, and repressed sexuality. The hypocrisy remained.

Without the means of supporting a baby, she would have had no choice but to give him up. He felt a great sorrow for her, and ashamed he could condemn her. That didn't make him feel like a great person. Often on the island, he stared at people of a certain age wondering if they were his parents, although there was no reason to suggest that they came from the island. Under the circumstances, it was just as logical to scan the crowd's at Penn Station, on Waterloo Bridge or Timbuktu. He wasn't going to hate his parents anymore, all he wanted now was to get to know them if they were still alive. Perhaps they married, and if they did, he probably had loads of siblings, half-brothers and sisters. That was a comforting thought, that he wasn't alone in the world, but would they want to know him, or spend time with him? He fell into a fitful, dreamy sleep.

When he opened his eyes, Teresa was sitting on the bed keeping a watching vigil.

'Pat, I'm so glad you're awake. Are you all right?

'I feel fine, how long was I asleep?

'Over two hours but it's OK. Everything can wait.'

'Even so, I need to do a few jobs.' He was hurting all over and careful not to sit up, he figured the least painful exit from the bed was turning over on his side and sliding feet first on to the floor. He completed the manoeuvre without wincing or crying out. He sat next to her.

'I had the strangest dream,' he said as she held his hand tightly in hers.

'All my dreams are strange. I don't understand them, but go ahead and tell me about it,' she said.

'I think the hypnosis session brought up the dream from somewhere deep in my head. It was sketchy, surreal, and jumping all over the place from one scene to another. I won't go down all the blind alleys it took me, I'll just tell you the main bits. It's loosely based on a TV programme. I watched it a few years ago about the Lebensborn experiment. It must have disturbed me a lot.

'The Lebensborn experiment, planned by no less a person than The Fuhrer, was social engineering on a grand scale. Only a sick mind could come up with it, and his jackbooted soldiers carried it out with determination. In the countries they occupied, he commanded them to impregnate as many women as possible with the stipulation that these unfortunate people were of sound mind, and body. The last part of the directive the soldiers ignored. The objective was to produce thousands of blue-eyed, fair-haired Arian children for the future of the master race.'

'My God, he was such an evil man. That was a terrible way to abuse women,' said Teresa, cupping her face in her hands in horror.

'If the children met the criteria, the Gestapo snatched them from their mothers to live in a special Nationalist Social Party institution. From that young age, they lived in a stage-managed environment, indoctrinated with precepts of the Third Reich. As they got older, the children who failed to meet the standard ended in the gas chamber.'

'Did they carry out medical experiments on the children?' asked Teresa.

'I don't know about that, but all this is leading up to my dream.'

'Pat, at times a good memory is a curse. I would say you remember everything verbatim from that TV, programme. Were the children united with their mothers after the war?'

'Few, it was almost an impossible task. Immediately, after the SS kidnapped the Lebensborn children, they stripped them of their identities, gave them German names, and effectively turned them into children of the Third Reich. There are heart wrenching stories of mothers after the war trawling Germany looking for their children they could no longer recognise. In later years, those children must have had difficulties adjusting to life because of their strange upbringing.

'Later in the experiment the SS ignored the dictate, 'only children with German fathers,' when the birth rate from the occupied territories was lower than expected. They needed more children, and to increase the numbers, they snatched Polish and Slav children with blond hair and blue eyes.

'That was a lesson in German wartime expediency. Even though they labelled the Poles subhuman, they saw no contradiction in kidnapping thousands of children from Warsaw, future fighters to swell the ranks of the super race.

'Now, back to my dream. I must have been three or four years old, and I was holding my mother's hand. We were somewhere in Holland admiring a windmill. Its sails were huge, and they made a whirring noise as they revolved. I wanted to stay looking at them all day but my mother was keen on getting us back home.

'There was something worrying her, I could feel her fear, but I couldn't see her face. Throughout the dream, I never saw her face; a blank space where I expected to see her eyes, nose and mouth, and that was frightening. Somehow, my mother was a non-person a ghost without substance as indeed my biological mother was in real life.

'Were you ever in Holland?' asked Teresa, swapping her sitting up position on the edge of the bed to lying back with her legs on the floor.

'No, but the film makers made the TV programme mostly in Holland.'

'We went by train from Paris to Amsterdam once, and we cycled everywhere. I loved those canals,' said Teresa with a faraway look in her eyes recalling the joie de vivre of a more carefree time.

He learned that French saying when he was in Paris on his honeymoon, and it described his feelings exactly at that time. He was full of, 'the joy of living.'

He would like to have asked Teresa who the 'we' were, but he let it pass. She had a life before he met her, and so had he. Nothing could change any of that. Rehashing the past was a waste of time and emotion. Still it was in his nature to feel curious, or perhaps he was jealous. He probably could not change that either.

'In my dream, symbolically the day changed from bright and sunny, to dark and gloomy as a thunder cloud passed across the sky.

Immediately, the scene shifted, and we were at home in our small kitchen. I was playing on the floor, and my mother was washing-up. A loud banging on the door startled her, and when she looked through the peephole, she said almost inaudibly, "Someone must have informed on us."

'In one movement, she rushed over, swept me up in her arms, and pushed me under the table. Then she spread a cover on the table that draped down to the floor. When she opened the door, I peeped out from under the cover, and saw the long shiny boots of a German World War II soldier with a rifle slung over his shoulder. I didn't understand a word he said as he pushed passed her into the room. Three Gestapo officers followed him.

'I noticed the terror in my mother's voice, and I wanted to cry, but I instinctively knew not to make a sound. There was danger all around, and I felt petrified that my loud breathing would alert them to my whereabouts. They were on a roundup mission, and wanted to add me to the ranks of the Lebensborn children.

'The soldiers searched the house, but luckily, they didn't look under the table where I was hiding. Before they left, my mother tried to convince them that she had no children, but I think they knew she was lying, and would bide their time.

'After that episode, I was virtually a prisoner in the house. Rarely would my mother chance leaving it, in case we ran into the Gestapo. The one exception was Sunday mass, and even then, if we saw goose-stepping soldiers we'd duck into a side street or up an alleyway until they passed.

'There we were, one Sunday sitting in the church as usual. The priest had turned to face the congregation with the host held high, and a look of reverence on his face when the doors burst open. Hitler's storm troopers marched up the centre aisle of the church escorted by a tank, and a fighter plane shooting at the congregation from overhead. Their marching steps sounded like a drum beat. They took up guard in front of the exits, and no one could get in or out.

'Two formal suited Gestapo followed them, and they searched seat by seat for blond, blue-eyed children to kidnap. As they came nearer to our seat, I was terrified. I couldn't hold out any longer, and my loud wail was like a homing signal to them. They came straight for me. My mother tried to protect me, but it was futile. They hauled me away leaving her crying, and screaming for someone, just anyone to get me back.

'Then I was in a Polish railway station with an impossible name, taken there by my captors. The SS had corralled the other prisoners on the platform. Dressed in rags, with shoulders bowed, and eyes staring at the ground, the prisoners seemed resigned to their fate. They were Jewish and Polish people, and for most of them that was the gas chamber. Apart from nervous coughing, shuffling of feet and the hissing of the steam engine stopped at the platform, there were no other sounds. An eerie stillness hung over the station as if populated by ghosts.

'I think many other groups like gypsies, and Catholics, wherever they came from faced extermination as well,' said Teresa.

'One Catholic made it to my dream. She was on the platform with a baby in her arms, and rosary beads wound around her fingers. She was silently mouthing a Hail Mary, and I wondered if I should say the rosary as well. My choice was five or fifteen decades starting with the Our Father and finishing with the Gloria.

'The train had a string of tar coloured cattle wagons attached to the engine. I might have missed a few but there were at least forty. Someone in the crowd shouted "Nazi pigs and murderers", and then all hell broke loose. The soldiers charged the prisoners and battered them with their rifle butts. Those at the back of the group received the worst abuse.

'I saw the woman with the baby knocked to the ground and trampled on. Her rosary beads went flying into the air, but she didn't let go of her child. Those in front rushed into the cattle wagons, and they carried me along with them. Dried lumps of cow dung coated the side of the wagon, and jammed tightly against it, I couldn't move an arm or leg. Stirred up by the tramping feet the dung on the floor was soft goo, and it covered my shoes and socks up to my knees. I was wearing short schoolboy trousers. The foul smell was everywhere, and someone was sick all over me.

'A whistle sounded, they slammed shut the sliding doors of the wagon, and we moved out of the station. Through a slit in the side, I could see the Polish countryside as we steamed south. At each country station, the train stopped, and we fell forward, when it started to move we went backward. They packed us so tightly into the wagons that it was impossible to fall down. I listened to the clicked-e-click of the iron wheels on the tracks, and tried to anticipate when the next clang was due. This happened when the wheels ran over a join in the rails.

'The dream went bizarre at that stage. Flying around with wings like an angel, I landed on the platform at Auschwitz to join the other prisoners getting off the train. Dressed in rags, the prisoner's band from the camp was playing on the platform to greet us. My mother was now by my side, holding my hand. Two armed soldiers positioned at the station exit beside a notice board showing a waiting list for the gas chamber. Jews went ahead of everyone else with one-week delay. On the list, the Poles followed with a two-week wait. For the other categories, including gypsies and handicapped people, there was an unspecified hold-up. Their turn came when there was space.

'The soldier's job was to form the prisoners into rows, on the right-hand side those suitable for work, and on the left the rejects for the gas chamber. When the soldiers signalled that my mother was fit for the work camp, she let go of my hand, and walked away without looking back. My destination was the gas chamber. My mother had abandoned me again.

'The smell of burning flesh was stifling as we shuffled up to the number one gas burner placed behind barred doors. The only warning of the activity taking place inside was the dark smoke emitted from the chimney. I was just about to walk through the gas chamber doors when I woke up.'

'Pat that dream was all about your parents abandoning you. It's doing your head in, and I think you should resolve it by finding out about them. Are you up for it?' Teresa turned her head to gauge his reaction.

The unexpected effect of her words on him shocked her. His face went white, and beads of sweat formed on his forehead, probably from the thought of facing something he had been avoiding for so long. Distressed he hesitated. 'Oh my God,' she had said too much.

'Pat, we don't have to start our search immediately. We can leave it for as long as you want. There's no hurry.' She was falling into the role of feeling she had to protect him.

'No, it's past time I found out. Next week is free before our trip to Birmingham and it's as good a time as any to start our search.'

'Well if you're sure that's what you want?'

'Yes I am, but we will need to get a replacement car. There's VW refurbishes around the corner. I'll give them a ring.' He dialled the number.

'Hello, I'm the undertaker, and my VW burned out. It's one with a split rear window, and they are hard to come by?'

'That's a vintage. I haven't seen one for years, and I wouldn't mind one of them for myself. Is it there with you?'

'Yes, it's a burnt-out wreck.'

'I'll come around to see it.'

When they descended the stairs, the garage owner and a mechanic were already in the yard examining the beetle. They shook hands with Pat and Teresa.

'I can rebuild it, and it'll be as good as the day it left the factory,' said the garage owner rubbing some of the ash from the carburettor with his hand.

'How long will it take?'

'Aha, about two weeks, we'll leave a car with you until it's finished.'

They agreed on a price, and before they left the yard, the garage owner said, 'I'm a big Harley fan. I'll restore that one for cost if you like. It'll be a labour of love?'

'OK, take it with you.'

As often happens, when men are discussing machines, they ignored any women in the vicinity.

'It would be nice if you at least asked me for my opinion. I have one you know,' Teresa said with a slight flush showing in her cheeks.

'Sorry about that. I didn't think you were interested. What is your view then,' he said lamely.

'You didn't ask in time,' she said, storming off.

In the VW, loaned from the garage they journeyed westwards to Galway, on the start of their mission to track down Pat's birth parents. Teresa sensed his tenseness, and understood his fear of the emotional roller coaster he was facing regardless of which way it panned out. It was not something he could take lightly. Driving through east Galway, to ease his anxiety, she decided to try to distract him.

'I bet there's lots of history attached to this part of the country,' she said, expecting him to take the bait. Given his prodigious memory, she expected a word for word account of some event or other that occurred in the area. He didn't disappoint her.

'We're not far away from Athenry,' he said, pointing to a road sign in Irish and English. 'An incident happened there during World War II the authorities kept secret until long after the war ended.'

'You like war stories?' she said, turning around in her seat to take in the other names on the sign.

'No, I hate war in all its forms, but you can't miss stories about it in the cinema, and on TV. It's such triumphalism about humans slaughtering other human beings.'

He slowed slightly to obey the speed limit. In these old Volkswagens, top gear was an overdrive, and they had a tendency to run on a bit. Teresa was talking,

'I couldn't agree with you more about wars. Humans are so primitive. If they could only sit down, discuss the problem, and reach a compromise,' she said, rolling down the window to let some cool air into the old VW. When it was built in the early 1960s, air-con was not available in European cars.

'The USA, B-17 bombers became affectionately known as flying fortresses and this is the amazing tale of one of them called 'Stinky'. It started its sixteen thousand mile journey in the USA with full crew, and four top brass military personnel on-board. The first port of call was the Caribbean. Next stop was Brazil, and then across the South Atlantic to Ascension Island. From there to the west coast of Africa, and they continued across the country to Khartoum. Onwards, they kept flying to Cairo and from there to the Rock of Gibraltar. This was their last stop before their final destination, a wartime airbase in England.

'That was the plan but things don't always go to plan. The passengers travelling with the ten man crew were the four highest-ranking officers in the USA forces; four-star generals.' Pat's phone rang. He looked at the number of the incoming call, the drug men were about to pester him again. 'What do you want?'

'Supplies are running low. Take a second coffin from Birmingham.'

'Let me think about it.'

'Don't think too long. I'll call back in ten minutes.'

The phone was on the loudspeaker, and Teresa had heard the conversation. Their trip had taken a more sinister turn. She felt uneasy with Pat's involvement with these gangsters.

'I'll call O'Neill for advice.'

'OK,' she said, but she was having some reservation about O'Neill's role in all this.

Pat went through the usual stalling at Pearse Street Garda station before he got O'Neill on the line.

'They want me to take two coffins from Birmingham this time. What do you think, John?'

'Do as they ask, Pat,' he said, sounding irritated by the call.

When he hung up neither of them spoke for a while.

'Pat I don't think we should take a second coffin. We are bringing in a lot of stuff already and even though the Garda got some of it, a lot goes missing.' She got out of the car to cool down, and he came around and stood by her side. The surrounding countryside was a patchwork of green fields separated by stone walls.

'It's uniquely different, basic, raw, and eternal looking,' she said, putting her arm around him.

'Very much the landscape of the West of Ireland,' he said, thinking about the decision he had to make. If he didn't agree it would be his first time going against O'Neill's advice. However, he wouldn't disregard what Teresa was saying, she was sincere and one hundred per cent behind him. His phone rang again. He ignored it, and eventually it stopped. He hadn't yet decided, and it wouldn't do any harm to hang tough and show this crook that he wasn't going to push him around. 'There's a lot in what you say. I'm going to refuse to take a second coffin and that's, that,' he said, shading his eyes against the sun.

'Will it be OK?' she said, tightening her grip on him.

'We're in the driving seat, as it were, no pun intended. They're short of the gung and they need us to take it to them,' he said but there was more to it than that. These crooks would not hesitate to silence her for good if he didn't comply with their wishes. He knew what they were capable off; he had only to think of what happened to his wife. He shuddered at the thought of it. He would need to exercise care and not push these thugs too far.

His phone buzzed again and this time he answered it.

'Well?'

'I've had a look at the hearse and there's no room for a second coffin in it. They're not made for that.' That was the end of the conversation.

'That was clever. I wouldn't have thought of it,' she said, hopping into the centre of the road and doing a few Irish dance steps. That released tension from her body, and she laughed. It was good to see her in a carefree mood. It was infectious and he found himself smiling.

Back in the VW, Teresa said, 'Finish the story about Athenry.'

'The navigator, Lieutenant. C. B. Collins plotted a course from Gibraltar to England using a chart, compass, and estimated speed as if on a ship. These were the days before effective radar, GPS and Satellite Technology. There were some radio beacons erected by both the Germans, and Allied forces. They were useful for distinguishing one country from another, but they didn't cover all of Europe. The inaccuracy of navigation was the reason the Allies switched from precision to carpet-bombing of Germany.

'Shortly after they left Gibraltar, the four-star generals advised the pilot to deviate from their plotted course to England, and fly west of Brest in France. Collins opposed this change in the direction, but the Generals outranked him. This change in the flight path took them out of range of the radio beacons, and within hours, they were effectively lost. They didn't even know which country they were flying over. Ten hours later, they saw green fields below them. Was it France, Germany or England? Eventually, the sight of Galway bay shimmering below answered that question.

'The pilot opted to land in a field rather than ditch in the Atlantic. Unfortunately, most of the fields had neat rows of stakes driven into the ground to prevent the Lufthansa planes loaded with SS paratroopers from doing the same. There was one field without stakes but it had a dividing stone fence build across the centre. Since he hadn't a choice the pilot decided to land there. He had other concerns as well. If the wheels sank in soft earth on landing, the plane would nose dive.

'He need not have worried. He throttled back to seventy miles an hour, just above stalling speed, but made the fatal mistake of coming in too low. The B17 hit the stone wall and the impact sheared off wheels and undercarriage. Luck was with the pilot on that January morning, and out of a potential disaster, he then made a successful belly flop landing. There was no loss of life.'

'That is a wonderful story, Pat. I hadn't heard it before.'

'Well there's more. The FCA our auxiliary army or if you like "Dads Army" surrounded the plane, and the Generals and crew surrendered their weapons. A charade designed to preserve Ireland's notion of neutrality. They took the military men to the local hotel where a party got under way with food and drink for everyone. Next day the Irish army drove the captured US personnel to their base at St. Anglo airport near Enniskillen. Aircraft mechanics from the airbase arrived in Athenry and took the B17 apart. They loaded it in manageable chunks onto trucks and took it back to the base. They, no doubt, repaired and reassembled it for its next flying mission.

'Ironically, the pilot flying 'Stinky' was Paul Tibbet who, later in his career, led the bombing on Hiroshima. The co-pilot, James McLaughlin, at eighty-six years old is alive and well.'

'Pat the extent of your memory is almost frightening. Your recall must be nearly as accurate as reading the TV script,' she said, hauling at the seat belt to make it sit more comfortably on her shoulder. It belonged to the generation of seat belts before automatic tensioning was invented. He loved these old cars with dodgy suspension and all, probably a male thing, but she preferred the current models with all mod cons. A new small Ford or a Fiat bambino was moving higher up on her shopping list, and he could drive whatever he fancied.

'All my memory does is to remind me that I'm not normal like everyone else. I have a condition that I'd prefer to be without,' he said, slowing to a crawl as they approached a tailback of traffic going into Galway City.

'Don't ever think like that. People would kill to have a memory like yours, and we are going to do something about your problem.'

'We'll see,' he said. There was a weary resignation in his voice, as if he felt there was no cure but she knew that with the right treatment his condition would improve. Maybe in the near future science would find a way to alleviate it.

Eventually, they got to centre of the city and drove around for a while until they found a vacant parking space in Eyre Square near the Bank of Ireland. As they walked towards the bank, childhood memories came flooding back and threatened to engulf him. His foster father had managed this bank so many years ago. It was only the beginning of the journey through his turbulent childhood, and was he wise to have started out on this journey? He wouldn't have without Teresa's encouragement. She slipped her hand into his. She was probably aware of the turmoil going on in his head. He felt women were like that, sensitive to stressful emotional states.

They joined the queue for the information desk and, when it came to their turn, the receptionist gave them a friendly smile. 'Can I help?'

He knew she was too young but he would ask her anyway.

'I wonder did you know Mr. Donnelly? He was the manager of this branch some years ago.'

She stopped for a moment to consider his question and then her eyes brightened.

'Ask the porter, he has been here for donkey's years,' she said with the same winning smile, pleased that she had solved their difficulty with such ease. They thanked her and stepped out of the queue, and the porter immediately came over. Somehow, as is the way of porters, he sensed that they wished to talk to him.

'Hello, can I help you at all?'

'Did you know Mr. Donnelly, my foster father? He was manager here.'

'I knew him well.' He stopped talking, and stared at Pat before continuing. 'I do believe he took you in here a few times. They lived up in Taylors Hill. It devastated him when they took you away. He and Mrs. Donnelly died years ago. They're buried up in the old Mount St. James Cemetery and their adopted daughter put up a headstone. She came after your time. She's a grand young woman. Call in, she'll be happy to see you.'

He recognised the large house standing in its own grounds, and set back from the roadway. As they walked up to the front door it was all so familiar, the garden, bordered with a boxwood hedge and the centre piece Cordyline Australis reminiscent of warmer climes.

The door opened before they got to it and a young woman rushed out flushed with excitement and threw her arms around him.

'I'm so glad you came Pat. The porter rang to say you were coming up,' she said through tears of joy and laughter.

'It's great to meet you,' he said a bit overwhelmed by her gushing welcome.

'This is Teresa.'

'Hello Teresa.' They hugged each other.

'Come on in, I have some food ready.'

They followed her into the house, which was almost as he remembered it. The grandfather clock was still in the hallway, probably beating out its lonely chimes day and night, as it always did.

In the kitchen, she had prepared a seafood lunch for them. He had always loved Galway Bay prawns, and she heaped them on his plate. She had insider information on his likes and dislikes from his foster parents.

'Oh my God, I forgot to tell you my name, it's Anne. The Donnelly's adopted me as a baby. They suffered a terrible loss when the social worker took you away, and they never managed to get over it. They grieved about it to the day they died. They wanted you back and, with both of us, their family would have been complete.

'It was the rules in those days caused the problem,' he said, thinking about the times he sat at this mahogany table to eat meals or to do his homework.

'The authorities wouldn't give any information about what they did with you, but that didn't stop my parents searching.'

She got up from the table and took down a yellow coloured Clark's shoe box from a cabinet shelf. He knew the type of shoes that fitted in the box without having to read it on the side; size nine brogues in light tan. Those were his foster father's foot size and choice of shoe and colour.

Before he set out for the bank in the morning, his final job was to polish his shoes. He made a big production of it using the shoe polishing technique taught in the army. In his younger days, he was a sergeant in the FCA. He brushed on a thick layer of polish on each shoe and, with a spit and shine, he buffed them to the first finish. Then with his index finger inside a soft cloth he polished each shoe inch by inch to a mirror finish. When he came home in the evenings he left his shoes in the hall, and Pat often looked at his reflection in them.

From the shoebox, she handed him a bunch of press cuttings, some from the local and national papers and others from the UK press. His foster parents had posted the notices trying to find him. Each text had the attached photo they had of him dressed in his school uniform, and standing outside the front door. In the later ads, they offered a reward for any information leading to his whereabouts. He was choking up and he didn't want to show it in front of the women. He needed to get away for a few minutes, to get his emotions under control.

'I'm not a great reader or I might have spotted these ads in the newspapers,' he said, standing up and pushing back his chair.

'I suppose the toilets are still in the same place?'

'No change,' said Anne, searching around in the shoebox.

'Excuse me for a minute.'

He headed for the small downstairs toilet, and it was such a relief to get out of the kitchen. He sat on the toilet seat holding his head in his hands. Fate had dealt him a bad blow. His life would have been so different had he remained in this house. Life isn't fair, and there's no sense regretting that fact. His phone rang and from the lit up screen, he knew the call was coming from Pearse Street Garda Station, and only one person would contact him from there.

'Hello John?'

'How did you get on with these gangsters?'

'I told them I'm not taking a second coffin from Birmingham.'

'Just like that, you refused?'

'I did, more or less.'

'You took a big chance. These are dangerous men. Don't get any ideas like that again without talking to me first.'

The conversation annoyed Pat. Who did this fella think he was? He felt tired of a dictator like O'Neill telling him what to do, and what not to do.

'Pat, are you all right in there?' Teresa was standing outside the toilet door.

'I'll be out in a second. O'Neill delayed me on the phone.'

'What's up with him now?'

'Just the usual talk about the Birmingham trip.'

'OK.'

In the hallway, he had another reminder of the past, the smell of Johnsons Furniture Polish as he walked pass the grandfather clock. His foster mother sprayed it liberally on all the wood in the house, and at times to clean the inside of the windows. It was powerfully evocative, a clean antiseptic smell like carbolic soap. All part of the childhood he experienced when he lived in this house.

In the kitchen, Anne held out his foster father's will to him. He didn't take it.

'Tell me what all this is about?' he said, sitting down next to Teresa at the table.

'I think you're going to get a surprise when you hear the contents. Your foster father felt convinced that one day you would come back, and he was right. The bank encouraged its employees to buy shares in the company at a reduced cost, and when he retired, he owned a lot of them. Before he died, he divided the shares equally between us, and deposited the certificates for safekeeping in the bank. At this stage, the shares are worth a fair amount of money. This is your account number.' She handed him another sheet of paper.

'I wasn't expecting this,' said Pat, looking at Teresa. She held his hand. She did that when she felt he needed support to cope with a situation.

'I know, but there's more. We are joint owners of this house,' she said hesitantly as if she wasn't sure how he would take it.

'No, this is your home. I don't deserve any of it, and anyway I have enough property to look after,' he said sounding determined.

'I won't change what's in the will now considering my situation,' she said sifting the papers in her hand until she found the document she was looking for. She didn't elaborate further on her circumstances, and he didn't know what she was referring to, but it was something in her life that she didn't want to reveal. Really, they were strangers to her, and she had an entitlement to her privacy. Their relationship was difficult to define, not blood relatives and hardly siblings but almost that.

'Do you work in the property business?' she said, shifting her gaze to his face.

'I'm an undertaker with two businesses, one in the West and the other in Dublin.'

'I didn't expect that,' she said taken aback.

179

'Most people react like that. It's something to do with working with the dead. You'll get over it,' he said smiling.

'This is something you haven't seen before, your birth cert,' she said, and handed the pro forma sheet of paper to him. It was yellow with age, and written by hand with a fountain pen in the spaces provided for the details of his birth. Reading the handwritten scrawl was difficult for him, and he passed it to Teresa. For an onlooker, it just seemed he was feeling too emotional to read it himself.

'Pat your father's name is Hickey, and your mother's maiden name is also Hickey, and your birthplace is Clifden, County Galway. The women were staring at him for a reaction, but he couldn't take in all this information. All his life he had agonised over not knowing who his parents were, and there it was in this document, but somehow it didn't feel like it was part of him.

'I'm going to need time to let it all this sink it,' he said, with confusion threatening to engulf him. Teresa gave his hand a squeeze to show she understood.

'You'll stay here tonight?' said Anne not prepared to accept a refusal. He was deep in thought, and a bit detached. Teresa replied for him.

'Of course we will, and you will have to come and spend time with us as well.'

'I would love to,' she said as both women set about the task of washing-up. Anne cleaned the dishes in the sink, and Teresa did the drying. No one spoke, and the work filled in the silence. Each left to their own thoughts; Teresa was regretting having encouraged Pat to start this search. There was still a lot to discover, and overall it might do more harm than good.

'Since we're this far, I think we should go to Clifden and try to find my parents, if they are still alive,' he said. He got up from the table to admire a picture hanging on the wall. He was standing beside his foster parents on the bank of the Corrib River. The photographer took the shot with a camera that was popular with both the amateur and professional at that time, the Polaroid Instamatic. The colour had faded to faint sepia but his foster parents were as real as in life. His foster father had struck his stern pose he thought made him look tough to the bank staff, and his foster mother smiled with her hand on Pat's shoulder as if to protect him.

Many times since, he needed that guiding hand but alas, it was never there. All these memories were making him sad and morbid, and he needed to snap out of it before he became a babbling idiot.

As the evening wore on, Anne tired quickly and by eight thirty, she was falling asleep in the chair.

'Anne, don't stay up for us. You look tired, maybe you should head for your bed?' said Teresa, looking with concern at her pale face.

'I think I will but it is such bad manners to leave my guests?'

'We're more like family, you don't have to worry about us,' said Teresa with a laugh.

Anne seemed groggy as she climbed the stairs to bed.

'I think she's not well. It is unusual for a young woman to get so exhausted,' said Teresa, moving over from the chair to sit beside him on the settee.

'There's something all right. She might tell us before we leave, and then again she might not. Don't forget that our presence here is a big shock for her.'

They were sleeping in his foster parents' bedroom and that disturbed him.

The next morning was dull and grey and a sea mist covered the city. It was the start of a typical May Day in Galway; later the sun would burn off the mist and expose a sky that cast shadows on the landscape much loved by poets and painters. With hugs and tears from Anne and promises to keep in touch they took the road out of the City for Clifden.

'That's an Opus Dei house,' said Teresa pointing to a large building they were driving past.

'What, how do you know that?'

'That surprised you. I've been here before and it's a long story.'

'Well, let's hear then.'

'Opus Dei is strong in the colleges and that's where they recruited me, along I may say with a few others. '

'Are they not some kind of secret society?'

'They used to be, but not so much nowadays. I see them as conservative Catholics, to the right of the Pope, and he loves them. They have ninety thousand members worldwide.'

'So that's what they are about?'

'They are powerful and controversial, with Politicians, Judges, Lawyers, Teachers, Civil Servants, and Businessmen in the organisation.

'Have they any place for an ordinary Joe Soap?'

'There is. About seventy per cent of the members live ordinary lives and they are the Supernumeraries. Twenty per cent, the Numeraries are celibate men and women living in the Opus houses. Associates, for whatever reason are unable to live in the houses but stay committed to the rules of the organisation. The final category is the Numerary Assistants, celibate women working as domestics in the houses.'

'What were you in the organization?'

'I was a Numerary living in.'

'What was that like?'

'They were very controlling worst than the army. I was up before six in the morning, and then a cold shower being careful with the towel so as not to commit a mortal sin when drying. God, they were neurotic about sins of impurity as if that was the worst act anyone could commit. This ritual we followed with half an hour of meditation before attending daily mass in Latin. They did not allow us to talk during our fifteen-minute breakfast and anyway we were wearing a Celise.'

'What in heaven's name is a Celise?'

Teresa laughed, 'You might well ask. One part of the Opus practice is something old and monastic. It originated in the 4th century and Christians and non-Christians alike did it as a mortification of the

The Coffin Maker

flesh or as they liked to call it putting the flesh to death. For that, we wore a Celise. It's like a piece of barbed wire wrapped tightly around our thighs.'

Astonished he was staring at her, and for a moment, he forgot he was driving a car.

'Look out or we will be over the ditch,' she shouted, stretching to grab the steering wheel and keep the car on the road.

'Sorry Pat, I had to do that or we were off the road. I got your attention with that revelation all right,' she said with a big smile.

'Did you draw blood? Not even farmers use barbed wire to keep their animals from straying nowadays. I think it is against the law.'

'Sometimes, but that was not the problem, it was just so uncomfortable digging in with ever movement.'

'There's so much going on in the church that I know nothing about,' he said, back in control of the car.

'The next part of the story is sure to shock you, and don't drive off the road when you hear it. With a small rope called the discipline we flayed ourselves across the shoulders and down our backs.'

'I almost can't believe it, self-flagellation,' he said, slowing down to look sideways at her. She was laughing loudly, delighted that she managed to shock him.

'All of this stuff is from the middle ages, and maybe we should leave it confined to history. I was so committed to the RC Church in those days that anything coming from those quarters I believed without question. Now I can't see any need for those Opus Dei rituals.'

'You always manage to surprise me. I never know what you are going to tell me next.'

'It's great isn't it that I can keep you guessing?' she said, leaning over and kissing him on neck. It amused her that he was finding it so incredible that this was happening in the Catholic Church. For her it was part of her girlhood search for divine enlightenment. She often thought the spiritual awareness she was looking for may be within her grasp and she was just missing it. That was for another day or perhaps it was a lifelong search. Now it was all about Pat; what were they going to find out about his family in Clifden?

'Do you think we have far to go?' she asked, never having been this far west before.

'A bit farther into the mountains for us yet, I think. I don't remember much about the last time I was here,' he said smiling.

'You were only a baby, and of course you must have been a beautiful baby.'

'Not beautiful enough for them to keep me.'

'You must stay positive, Pat. That's not the reason.'

'Well – I'm nearer now than I have ever been to finding out.'

'Don't prejudge it, Pat. I'm sure it will all work out.'

'I hope you're right.' They drifted into silence and with the heat inside the car, Teresa fell asleep.

He turned down the music on the radio, a Motorola fitted to the VW before it left the factory in Germany. Compared with modern versions the reception on the valve set was poor and in the Connemara Mountains, it crackled more than usual. He had more problems to contend with than radio reception.

He should have given this project more thought; he could not just arrive up on his mother's doorstep and say, 'I'm Pat the illegitimate son you gave away and forgot about.' From the small bit of understanding he had of life he knew the last part wasn't true, no mother ever forgets her child. He would be discrete, drive around Clifden and get as much information on his family as he could without raising suspicion. Was that possible in a small Irish community? Probably not, instantly a neighbour would let them know a stranger in town was enquiring about them.

The best approach to his mother might be through a family member like an aunt or some other close relative. That way he could find out if she wanted to meet him or not. Getting it over in one visit was too ambitious and in his head he was downgrading the trip to a fact-finding mission.

Teresa was sleeping soundly and it amused him listening to her incoherent mumbling. The sounds came out in a rush and he found it impossible to disentangle her word salad.

His phone rang and Teresa, restrained by the seat belt tried to jump up. This thug was calling again.

'The reception is bad where the hell are you.'

Pat ignored the question and said, 'What's it now?'

'Get to Birmingham the day after tomorrow and we don't give a dam if you bring the doll with you or not. Just remember for your own good and hers no tricks.'

That was the end of the message.

'That means we are on the road again in two days, Pat. You are going to feel exhausted,' she said, loosening the seat belt and repositioning it across her shoulder.

'I expected we were going to get a week free from these crooks, but not so. We will need to get back to Dublin by tomorrow night at the latest,' he said, turning off the radio, the crackling had increased to an annoying pitch.

'We should have finished our business here by that time,' she said, laying her hand on his arm to reassure him that everything would be OK.

They came over the brow of a hill, Pat hit the brakes hard and brought the car to a stop. Clifden was below them nestled in the hollow between the hills.

'That's a beautiful scene. I could look at it forever. You're lucky that you can call this your birth place.'

'Look at the church spire with the hill in the background. They probably baptised me there. It's just like a postcard.'

'Let's drive down there and find out,' she said, acutely aware that his life did not start out with baptism. Since they were on a religious theme it was the ramifications of his conception and how he would cope with the information that was worrying her. As if dealing with the thugs was not enough for him, she had added another layer of stress by coaxing him to search for his birth parents. She had no right

185

to do that and the guilt of this trip was hanging heavily over her. How much can one man take? Please God for Pat make this outcome a good one.

On the road in to Clifden, they passed an elderly man out for a stroll and Pat stopped to talk to him, on the off-chance, he might know something about his family. Pleasantries about the weather were exchanged before it was time to ask the big question.

'Do you know a family called Hickey anywhere about here?'

The older man lifted his head, stared at Pat's face for a time and didn't say anything. Teresa felt whatever he knew he was not going to part with easily.

'I'm one of the family,' said Pat, losing his anonymity and immediately regretting it. He might as well have stood up in the main street and shouted it out for all to hear.

'The auld memory is not as good, it's old age but I'll tell you who'll know, the retired parish priest. He has been in this parish since he was a curate and that is not today or yesterday. He lives in the big double-fronted house up there on the left. He takes a few hours rest in the afternoon and you'll need to ring the housekeeper for an appointment.'

They thanked him and drove on.

'Pat we didn't expect this would be easy, ring the housekeeper and we'll go and see this man,' she said, dialling directory enquiries on her mobile phone and asking for the parish priest's number.

'I know but it's typical; that's the way we deal with this kind of difficulty in Ireland. The priests will solve the problem.'

'Not anymore, times have changed.'

She wrote down the number from enquiries on a scrap of paper.

'Shall I ring it?'

'Fire away.'

'The phone buzzed for a few minutes before the housekeeper answered.

'Hello.'

'Can we see the priest any time today?'

'Father Higgins went for tests to the regional hospital this morning. You will have to wait until tomorrow. Will I give you a time?'

She sounded old and frail.

'OK, As early as possible.'

'Will ten o'clock do?'

'That's fine.'

'What's the name?'

Teresa hesitated and looked to Pat for direction but he looked bewildered. She had two surnames to choose from now, the new one Hickey and the old one O'Donnell.

'Pat Hickey,' she said.'

'Has he seen Father Higgins before?'

That was a loaded question - he possibly baptised Pat but that was long ago and, in truth, he never had a discussion with this priest.

'No.'

'Well, when he sees Father Higgins he can tell him what's troubling him. Goodbye now and God bless you.'

'Bye.'

'Pat I felt confused and used your Clifden surname. Was that OK?'

'That's fine. I was expecting we would get back to Dublin tonight but that is not going to happen now. We need to book in somewhere.'

'Why don't we try the "Alcock and Brown" in the Market Square? I saw an ad for it on the road in and their prices are reasonable.'

'OK. Ring them up.' The reservation made they drove up to the hotel and after a meal settled in for the night.

Tired they were soon asleep but it did not last long. Pat was restless, muttering, tossing, and turning in his sleep. He woke Teresa and she could not get back to sleep again. This was a disturbing trip and she couldn't get it out of her mind. She sat up in the bed, rested her head against the headrest, and started to meditate, her cure for insomnia.

Eureka. In a flash of insight, it hit her with the force of a proverbial ten ton truck.

'Oh my God, not that of all things. He is going to be so distraught,' she whispered to herself.

It was the love people rarely speak about, and the joy of the chat show hosts when a participant openly discusses their personal experience of it. The clue was the identical surnames of Pat's parents. Was he the product of an incestuous union between brother and sister?

She was as wide awake now as if it was midday, and she would not get back to sleep again. Without disturbing him, she slipped out of bed. A cup of tea would help to revive her. Carrying the half-full kettle, she unlocked the bedroom door and stepped into the deserted hallway where he wouldn't hear the sound of the water boiling. In her nightdress, she hoped no one would see her, and they would not, unless they were hopping from bedroom to bedroom like a French farce.

With a cup of tea in her hand, she sat by the window with the curtains open and watched the sun rising in the east, gradually lightening up the town as if moving from building to building. It was a beautiful moment, but she couldn't enjoy it with her mind full of what could be a startling revelation.

Her speculations were probably wrong, and it was likely only a coincidence that his parents had matching surnames. How she hoped and prayed that was the case.

By now, her relationship with Pat had deepened, and they were as one in many ways but this theory on his parentage, she would keep to herself. Already traumatised by the abuses he had suffered, this new shock, if true, would affect him for the rest of his life, like an incurable open sore that constantly oozed puss.

She had seen the long-term effects of incest when she worked in the Prison service, and had attended a one-day course given by an expert in the field. Her recall was not anywhere as good as Pat's, but she did remember some bits of the lecture.

The lecturer described incest as a Genetic Sexual Attraction or GSA for short. He talked about examples where siblings developed deep attraction to each other and were planning marriage until they discovered that they were brother and sister. He said a child born of such a union was at risk of developing either severe mental or physical illnesses or a combination of both. Faulty genes cause many serious conditions and when both parents are carriers, the child is almost certain to inherit a problem. She could not remember much else about the condition. Down the line, what health problems were awaiting Pat?

'You're up early,' said Pat, sitting upright in the bed and looking drowsy.

'Sleepy head, you missed a lovely sunrise, and it is time to get up for breakfast.'

Pat's phone rang and on the loudspeaker, they heard the familiar voice.

'Fill the coffin with gear and don't bring any corpses with yea from Birmingham.'

He felt he had pushed them as far as he could and any further reluctance on his part would risk retaliation. Give in to their demands and put a price on it. That is the way they understood life.

'Right but it's going to cost you.'

'I'll be glad when this business with the drug dealers is over,' said Teresa aware that they were risking death with every transaction with these crooks. She wouldn't push her point for now but to her way of thinking there was a lot wrong with all of it.

'I'd better ring O'Neill,' he said as he got out of bed and dressed.

'John, they called again. This time they want me to fill the coffin with dope and no corpse. If the customs open it, I'm caught red-handed.'

'It's safer to do what they want. Leave the customs to me. We are getting nearer knowing who the big fella is and those that drove your wife off the road. You're doing a good job, and before long we'll have them all in prison. Bye for now.'

'Goodbye,' said Pat, aware that O'Neill was buttering him up, encouraging him to continue supplying the drug men. He had to admit that they were close to exposing the head of the gang.

Following breakfast, they drove up the hill to the priest's house on the outskirts of the town. Teresa rang the doorbell and the sound echoed through the hallway. They heard the hollow sound of heavy footsteps on a bare board floor and through the glass hall door they saw the housekeeper coming slowly towards them. Stooped, she dragged one leg behind. His mind started play tricks with him, and he imagined they stumbled on a gothic horror film like he'd seen on TV. He had a sudden urge to run for it. She opened the door slowly and looked at them with suspicion.

'We made an appointment yesterday to meet Father Higgins,' said Teresa, moving closer to the housekeeper in case she had hearing difficulties. The housekeeper's mood seemed to change and she smiled.

'You're welcome, come on in. If I could remember an appointment I made yesterday it would be a miracle,' she said, walking ahead of them to a room at the back of the house. The priest was sitting in a reclining chair wrapped in a rug. He shook hands with them with fingers swollen and deformed from arthritis.

'Sit down and take the weight off your feet. Maybe this young girl would pour the tea, and I am partial to a chocolate biscuit.'

He meant no harm, but if a younger man had said that to her, she would have told him to get his own tea, and what did his last servant die of. She filled the cups, added milk and passed them around.

'What about my biscuit?'

She held out the biscuits he placed the cup and biscuit on a small card table beside his chair. He showed no interest in eating or drinking. It was most likely a social ritual he used to put people at ease before any serious business began.

'You probably have guessed why we are here - to find out if you knew my family,' said Pat, taking a drink of tea.

'That I did. They were decent people and strong church goers. Over the years, I got many inquiries about families in the parish. People keen on tracing their ancestors from as far away as America and beyond. I always started by referring them to the Bible, Mathew 1.

'The beginning of this chapter is about genealogy, and biblical scholars have different interpretations. Of course, it is arrogant for a humble country priest like me to explain any part of the bible, but here it is. Its significance for all of us concerns the people mentioned in Mathew 1, not all of whom were whiter than white. Some had committed all kinds of sinful acts, but they deserved their place in the family tree in the bible.

'It's the same for all of us somewhere back there in our family history, we are going to find sinners as well as saints. Expect it or else don't start searching among the withered bones of your ancestry, unless you prepare yourself for some shocks.'

'Good advice. Sometimes it's better to leave things as they are,' said Teresa, dreading what was coming next if Pat decided to continue with this search, that she was largely responsible for starting.

'Your analogy is good and there's no doubt that caution is the best policy in a search like this. That's my preaching over for today. It is your decision Pat?'

Teresa felt the Priest was apprehensive, as if he would prefer if the episode unfolding wasn't happening.

Pat didn't hesitate. 'Tell me about my family warts and all,' he said, leaving his cup and saucer back on the coffee-table.

'First of all I have to apologise for my handling of matters after your birth. I am deeply sorry for the part I played. Priests were like gods in those days. The congregation thought they knew about life and death and everything between. That was not so in my case. I was young and unsure of myself with little experience of the world. I should have stood up to the bishop, but I did not have the guts for that. My job was to get you to the orphanage, but you should have remained with your mother.

'With all the revelation coming out about the abuses in the church I sometimes think; is it not great to have lived so long and to have done such little harm. Then I think about you, and I feel culpable for the part I played in your life. The guilt will never leave me.'

The priest seemed smaller and older than before and his voice had grown fainter.

'Tell me the whole story,' said Pat, leaning forward in his chair so as not to miss a single word.

'I first met your father when he came to talk about his vocation to the priesthood. He was a serious young man and in my view eminently suitable for the work, and I told him so. I set up a meeting with the bishop who arranged for his entry into the seminary, St. Patricks Maynooth. Because I had advised him, and since he came from the parish, I kept a watching brief on his progress. He was a good student. I attended his ordination, and here is one of the photographs taken on that day. You won't recognise me as the young curate on the left with long black hair.'

With a wry smile, he handed the photograph to Pat. Flustered, with Teresa gazing over his shoulder, this was Pat's first sight of his father and his relatives. It seemed a joyous occasion, and they were smiling for the photograph. Teresa held Pat's arm tightly.

The priest closed his eyes as if taking a breather before continuing. She had seen many older people do that. With their eyes drooping at first then their heads falling forwards as they went into a deep sleep waking up later having forgotten what the previous conversation was about. With his slack translucent skin, the priest looked comatose or dead rather than asleep. God forgive her for thinking such a thing.

In the photograph, his father, dressed in white vestments, looked similar to him in height and build and the older couple were probably his grandparents. The younger women were likely his aunts. He would ask the priest later. The facial features in the old photograph were hazy and poorly defined, but he felt he resembled his father.

'Do I look like him?' She took the photo from him and held it up to the light from the window.

'It's hard to see the faces, but I think so.'

She handed the photo back to him, and she pondered on which aunt might be his mother. There was no way to tell that.

'How do you feel now that you have discovered your father is a priest?'

'Relieved that he didn't want rid of me. If anything, they took me away from him. The priest hasn't told me yet about my mother but that will come when he wakes up, and I feel sure they put her under the same pressure.'

The revelation coming later might be easier for him if she talked about incest but how would he feel if his birth had nothing to do with incest. The priest woke up and, bemused, looked around for a few minutes.

'Where were we before I fell asleep?' he said, directing his gaze at Teresa. He seemed unable to recall their previous conversation and the reason they were sitting across from him. She could excuse him for that, as she knew from her studies it was just age related cognitive decline. It comes to us all but with any luck, she and Pat were a long way from that stage.

'You were telling us about Pat's father's ordination in Maynooth?' she said, hoping that would be enough to jog his memory and bring him back to the present.

'I remember now. Your father's first parish was in Ballyfermot in Dublin, and he worked there as a curate. He came home a lot and his sister Mary, your mother, was a lovely young woman.'

'Did I hear you right?'

'Yes it was a case of incest. When I heard about it, it was my duty to tell the Bishop. Straight away, he transferred your father to an American parish and arranged for your mother to work in an unmarried mother's convent laundry. All he was worried about was saving the Church from any whiff of scandal. Your mother wanted to keep her baby, but she had no say in the matter. The infinite power of mother church took over.

She never came back to the parish but joined a Cistercian order; I think it was in County Wexford. Of course, it was an enclosed order with little contact with the outside world, and she died there. She was a good woman, and I'm unable to imagine the depth of despair she suffered at losing you.'

The priest went silent and Teresa saw his eyes misting over. She was at that stage herself, but her main concern was for Pat. Emotion had overcome him and he was crying silently into his hands.

After a few minutes, the priest felt composed enough to continue. In your father's California parish, he was responsible for teaching religious doctrine in a Catholic high school. One day like any other day, a disturbed student took a loaded gun to school with the sole purpose of getting even with some of his classmates. Your father tried to reason with him, but he shot him dead. I have all the cuttings from the papers along with photographs for you in the folder on the coffee-table.'

'Are any of my relatives still living here in Clifden,' asked Pat, through his distress.

'No, I'm afraid they are all dead. If you would like to visit the cemetery on the way out of town, you can see your relatives' grave stone. It's near the entrance. They were all well-respected people about here. I'm so sorry Pat for the mess that we made of your life, and I'll carry the guilt to the grave.'

'It was the time you lived in, and you must forgive yourself. I'm more satisfied that I've heard the full story, and it's important for me to know that my mother wanted to keep me. That's enough to keep me going. Thanks, Father.'

'I'm so glad you came, Pat. I somehow knew you would. Come and see me any time and call me on the phone as well.'

They shook hands with him and took their leave. Teresa looked back from the doorway, and he had already fallen into a tired sleep. Later they learnt that he had died less than two days after their visit. Had he been holding on for Pat to call and see him?

22

The following morning Pat was up early preparing for the journey to Birmingham. He loaded an empty coffin into the back of the hearse and checked the engine oil and tyre pressure. A breakdown on a motorway would attract too much unwanted attention to a hearse loaded with drugs.

He briefly considered joining the AA but that was only for nerds who couldn't even change a wheel. He felt his knowledge of the mechanical workings of the hearse went deeper than that and there was little he couldn't repair if it came down to it.

Most undertakers kept their hearses in good mechanical condition. From experience, he knew that a hearse breaking down on the way to the cemetery with a corpse on-board should never happen. It compounded the grief of the relatives, they felt and they were being disrespectful to the dead person, and it was their fault. It was a strange phenomenon and happened to them only once when his father was driving an old hearse they owned. Neither he nor his father expected the level of distress caused to the relatives of the deceased. To try to mitigate the damage they took a hit and wrote off the cost of the funeral.

Teresa was still in bed awake and feeling tired, drained by the emotionally charged visit to Galway. Was Pat better to know about his parents or should the secret of their wrongdoing have remained hidden from him? What was the adage, she couldn't remember the exact words but the sense was - it's not what happens to you but the way you take it.

Over the next few days, she would know how well he was dealing with the revelation that would cause most people to crack. The suffering in his life had made him stoic, but this could put him under severe mental distress. He wouldn't go down if she had anything to do with it, and she was experienced in this area. Helping people to cope with the horror of their lives was what she did in her previous role in the prison service under the broad label of religion.

She heard him moving about the yard and decided to get up and help him prepare for the trip. It was a pity they didn't have a few days free to take a holiday and go away somewhere to clear their heads.

When he heard her downstairs he came into the kitchen from the yard.

'Morning, I thought you weren't going to get up at all today.'

'No chance of a long lie in this place. It's busier than Waterloo Station.'

'Time is money, as they say,' he said, sitting down at the table.

'Have you had any breakfast?' she asked.

'No not yet.'

'What do you want porridge or flakes?'

'Any cereal is fine,' he said, putting his elbows on the table and staring out the window into space. With cornflakes, bowls, spoons, cups, milk and a teapot of tea, they started to eat. There was a silence between them, the elephant in the room was yesterday's trip to Galway, and they were reluctant to talk about it. Finally, she said, 'Pat are you feeling OK?'

'My head is in a jumble, incest of all things. I feel tainted by what they did. It just keeps going around and around in my head. Why me? Have I not had enough already?'

'We don't know why life is so skewed - some people seem fated to suffer. In the convent, we had a technique of dealing with disturbing thoughts. Just say, cancel, cancel whenever something troubling comes into your mind and don't give it any further house room. A new thought will take over immediately. Will you try that?'

'I will,' he said with little conviction. She felt he wasn't fully listening to her and anyway what she was suggesting wouldn't work in his case. He was in a stalwart macho mood and would suffer on.

She had seen it before with men in prison. It was as if they were saying, hit me with whatever you've got. I can take it, and I don't need help from anyone.

She couldn't blame him for that. She guessed that, combined with activity, it was the strategy he used to cope with his turbulent life.

'Pat have you heard the saying let go and let God. Sometimes when you're at the end of your tether the only way is to hand it over to the good Lord. Let him deal with all your troubles.'

She was preaching again. Old habits die hard and if she could only hear herself, it probably sounded like the ramblings of an overzealous religious type. She had promised herself that she would never get like that, and here she was slipping into type.

'That's easier said than done. Right let's make a start' He almost jumped up from the table.

Soon they were driving into the Dunlaoghaire ferry port. A deck hand directing traffic waved them on to the car deck of the ferry. He ushered them to a secluded spot in the bows and when they got out of the hearse, he covered it with an opaque plastic sheet.

'I'm trying to make it invisible. It's surprising the number of drivers feel spooked, when they see a hearse with a coffin inside,' he said. He continued tying the ends of the sheet to the deck to stop it from blowing away with the gusts of wind sweeping across the boat.

'Awe, tell me about it. People don't like reminders of death; they think they're here forever. How do you feel about working around hearses?'

'Not that keen on it, especially at night when there's nobody else down here but myself. It spooks me out but, a job is a job,' he stood up and looked at Pat for a feedback. Pat smiled.

'Stick it out. Jobs are hard to find with so many on the dole.' They nodded in agreement.

'We booked bunks, where do we go to get them?'

'To the reception on the next deck, take the stairs over there.'

'Thanks,' said Pat.

They had to wait in line at the reception desk and when their turn came the harried receptionist scanned the computer for their reservation. She found it and printed out a receipt with their cabin number on it. She handed the paperwork over to another employee, and she led them to cabin number fifty. Travelling on his own he never bothered with a cabin but on this trip he felt pleased Teresa had booked one for them. He hadn't slept well and it was an opportunity to grab some rest if not sleep.

The cabin was small and he couldn't with any stretch of the imagination describe it as luxurious. The bunks were one on top of the other with an en suite toilet at the end. Two people couldn't overtake each other in the passageway, unless one sat into the lower bunk. Such were the joys of tourist accommodation on a ferry crossing.

'What bunk would you like?' asked Teresa giving him a reassuring peck on the cheek.

'It doesn't matter. I'll take the upper one to save you climbing up there,' he said, stretching up to catch the guard rail on the top bunk in both hands.

'That suits me fine, give me a shout when we get to Holyhead.'

'Will do,' he said, swinging himself up into the bunk. She closed the porthole curtains. With the gentle rocking of the ferry, she was soon asleep. He wasn't so lucky. Deep sleep evaded him and he was awake for most of the crossing. There was too much worry on his mind.

The rattling of chains and the noise from a whirlwind of activity heralded their arrival in Holyhead. There was no need to call her with that din going on.

'Are we in Holyhead?' she asked, sleepily.

'Yes we are. I'm coming down out of here and don't stick your head out. There's the old yarn about the fella in the top bunk feeling sick and shouting, "Watch out." The second fella stuck his head out of the bottom bunk and said, 'What?" as the vomit came down. Do you feel like eating anything? We have a fair bit to drive to Birmingham.'

'My stomach is all over the place after hearing that. Perhaps something light. I wonder who makes up those jokes. I haven't met anyone who admits to it, although they can be funny.'

The ferry trip hadn't increased their appetites and in the restaurant they made do with coffee and croissants.

Down on the car deck the crewman was waiting for them.

'You're the last out. It's straight ahead through Holyhead, and the weather is good for once.'

They said goodbye and joined the tailback through the centre of the town. Free of the traffic jam they were on the open road heading for Birmingham. Pat knew the route without having to think about it.

If she knew what was going on in his head, she would give him one of her knowing smiles and tease him about his photographic memory. When he glanced at her, she was fast asleep with her chest rising and falling, keeping rhythm with her breathing. Motorway driving was boring and he would need to stay alert and not fall asleep. He turned on the CD player - country and western music blasting from the speakers would keep him awake.

He turned into Fillinghane & Cagney City Funeral Directors, waking Teresa as he drove into the yard and parked at the back entrance door as he always did.

When he stepped out of the hearse a searchlight lit up the yard and a noise like an air raid warning sounded. Instantly, armed men with machine-guns, barking out orders surrounded them, dressed all in black down to their face masks and baseball caps. The laser beams of their guns shone direct on Pat and Teresa.

The noise was to distract them from any thoughts of making a run for it. He knew they were a SWAT team. He had watched their antics on a TV series, and they had a reputation for shooting first and asking questions later. That's if the stories on the TV were believable which they probably were not.

He always suspected he would meet a bad end and this fitted in with his life: an awful start with a worse middle and a violent finish. Nevertheless, he was shaking as the adrenaline coursed through his body preparing him for flight.

A loudhailer cut through the noise and halted his racing thoughts,

'Will the passenger step out, and both stand against the vehicle and raise your arms. Place your hands to the roof where we can see them.'

Pat stretched up his hands to the roof of the hearse, and it was cold when he touched it with his sweaty fingers. He shuddered slightly when the barrel of a machine-gun pushed into his back, and he almost jumped when a female voice said, 'Have you any sharp needles in your pockets or anything that could do me harm?'

'No. Nothing.'

Then she began frisking him for hidden weapons. He hadn't expected a woman on the team. He had assumed that SWAT teams were exclusively male. She stopped at his back pocket and patted it twice,

'What have you got in this pocket? Is it a hip flask?' she asked.

'No. It's a silver pocket spittoon. It's disgusting but they were all the rage in the 17th century. It's so unusual that, when I saw it on a market stall here in Birmingham, I had to have it. The circular door on the front pivots opens to reveal the main body of the container for spitting phlegm into. The user can get rid of it later. I don't use it but carry it around for the novelty. I think it's silver-plated but rich Chinese had gold ones to advertise their wealth.'

'Never heard of them, it's gross all right, but it's real silver. It's stamped on the back,' she said, turning it around and passing it to what he presumed was a senior officer. Minutes later he returned it, and she put it back in his pocket.

'We are looking for bombs or germ warfare material, and people can do whatever they like with their phlegm,' she said, deftly patting down his legs to his ankles.

'That's generous of you.' He didn't mean to say it, but somehow it came out.

She laughed quietly. 'That's the kind of people we are, full of heart.'

She stepped back from him and shouted, 'Clear.'

Gloved hands caught his arms and hauled them roughly behind his back for handcuffing. They were taking no chances with him, marching him to a white Ford van and manhandling him into the back of it.

Teresa froze when the searchlight came on and the noise started up. Everything went into slow motion. She tried to follow instructions but her fingers couldn't open the seat belt. A figure leant across her and unclipped the belt and handcuffed her hands behind her back. Two other darkly clad figures lifted her out of the seat, and hauled her backward to a Jeep with blacked out windows. They were destroying the heels of her new shoes, dragging them on the abrasive tar macadam of the yard. She tried to protest but no words came.

They bundled her into the back seat, closed and locked the doors.

The sophistication of the surveillance equipment in the van surprised Pat. Banks of monitors were showing pictures from both inside and outside the morgue. One infrared camera focused on Teresa sitting in the darkened Jeep. She looked scared but at least he knew where she was, and she was safe.

'Why are you here?' the interrogator asked, staring at Pat with unflinching eyes, his pen poised over his notepad. This was one of the techniques taught on police training courses for interviewing suspects. Teresa had told him about it from her prison experience. She'd called it passive intimidation.

Pat decided to come clean and explain his reason for being here, otherwise he could end in prison for a long time on a drug charge.

'I'm working with the Garda in Dublin. They are trying to find who is the 'Big Fella' bringing drugs into the country. They badly want to get him. I'm involved on a personal level. They ran my pregnant wife off the road. She was killed in the crash. I won't forgive them for that.' Pat was choking up, and he stopped talking.

In sympathy with what he had just heard, the interrogator's mood changed and the hardness went out of his voice.

'Give me the name and telephone number of your Garda contact in Dublin.'

'Detective John O'Neill, and he is in Pearse Street Garda Station. The telephone number is on my mobile sitting there in front of you.'

The interviewer handed the phone to a colleague.

'We are going to ring him now. By the way, who planned this, and what happens when you get here?'

'I get a phone call from the drug men telling me to come to this morgue to collect a John Doe body, always with the same name Patrick Murphy. The coffin in the hearse has a false bottom, and that's where the drugs go.'

'Predictable, there's no other name more Irish than that one. What happens to the drugs when you bring them to the other side of the water?'

'Detective O'Neill makes the bust after the mob picks them up.'

Abruptly, the interviewer got up from the desk and knocked over the chair he was sitting on. He took a piece of paper from his colleague with O'Neill's number on it and left the van. Pat suspected that he was going off to ring O'Neill for confirmation of what he had heard.

Here was the rub, what if O'Neill decided not to confirm the details of the story? O'Neill, determined, to protect his anonymity, might leave Pat swinging in the wind facing the prospect of a long prison sentence.

Pat would try to save Teresa. She had no involvement in O'Neill's scheme to import drugs that he hoped would lead to discovering the identity of the gang leader.

This arrest exposed the weakness in Pat's position as an undercover Garda agent. He should have seen it coming and demanded some guarantees from O'Neill if this arose. It was too late for that now. He would just have to sit tight and hope for the best.

It seemed a long time until his interrogator returned, even though the minute hand of the clock on his desk had barely moved. Pat's shirt, drenched in sweat stuck to his back. The interviewer showed nothing in his face as he righted the chair and faced the back toward the desk, straddled it, and rested his hands on the top. He looked at Pat for a few seconds. It felt like hours, and then he spoke in a less combative tone.

'Detective O'Neill confirmed that you are collaborating with him. We don't want to blow your cover, continue as normal. Wheel the coffin inside and collect the body. We have taken several workers into custody and charged them with drug trafficking, but we also suspect some of the others. The burden of proof lies with us and sometimes it is difficult to get evidence that will stand up in court. It will be of interest to see who comes to help you. Leave as soon as you load the cadaver, and we cannot allow you to take any drugs.'

'Ok. Is Teresa coming with me?'

'No, there's a problem. As a student she was part of a peace march that got out of control. She got a conviction for disorderly conduct and didn't pay the fine. People who break the law think they can get away with it but the record stays.'

A woman came up behind Pat and removed the handcuffs.

'We are holding your girlfriend in custody. Don't worry too much. It's not a serious offence, little more than a student prank, and we hope she'll get home soon.' With that she was gone.

Pat removed the coffin from the hearse and pushed it into the morgue. Two men came forward and directed him to a body covered in a white morgue sheet. The big toe sticking out had the name tag Patrick Murphy attached to it. They took off the sheet, and he would bet the Oriental corpse that lay there had no Achill Island connection or even Irish ancestry. They lifted the corpse into the coffin and screwed down the lid. The respectful way that undertakers treated the dead was well-known. They might be drug dealing crooks, but their training as morgue attendants took precedence when dealing with corpses.

'We have nothing else for you today. The filth is all over the place, watch your back,' one of the men whispered as he busied himself around the coffin.

Pat nodded his head in acknowledgement and the three of them carried the coffin to the hearse and loaded it on-board.

'Could I see Teresa for a few minutes?' Pat asked the female officer standing close to the Jeep.

'I'm afraid not. She's in the custody of the local police and her next port of call is to a remand centre. We will let her know you that you are thinking of her. Give it a week and you lovebirds will be together again. Someone will go and talk to her now.'

With that she walked toward the Jeep.

His interrogator said, 'You need to get out of here.'

Pat didn't want to leave Teresa behind, but the tone of his interrogator's voice made it clear he was ordering him off the property. It was not negotiable. Unhappy with the way things had developed, Pat drove out into the busy city traffic and with his mind working overtime.

He would arrange for the best lawyers in the country to work on Teresa's case. If he hadn't a corpse on-board he would have stayed on in Birmingham to bring her back home when they freed her. He had no doubt that they would release her soon but there were no certainties when it came to the law. With the best legal representative, even the worst offenders often walked free. He hoped and prayed he was right that Teresa would soon get out of there.

There was another possibility that they would give her a long prison sentence. He gave it no thought. She was always telling him not to dwell on negatives and only imagine positive results. He found that difficult and maybe it was easier for a clever person. He wasn't that. As he drove along, he had become used to having her sitting beside him. He was missing her chattering away perhaps trying to educate him about the many things he knew little about. It was going to be a lonely road back to Dublin. He had toyed with the idea of asking her to marry him, since they met, but he couldn't make up his mind if she was the one for him or not. Now he was sure about it. As soon as they released her, he would go down on one knee and ask her to marry him. If she refused, he would feel gutted although everything about her was saying to him that she was ready to marry him. He wanted her by his side for the rest of his life. He was going to take a chance whatever the consequence. He was going to ask her. He had to know.

Teresa was sitting alone in the dark, trembling. She was trying to put it out of her mind, and, unless she managed to control her emotions, she would end up a basket case. From experience, the best way was to try to tap into the reason and logic in her head and divert her thinking from events going on around her. It was an effort of will, but she started to examine the circumstances that had landed her in this mess; from helping prisoners to being one. Why had they not picked up on the unpaid fine when they carried out a clearance security check on her to work in prisons?' The answer might be simple. Perhaps they ignored minor infringements when it came to nuns, or in the search for previous they used her convent name, Sister Genevieve.

She was a great reader, and the Reverend Mother nicknamed her the dedicated bibliophile. With all the fixes she got into, she sometimes felt her life wouldn't be out of place in fiction she read. In truth her present predicament was bordering on the bizarre. Perhaps book readers were like that, moulding their lives around the make believe stories they read. If they were all making up their lives from whatever story they fancied, where had reality gone, if there even was such a thing?

The backdoor of the Jeep opened and a policewoman in usual Bobbies gear removed Teresa's handcuffs. She shut the door again and sat in the driver's seat. One of the SWAT team slid into the passenger's seat beside her, removed her balaclava and turned her head around to address Teresa.

'We verified with the Dublin Garda that your friend is helping them with a drug problem. We released him. Regrettably, we are holding you on remand, but we hope only for a few days or a week.'

She looked across at the other policewoman who hesitated and then nodded in agreement.

'I explained this to him, and he understands.'

'Can I see him for a few minutes?'

'That's not now possible,' she said, abruptly signalling the end of the conversation. She pulled her face mask down and left the Jeep.

Teresa's escort started the engine and said 'I'm taking you to a holding cell in Quinton Police Station here in Birmingham.'

Teresa felt herself becoming detached, entering a semi-dream state, seeing everything from afar and feeling as if she was not part of it. It was all vague from there on; when they lifted her out of the Jeep and took her to a prison cell to her appearance in court and her sentence of a two-week prison sentence and a fine.

She came back to reality with a jolt in the prison van taking her to Styal Prison in Cheshire.

She wasn't alone, with three other women prisoners travelling with her. Their eyes fixed, staring ahead to show no weakness. From her previous incarnation in the prison chaplaincy she knew these types. This was not their first time taking this trip. Nevertheless, she felt great compassion for them.

She knew the breakdown of their likely offences by heart; drug offences for over a third of them, twenty per cent of them having carried out violent acts, mostly against their abusive partners. The rest involved in stealing and robbery of some kind to try to get money to feed their habit and provide for their children, and yes just about all of them have children. The most damning statistic of all is that eighty per cent of all female prisoners suffered from mental health problems.

Nevertheless, she was now one of them, and she would have to watch her back and play by their rules in the prison regime. How she wished Pat was here to talk it over. The more she thought about him, the more emotional she got. To her horror, she started to cry. She would have to show her toughness inside the prison when they tested it. That's where bullies rule.

The prison van stopped at the gatehouse, and the driver produced his ID card. His details were noted in the gate book by the security guard.

'I know most of the faces you have on-board. Former guests of ours, we are so lucky with the quality we get in here. Have you any fresh meat?' he said.

'One new one,' said the driver, pointing to Teresa.

Before waving the van on, the security guard painstakingly wrote down each name, hesitated a moment and then put an asterisk beside Teresa's. The prison officers were waiting for them at the next stop, and they marshalled them into the reception area.

'Take off your clothes and put them into the plastic bag on the floor. Pick the correct one with your name on it. You'll get your possessions back when you leave here,' one of the officers barked, reading from a typed sheet.

Then to Teresa's horror and in full view of everyone, the officers started to strip-search them. When it came to her turn, she closed her eyes and tried to imagine being in a nicer place as a female officer roughly prodded and poked her.

Complaining about the way they were abusing and humiliating her wouldn't achieve anything apart from marking her out as a trouble maker. The other prisoners in line received the same mortifying treatment. That should have consoled her, it wasn't personal, and they were not singling her out. Somehow that thought didn't help. In a few hours, she was going to have black and blue marks all over her body. She felt violated and dirty.

Next, to the showers and she scrubbed her skin until it glowed white, trying to remove the grime she imagined was sticking to her from the brutal search. In some small way, she now understood how rape victims felt. Before marching to the healthcare section for examination, the sewing room staff distributed prison clothing for them to wear. One size fitted all but if given permission from an officer, they could later visit the sewing room for alterations. It was small comfort, but she felt relieved that all the medical staff were female.

Her accommodation was sharing a two-person cell in the housing block. She would have preferred a single one but this wasn't the worst. She could have ended in the dormitory sleeping cheek by jowl with others in rows of bunks.

A prison officer escorted her to the second-floor landing, unlocked the door to cell number nine hundred and ninety-nine and pushed her inside. She closed it again with a clang and locked it. The prison officer didn't speak or acknowledge her. It seemed like she was a non-person, a piece of garbage discarded and locked away out of sight.

In the dim light, she became aware of sobbing. It was coming from the lower bunk where her cellmate, a young woman, was curled up in the foetal position. She guessed the girl was about twenty years old.

She hesitated for a moment then said, 'I'm Teresa,' and held out her hand.

The girl opened her eyes, and took Teresa's hand in a limp grip, and said in a deep Geordie accent, 'I'm Leanne and I'm missing my children terrible. I need to get out of here, or I'll go mad.' She started crying again. She was so pathetic with her eyes red from crying and tears running down her face.

'How long are you here for?' Teresa asked, wondering if there was a way she could console this girl; someone who was little more than a child herself.

'I was so stupid. I was a mule for my partner. The customs officers caught me with the goods coming off a plane from China. I got ten years, and that bastard, the father of my children, doesn't even bother to come and see me. He'll now have another silly girl like me pregnant, and doing his dirty work for him. When she's caught, he'll still be out there, scot-free.'

Making heart wrenching sounds she was sobbing again. Teresa felt there must be a more humane way of dealing with mothers who break the law rather than imprisoning them away from their children.

This was dreadful and she felt powerless to help, what could she say that would make any difference in this situation? She climbed into the top bunk and cried herself to sleep.

Next morning they assigned Teresa to a job mopping the walkways and landings outside the cells.

'What job have they given you?' asked Leanne, 'I'm working in the kitchens.'

'Mopping.'

'Watch out for Grizzly. I hit her first and that's the way I handled her. Show her you won't stand for any nonsense. She has half of them scared of her,' said Leanne, her words belying her innocent face.

'I'll keep an eye out for her,' said Teresa, aware of the gangs and the gang leader culture in prisons. It was the survival of the fittest, and it was the last place on earth she wanted to be.

'The screws are lesbos, and sadists, and don't bend down with your back on them,' said Leanne with venom as passed on her wisdom of the dangers of life on the inside.

'I have a lot to learn,' said Teresa as she contrasted her experience of working in the chaplaincy to being a prisoner. The cliché, chalk and cheese seemed to describe it accurately. The prison officer stood nearby on Teresa's first day working next to Grizzly. There was no incident, apart from the look of hate on her face whenever Teresa glanced in her direction.

Paired together again next day, Grizzly waited until the officer took a toilet break and then she attacked. She rushed at Teresa with the mop held in front of her like a battering ram. Just in time Teresa stepped aside grabbed the mop head and pushed it back with all her strength. Grizzly looked confused, she wasn't expecting that and doubled up in pain as the mop handle hit her hard in the stomach. She was gasping for breath when Teresa hit her with an elbow in the face. Blood gushed, and sprayed everywhere, and Grizzly moaned as she fell to the floor. She had learned well, it was similar to what Pat's evil twin did in the pub. Heavens she hated violence and was now somewhere between fainting and throwing up but she was determined to stay on her feet. She had never hit another human being and it was frightening. They handcuffed her, and a prison officer she hadn't seen before rushed her away to the isolation unit reserved for violent inmates. They took Grizzly to the infirmary for medical treatment. The prison officer uncuffed her wrists, and pushed her into the padded cell.

'Make up the bunk.'

When Teresa bent down to spread out the sheets, the officer started to grope her from behind. Almost without thinking Teresa swung around and in one movement punched the officer in the face and kicked her knee. She heard a breaking and tearing sound from bones and tendons. It was the only way she knew how to defend herself, by following the example of the evil twin. Perhaps she had overreacted.

Angry, and in pain on the floor the officer blew her whistle and within seconds reinforcement arrived. Teresa was roughly straitjacketed and rolled onto the bunk. The officers left, closed and locked the door behind them. She hadn't known they still used this obsolete restraint that should have been consigned to the dark ages. She had skinned her knuckles punching Grizzly.

Lying on her hands was so uncomfortable, and soon the numbness, and pins and needles caused by restricted circulation started. She tried to remove the straight jacked by pulling, twisting and turning but it was a futile gesture. She screamed with frustration. There was no one about to hear her cries.

Her watch was on her wrist tied behind her back, and she didn't know how long she was lying there. It seemed forever until she heard a key turning in the lock of the cell door. The prison warden came in, and her manner was strict and her speech formal and direct. She ordered her officers to remove the straight jacket.

'I'm sorry this happened to you. Plastic restraints have replaced straight jacket's to stop prisoners from hurting themselves or others. We haven't used that thing for years. Are you OK?'

Teresa was rubbing the circulation back into her hands.

'I think I'm Ok.'

The warden waited a few minutes before saying, 'Take your time, and tell me truthfully what happened here?'

'The prison officer pushed me in here. She then told me to make up my bunk. When I bent down she groped me from behind, and I hit her to stop the assault.' The warden was silent for a while, writing in her diary.

'As is your right, you can take this matter further. We will arrange a solicitor for you.'

'No, I just want to complete my two weeks sentence and get out of here.'

'OK, this is not the first time inmates have accused this officer of this type of incident. I previously recommended to the Home Office to transfer her to a male prison but nothing happened. I phoned them again today and they have agreed to move this officer. Tomorrow she is leaving here. We are moving you to single cell occupancy, and your new job is in library services.'

With that she left the cell. They had given her the best accommodation and a plum job but it was going to be a long two weeks with Grizzly still out there. God, how she wished Pat were here.

23

Pat arrived back in Dublin, and his first task was to contact Teresa. He texted and telephoned her, but there was no answer, either it had run out of charge or else the prison authorities had confiscated it. He imagined the latter was the case, and he heard it rumoured that drug lords were running their criminal empires from their prison cells using mobile phones.

He rang the prison and talked to a receptionist. She told him they had restricted Teresa from either receiving or making phone calls, and suggested that he try again in a few days.

He decided to ring O'Neill to ask him for a favour, to plead with the Birmingham police to release Teresa.

He went through the usual stalling before getting through to O'Neill.

'Hello John, the coffin maker here.'

'That was a right balls up. Are you back?'

'I'm back, there're holding on to Teresa. It's about some student prank in London years ago, and she didn't pay the fine, but it must have stayed on record. Can you do anything?'

'I'll see what I can do. Have you any gear with you?'

'No just a corpse.'

'OK leave it with me.'

'Bye,' said Pat but O'Neil didn't hear it, he had put down the phone.

A plan to dispose of the body was forming in Pat's head. Late in the evening he could check the graveyards around the city until he found an open grave, made ready for a burial the following morning. He would bury the John Doe body in the bottom of the grave, and it would be invisible when they buried the next coffin there in the morning.

He didn't feel what he was doing was totally respectful, but it was an emergency to get rid of an unwanted body. What a terrible end for this unfortunate homeless Asian. He would get Teresa to pray for repose of his soul. He had a feeling that her prayers were more readily heard than his. He couldn't imagine what she would say if she knew what he was thinking.

In the evening, he found what he was looking for in Mount Jerome cemetery, an open grave with a digger parked nearby. Under the cover of darkness, he drove the hearse to the cemetery with the John Doe body in a body bag in the back. Using the digger he went down three more feet until he hit bedrock. That would have to do, going deeper would require explosives.

With the digger bucket, he lowered the body into the grave and covered it over with clay and damped it down. Life and death was a shocking mystery and how he missed his father at times like this. He would have said something wise that could explain it or else fudge it.

His days without Teresa seemed somehow without purpose. Here, he was grieving for another woman thankfully far from dead. He tried to rationalize that she would return after a few weeks in prison, and that was true, but he was missing her, as if she was gone forevermore. He had experienced a loss like that when Marie died in the accident, and the memory would remain imprinted on his mind forever. The loneliness of losing someone he wanted close was almost unbearable. He would have to snap out of. The way forward was a distraction, to direct his energies into work.

The surprise, when it came, was a pleasant one, and there never was a more welcome call, Teresa phoning from the airport.

'Hello I'm here, and it's just great to be back. How are you?'

'I'm fine. I'll come out and collect you.'

'There's no need, I can take the airport coach and save you the bother of driving through the traffic.'

'I'd like to do it. Have a cup of coffee while you are waiting. I'll meet you in the restaurant.'

'OK then. I have loads to tell you. Out of the blue, they just release me, and didn't give any details except to say, "The incident, we were holding you on is no longer on record." Isn't it great that I don't have to think about it anymore.'

'I asked O'Neill to talk to them.'

'Oh, that might explain it, although I don't think he has that much power.'

'I don't care how it happened. I just wanted you back.'

'Well I'm here now. See you shortly.'

'Bye.'

In a crowded Dublin airport, he found Teresa sitting in a quiet corner of the restaurant. With the hustle and bustle of passengers entering the café and others rushing away to catch their flights, he had to take the long way around to reach her. They hugged and kissed, and he felt embarrassed until he realised few people were aware of them. In this throng, it was just about possible for a naked person to run amok among them and be hardly noticed.

They eventually released each other and sat down.

'I had an eye-opener in that prison. It wasn't the same as working in one. There's no one there to protect you. I had a run-in with the prison bully and a lesbian prison guard tried to assault me sexually. It's over now, thank God, and I'm so glad to be out of it. Enough talk about me what about you?'

'I had to get rid of a corpse. I took it with me so as not to blow our cover. That one was a close call and without O'Neill backing, we were in bad trouble.'

'I don't trust O'Neill. I think he's working with the drug gang. A lot of drugs go missing after he gets his hands on them. It says in today's paper that he is about to pounce on the people who are taking drugs into the country. I think he is ready to drop us in it.'

'I trust him. We are working for him, and we are not crooks. I'd say he means the couriers the drug lords make use of, and there's no shortage of them.'

'We are out on a limb here, and I think we need to protect ourselves. If you agree, we'll contact his Superintendent just to make sure everything is OK. I can set it up.'

Pat thought about it for a while.

'It's a good idea. It won't do any harm to let somebody else in the force know what's going on.'

'I'll start on it right away. It might be hard to get to see him.'

Now was the time to ask her, although it was more urgent in his head when she was away from him. He felt nervous about it, worse than facing the criminals. He was warm and sweaty with pulses beating in his chest and ears. Was it the start of a heart attack? If it was, the timing wasn't great, just as he was about to ask the big question. He went for it.

'Teresa, I have been thinking about it for some time, and it wasn't a hard decision to make, will you to marry me?'

A couple at the next table heard what he said; they applauded and came over to congratulate them. They shook hands and then they were gone. Few places are as transitory as an airport. The people there are impatient to be somewhere else, and the stopover is nothing but an inconvenience.

They might have jumped the gun, she hadn't answered yet, and with the time she was taking it might be a negative reply. Then she crumpled the paper serviette in her hands and covered her eyes with it. She was crying, and he wasn't sure if it was joy or sadness. He could hardly breathe as he waited for her answer.

'Pat I would love to, but I can't marry you, there's something.' She was sobbing loudly.

'What's annoying you Teresa?'

'It's bad, and I feel so guilty. It ruined my life and was the reason I took drugs and the reason I didn't protest when my family shoved me into the convent. I deserved any punishment I got.'

She stopped talking, still holding the serviette to her eyes, and her chin dropped forward on to her chest in despair.

He waited for a few minutes and said, 'No one deserves that. What is this thing you did?'

She didn't say anything for a long time. Then between sobs she blurted out, 'I had an abortion in Paris. I'm from a strict Catholic upbringing and I'm tortured with the thought of the mortal sin I have committed. I am sure I will never manage to have a family after all that. It's what I deserved and why I won't marry.'

'I'm sure that's not true. Did you not go to confession?'

'No.'

'We'll sort it out some way.'

'Pat can we leave it for now?' She stretched her hands out across the table and held his tightly.

'OK, park it as the Americans say. We can talk about it again.'

A great wave of sadness emanated from Teresa and seemed to engulf them as they sat there in silence. The table cleaner came along and placed their empty cups on a tray and sprayed cleaning fluid on the table-top and wiped down with a cloth. The message was clear it was time to leave and make way for the next customers. This was a place for people in transit and not a café for students or others who wanted to loiter all day over a cup of coffee. The owner wanted a quick-change over. Get new bums on seats as quickly as possible, and that equated to higher profits.

'I'll go up and pay, and we'll head for home,' he said.

He respected her wishes, but the sooner she resolved this problem that was holding her back the better, as it was making her miserable.

On the drive home, Teresa looked despondent, and he had no doubt that his proposal of marriage had re-energised her old demon, her abortion. If distraction worked for him, it might work for her, and in the apartment he asked, 'What about ringing the superintendent?'

'I'll do that now,' she said without much enthusiasm. It was the first time he had seen her as low as this, but he didn't think discussing the problem would help. She didn't seem ready for that, and he felt concerned that she might leave him if he pushed it.

'Hello, you want to speak to the Superintendent. Can I ask what it is about?'

'It's confidential.'

'I deal with all of his confidential stuff, and unless you tell me what it's about, I can't make an appointment for you.'

'Pat, she won't make an appointment, unless we tell her why we want to meet him?'

'If that's what it takes, then, tell her but not too much.'

'It's about my partner Pat and Detective O'Neill.'

'Hold on a minute.' There was silence at the other end of the phone and Teresa guessed that she was talking to the Superintendent.

'Putting you right through.'

'Hello this is Superintendent McGing. You wanted to talk to me?'

'I'll put you on to my partner. Here's the phone, Pat.'

'Hello Superintendent. It's a long story. I'm an undertaker, and I'm helping Detective O'Neill to try to catch the big drug fella.'

McGing was silent for a minute or two as if trying to make sense of what he had heard.

'Let me see…I'll meet you downstairs in Bewley's Café in about an hour.'

'OK.'

'By the way, what is your name?'

'Pat Murphy.'

'And the girl you have with you?'

'Teresa.'

'OK.' with that he went off the phone.

They entered the crowded Bewley's café and had to share a table until the Superintendent came through the door. Without the braided uniform Pat would never have guessed he was a Garda. Small, rotund with red jowls, he was hardly anyone's image of a top Garda. Pat raised his hand, and he came over and introduced himself.

Two men in plain-clothes came in the door behind him, and few would mistake them for anything but Garda. Police the world over had that look about them, as if they expected mayhem to break out any minute. Their watchful eyes surveyed the room in front, behind and to both sides, and their pockets bulged with the dim outline of pistols.

'I booked a room on the third floor. It's quiet up there, let's go,' said the Superintendent with the confidence of a man used to telling people what to do. He didn't expect a refusal.

Before getting into the lift, he ordered tea, coffee and cakes from a nearby waitress and asked her to bring it up.

The plain-clothes Garda moved towards the lift but didn't get in. Pat guessed that they would wait for the next one pretending that they were not the Superintendent's armed escort. They were silent going up in the lift, and the third-floor room was vacant. He had probably carried out many other confidential interviews in this place.

The waitress came up with their order, and placed the tray on the table before they had time to settle into their seats. Teresa passed around the cups and filled them with coffee. The superintendent refused the offer of a Danish pastry. He took a sip of the coffee, placed the cup back on the saucer and pushed it away into the centre of the table. Drinking coffee and socialising was not what he had come here to do. He took from his pocket a small notebook, snapped off the band to open it and, with pencil poised, he was ready to begin.

'Before we start, give me your details - names, address and telephone numbers.'

Teresa gave him the information, and he wrote it down holding the notebook in his left-hand and writing pedantically with his right. It wasn't difficult to imagine that this was the way he worked on the beat when taking notes in his little black book. That was doubtless a long time ago.

'What is your connection with Detective O'Neill?'

'I'm helping him to find out who the big fella is. I bring coffins over from England with drugs hidden in the bottom. When I pass the stuff on to the crooks, Detective O'Neill follows their movements hoping to get to the big fella, but it hasn't happened yet. He raids them before they get a chance to sell on the drugs. The big fella is good at staying hidden.'

'Mm…I didn't know any of this,' said the Superintendent as he finished writing and started tapping the eraser end of the pencil on his notebook.

'Teresa felt concerned that nobody else other than Detective O'Neill knows we are working with the Garda. She's puzzled as to why the TV reports on the amounts of drugs seized is less than what we bring over and give to John O'Neill,' said Pat, sweating caused in part by the temperature of the room but also from the presence of an authority figure, a throwback to his orphanage days.

'Clever young woman,' said McGing before lapsing into deep thought, tapping away with the pencil, the only sound in the room.

The sound annoyed Pat. It was like the drumming of a woodpecker beak against the bark of a tree trunk, but there was not a lot he could do about it. This self-important man wouldn't take kindly to someone telling him to put a stop to it.

Teresa was looking at Pat, sending him a silent message he couldn't decipher as they waited for a response from McGing. It was one of those moments where he would either accept or reject their story, and as they had no verifiable proof, it could be the latter. Maybe telling him was not such a good idea after all.

McGing took his time and his heavy eyebrows, dark and flecked with grey, were almost touching each other with the depth of his frown when he spoke.

'Usually when I hear a criticism about one my officers, I explain to the accuser that they need proof. Then I advise them to report the matter to the complaint's authority. I am not going to do that in your case. You see, we have investigated O'Neill several times, and until now, we have had no proof that he was doing anything illegal.'

'That's a relief, we thought for a minute you didn't believe us, and that you were going to arrest us.'

'O'Neill has been leading us a merry dance. We know his Sergeant's pay couldn't buy him the life he has. He lives in a mansion on the Southside with a swimming pool, tennis courts and an artificial grass football pitch. He's off with his wife at weekends to wherever you can name, Paris, London New York or whatever. Now it's important that we catch him in the act. Don't in any way let him know that we are on to him. Just carry on as usual and let me know about it, and when the time is ripe, we'll spring on him.'

'I will tell you everything that's going on.'

He handed Pat a business card. 'That's my personal mobile number and don't hesitate to call me day or night.'

'I won't.'

'Stay on to enjoy the coffee and cakes, and I want to thank you for letting me know all this.'

He shook hands with them and left.

24

Pat felt annoyed by what he had heard from Inspector McGing, and after the meeting, he and Teresa returned to Ringsend.

'I'm a eejit letting O'Neill fool me like that. He has me wrapped around his little finger. I should have listened to you, but no I always know best.'

'No don't say that, Pat. You thought you could at least trust a Garda. How could anyone guess O'Neill was a crook? We're lucky not to have to have finished up in gaol.'

'This new Inspector fella, what do you think about him?'

'I'd say he's all right. We have to put our faith in somebody, and I don't think he would risk his career. Will I make tea?'

'All right…we'll have to wait until we hear from these thugs again, and then let McGing know about it.'

Two days later the call came from the drug men.

'The big fella wants you to see you in Greenore tomorrow. Bring two coffins. We'll meet you in the Greenore Inn car park.'

'Where are you intending to take me after that?'

'To the yellow bungalow just past the pub.'

'What kind of set-up is that?'

'It's no set-up. He has a surprise for you. Bring the gun with you if you like.'

There was no time for any more talk, he was gone.

'How did they know I had a gun?'

'O' Neill must have told them. The whole thing sounds dangerous. I wonder if you should go at all,' said Teresa, looking worried.

'I'll talk to the Inspector.'

He dialled McGing's mobile, and he answered immediately.

'Hello.'

'This is the coffin maker.'

'You've heard from them?'

'They want me to take two coffins to Greenore.'

There was silence on the other end of the phone. Eventually, he answered. 'That's OK then, do it.'

'They told me I could bring my gun.'

'You have one?'

'A Glock pistol.'

'A Glock Safe Action Pistol, where did you get that?'

'O'Neill gave it to me.'

'Parcel it up and leave it in at the station until I have a look at it. I'll leave another one out for you.'

'I'll do that.'

He rolled the Glock in bubble wrap, and covered the outside with brown paper and duct tape so it didn't look like a pistol. The Ban Garda at the desk checked with McGing before she accepted the package.

'You can't be too careful with the cowboys we have around here nowadays. A parcel like that could have a bomb it. Dublin is like Dodge City in the old days, every crook here is a gunslinger.'

She handed them an envelope with a harp motif in the top corner.

'The Inspector left that for you. Sign here to confirm that I didn't break the seal.'

Back in the VW he opened the envelope. The pistol inside was identical with the one he handed in at the desk, except it looked newer. The bullets didn't look the same. He thought bullets for a particular gun had to be of the same calibre and shape, but then again, he didn't know much about that. Doubtless, there were hundreds of firms out there manufacturing guns that looked vaguely similar, and probably a different company made the gun and the bullets O'Neill gave him.

'I hate to see you with that thing. I loathe guns.'

'I have no intention of using it, but it's for protection. The thugs might be slow to starting a war when they know I have it.'

'I'll be glad when we are rid of it, forever.'

'Amen to that, and I think we are getting nearer that day.'

'Not before time.'

'We should leave early for Greenore tomorrow,' she said, opening the car door to get out.

'I'm going on my own tomorrow. It's far too risky having you along.'

'If you're taking the risk, then I'm going with you.'

'It's for your own good. I don't want you there.'

'Good God just listen to you. My parents, my teachers, the nuns were always using the same mantra. "It's for your own good," 'I'm not a child needing chastisement…'

'I'm not saying you are, but it could get ugly.'

'…and I suppose I need protecting. It may be news to you, but I can look after myself.'

'I'm not going to argue, you are not going in that hearse tomorrow, and that's the end of it.'

'Neanderthal just like the rest of them. Let me out of here.'

With that she jumped out of the car and rushed upstairs to the bedroom. She was furious with him. She dumped her clothes out of the drawers on to the floor and rolling them into a ball and threw them into her suitcase.

The activity dissipated her anger, and she sat on the bed for a few minutes and cooled off. She had overreacted. She knew he had her best interests at heart, and she should have been more aware of that instead of flying into a fury.

She sat quietly for a few minutes thinking. He needed her as much as she needed him and a devious plan was forming in her head. She would pretend she was agreeing with his decision while preparing an alternative. She was going to get to Greenore tomorrow whether he liked it or not. She emptied the suitcase and folded her clothes neatly back into the drawers.

She could see him busy in the yard as she waited patiently for him to return to the kitchen. His phone rang as he stepped inside.

'McGing here, I have given the Glock the once over. It's a gun used in more than a few robberies in the city. We had it locked away in our evidence room, and O'Neill must have stolen it out of there.'

'He didn't tell me that. My finger prints are all over it,' said Pat, feeling concerned that O'Neill was planning to have him tried for robbery and drug dealing.

'Don't worry about that. I'll clean it forensically. By the way, only use the bullets I gave as any other type could be dangerous with that gun.'

'It was a blessing that we went to see you.'

'Anytime, just make sure to tell me everything that's going on,' said McGing.

'OK.'

'Pat, I'm sorry for the way I acted,' said Teresa, 'I know you have my best interests at heart, am I forgiven?'

'There's nothing to forgive. I'd better tell O'Neill where we're going to keep up the pretence that we're working with him. I'm sure he knows all about it already.'

'It's all getting more difficult. I hope we get out of it all right,' said Teresa not relishing the thought that they were dealing with a rogue Garda as well as the crooks. It could all end in tears as her mother was fond of saying.

Pat was getting ready to talk to O'Neil. He would need to put on a good performance, not to let slip either by what he said or by the tone of his voice, he suspected he was a crook Garda. He dialled the number.

'Hello John the coffin maker here.'

'What's happening?'

'They want me to take two coffins to the Greenore Inn car park tomorrow.'

He held the phone away from his ear waiting for O'Neill to answer. It was a habit he developed since he heard mobile phones emitted harmful rays of some kind

'That's a strange turn of events; two coffins I wonder what they are for? There's danger written all over it. I think it's time I pulled you out of this. They might be planning to shoot you. I can't put civilians in that much danger. It's over and done with.'

'Oh no, I'm going.'

'You're not listening to me. They could kill you if you go up there on your own.'

'I know. It's at my own risk then.'

'Maybe I should give you backup, some of the lads that I can trust?'

'There's no need. I'm going to be fine.'

'I wish I could believe that. At least don't bring the girl with you; she doesn't deserve to die this way.'

'No I'm not taking her with me on this trip.'

'I can't put it any stronger, here's my mobile number and contact me any time if it starts to go wrong.'

Pat wrote it down. O'Neil hung up.

'That was a strange conversation. Listening to it, you would think he cared about us,' said Teresa, frowning.

'He's good. Maybe he suspects we are on to him, and he wants to stop using us. We are past our sell-by date, and it's safer to get another sucker to bring in the drugs for him.'

Another thought had entered Pat's head. He might have made a serious mistake in turning down the peaceful way of ending this drug arrangement with O'Neill. Though, he would never get to know the identity of the big fella, if he had accepted that approach. That would annoy him for the rest of his life, thwarting his aim of bringing his wife's murderers to justice.

Teresa was being deceitful. Fifteen minutes after waving goodbye to Pat at the start of his journey to Greenore, she started up the VW and headed for the same destination but along the shore route. This ensured that he wouldn't know she was following him, and while it was longer, she would probably get there before the cumbersome hearse.

She didn't drive particularly fast, but she arrived well before the hearse and parked round the back. Peering around the corner of the building she saw two men sitting in a Jeep smoking and drinking beer, holding the bottles by the neck as they drank.

Drunken crooks were more dangerous than sober ones, and she wished she had a gun to support Pat. Even though she didn't rightly know how to use one, although she thought it must be simple from watching films: point it at the target and squeeze the trigger.

She ducked back out of sight when the hearse came lumbering along and drove into the front car park. Minutes later, one of the thugs came over and talked briefly to Pat, before getting into the passenger side of the hearse. Not to lose them, she was going to have to follow them closely.

To disguise the identity of VW she bent down and smeared the number plate with squishy black goo from the yard. She pulled a face at the thought of what might be in it.

The hearse was disappearing into the driveway of the yellow bungalow when she steered the car out of the car park and on to the roadway. She drove past the bungalow, and parked in a lay-by a hundred metres or so further on. She was reaching over to the passenger seat for her handbag when there was an almighty bang on the driver's window. It shattered, and bits of broken glass went everywhere. She turned her head quickly and looked down into the barrel of a revolver. The thug holding it yanked the door open, hauled her out to the seat and dragged her along the rough ground before hauling her upright.

'Not a word out of yea, or you're one dead chick.'

Her knees were tearing into a bloody mess and her trousers were in shreds. She wanted to scream but only a gurgling sound came from her throat.

Meanwhile, Pat was following instructions and drove around to the back of the yellow bungalow and then into a field where four shipping containers were sitting on concrete blocks. Steps led up to the locked doorways. They were well past their working lifetime on ship decks with patches of rust showing through their weathered paintwork. These were the gang's storage units for contraband or else holding cells for those who had crossed them. He hoped O'Neill's dark warnings were not coming true, and he was glad he had the Glock pistol in his trouser pocket.

The thug went up the steps, and produced a handgun out of nowhere, he thumped the butt hard against the door. It opened, and he shouted at Pat, 'Up here pronto.'

For a second Pat thought about running for it but he knew he wouldn't get far before they shot him. It might be a better death than the one waited inside. They probably didn't have a quick and painless demise planned for him, more likely a drawn out sadistic and torturous end. If it came to it, he still had the gun, and he might have to use it.

'Come on, what the hell is keeping you?' The gun was pointing direct at him from the top of the steps, and from that close-range, the thug wouldn't miss. Pat climbed the steps slowly, and the idea of mounting a gallows to hang by the neck crossed his mind, but there was no executioner's noose up there, though it might be worse.

Pat stepped across the threshold into the dim interior of the container lit by a dull bulb attached to the roof, swinging from side to side on its flex each time the door opened. He smelt blood, undertakers well knew that aroma, and in the gloom he could make out two figures, bound and gagged and tied to chairs.

As he moved closer he could see their faces battered and covered in blood with their chins hanging down on their chests. He could barely recognise them but they were the crooks who had driven through his showroom window. A baseball bat, the Belfast peacemaker, lay on the floor beside them, the striking end covered in dried blood.

'These are the men you wanted. They drove your wife off the road. It's down to you to finish them off,' said the tall crook standing over the battered men before he yanked off their gags. He slapped one of them viciously across the face.

'What have you to say for yourself?'

The man raised his head and hesitantly through swollen lips he whispered, 'I know my time is almost up and I'm going to tell you the truth. I can't tell you how sorry I am for causing the death of your wife. I did not intend that to happen. I drove up behind her to scare her on orders from the big fella. I got too close and rammed her bumper, and that sent her flying off the road to her death. I'll never forget the terror on her face as she went over the edge, and not a day goes by but it haunts me.'

A commotion started outside the door. They flung it open and the bulb danced up and down from the sudden external rush of air. The crook holding her by the hair pushed a dishevelled Teresa into the container. She stopped struggling and kicking when she saw Pat and shouted, 'Bastards.'

'What have we got here - backup?' said the tall thug, he laughed mockingly.

'We are glad to see you and everything should be easier from now on. You don't know it but you are helping me.'

She was the last person in the world Pat expected to see and it had lessened his options. They could threaten to hurt Teresa if he didn't do as they asked. His priority now was to get her out of here safely and he might not achieve that without shooting somebody. Why could she not have stayed away as he had told her.

'Orders from the big fella,' he said to Pat, 'shoot those two and take them away in the coffins.

He pulled a second gun out of his pocket.

'This one has two bullets in it, one for each of them.' He handed the pistol to Pat.

'Don't do it Pat, it's murder and you're not a murderer,' Teresa shouted before one of the thugs hit her across the face. Blood poured from her nose and eyebrow. Pat rushed towards the thug, but the others held him back and his punch never made contact. For a fleeting second he wished the terrible twin was here and these bully boys wouldn't be standing on their feet and giving orders for very long.

'What the hell did you hit her for?' the tall crook shouted, 'If you try that again I'll blow your bloody head off.'

That ended the confusion in Pat's head of who was in charge. This thug was the boss and it wasn't an idle threat he looked more than capable of carrying it out. The eczema scarring on his face heightened the aura of evilness that surrounded him.

The thug who hit Teresa was holding her tightly by the hair and pulling on it. When the boss threatened him he relaxed his grip and she decided to take her chance to escape from his clutches. She stamped down on his toes with her heel and he shouted in pain and let go off her hair.

Free from his clutches, she ran for all she was worth but they didn't design her heels for running. The thugs easily caught up with her, and dragged her back to the container. That was not a good move on her part, if she had thought about it where could she run to. She was making their situation worse.

'Take her down to the house, we have a first aid kit there. When you're finished with that gun, leave it on the table,' the boss said. The two thugs caught Teresa under the arms and carried her towards the house. She shouted to Pat, 'Don't do it. Don't murder anyone.'

'I'll bring the hearse in closer to the door,' Pat said starting to walk towards it.

'Leave the gun on the table when you're finished,' the boss said as he headed in the direction of the house.

Pat reversed the hearse as near the door as he possible could, raised the tailgate and removed the lids from the coffins.

Inside in the container the two battered men were just about conscious and unaware of what was happening.

He looked around and spotted an upturned crate in the corner of the container it would serve his purpose. He pulled it away, took out the pistol and fired a shot through the floor where the crate had sat. The noise was deafening and they would hear it down in the house. He waited for half a minute and fired the second shot, aiming at the same part of the floor.

In the semi-darkness the light from outside shone through the two bullet holes. A dead giveaway, he didn't want the crooks to see those holes or they would know he hadn't killed anyone. It was a simple matter to disguise them. He pulled the crate over the holes and it blocked out the light. He untied the captives and dragged and half lifted them into the coffins.

With their distressed breathing their chests were rising and falling rapidly and the other thugs would see this when they looked into the coffins. From the drawer under the coffin pedestal he pulled out two sheets he used for protecting the varnish finish on his most expensive caskets from the sun and stretched them over the battered thugs up to their shoulders. That would have to do and he closed down the tailgate and drove down to the bungalow and blew the horn.

Teresa came rushing out, followed by the leading thug. Pat opened the passenger door for her. She looked into the coffins and recoiled in horror, clutching her face,

'O my God you have killed them?'

'They're dead meat now and I have never seen them look better,' said the thug, looking over her shoulder through the side window of the hearse.

'Get in,' Pat said gruffly to Teresa. She hesitated and the thug lifted her bodily, shoved her into the seat and closed the door. Pat pulled away fast.

'Where is the car parked?'

'Up to the right,' said Teresa weakly.

He stopped beside the VW, out of sight of the bungalow and pulled down one of the sheets covering the injured thugs.

'Look I didn't kill anyone.'

'O thank God, Pat.' She hugged him and cried with relief.

'We need to get out of here fast in case these crooks find out we tricked them. These men need to get to a hospital and I think we'll take them straight to the Mater on our way in.'

'They smashed the window.'

'Don't worry about that, it's not too hard to fix. Get going to the Mater and I won't be far behind you.'

'OK.'

He couldn't keep up with the VW and she was soon out of sight. He was so relieved that she was safe, but he felt cold and realised that he was covered in sweat with his shirt pressing against the seat stuck to his back. He shrugged his shoulders and that helped a bit, and turned on the heat. To say he had been scared was an understatement but it was more about Teresa's safety than his own.

He drove straight to the Mater Hospital A&E department and parked outside the door. Teresa was there before him and had alerted the staff to the condition of the thugs in the coffins. They came rushing out with trolleys.

'This must be the first time we have had patients coming in coffins,' said a porter as he helped to lift the thugs on to trolleys.

'We're good - we bring them back from the dead,' said another.

Before they left the hospital, Pat asked the Nursing Manager to let him know when they were discharging the thugs, he would call and collect them.

Two days later the telephone call came.

'Hello, this is the Mater casualty. The men you asked me to call you about have discharged themselves from the hospital. One of them said to thank you and that he owes you big time.'

'When did they leave?'

'They left this morning, in different taxis.'

That was bad news, if the gang caught up with them when they were supposed to dead it would jeopardise discovering the identity of the big fella, neither would the gang take kindly to being duped. It was something he noticed over the years and he wished it were otherwise that the people you go out of your way to help are often the same people that cause you the most difficulty. That couldn't be right, he would discuss it with Teresa sometime but now he had bigger problems on his hands.

His phone rang again and this time it was an unexpected call from a new number in Galway. He answered it immediately,

'Hello.'

'This is Sweeney solicitors here in Galway. We are representing your adopted half sister. She didn't tell you when you visited but she was suffering from a terminal cancer. I'm very sorry to say she has passed away and was buried yesterday. She didn't want to cause you the trouble of having to go through it all, she was that kind of gentle person.'

He stopped talking for a few seconds to let it all sink in.

'You are the only beneficiary of her will and in it is the house and a considerable amount of money on deposit in the Bank of Ireland. You can call into our office to sign the necessary papers or I can send them on to your solicitor in Dublin. Either way there's no hurry, you might want to take a few days to think about it.'

'No I can tell you now that I want to go to Galway to visit her grave. I wish she had told me. It's terrible that she had to go through that on her own.'

'She had some good friends that were with her at the end. Again I'm very sorry and drop in to see us when you come down.'

'Pat I'm so sorry,' said Teresa, crying as she put her arms around his neck and pulled his head on to her shoulder. Pat did something he hadn't done for a long time. He cried.

25

A week passed before the crooks telephoned again and this time the thug on the line seemed more conciliatory - almost friendly.

'The big fella says you are one of us now. With Birmingham gone, he has a load for you in Paris. When you get back, he'll take charge of the stuff himself. They'll get in touch with you over there on Thursday.'

'Do I have to be there on Thursday?'

'Are you bloody stone deaf or something, that's what I said.'

In seconds, he had reverted to type, the aggressive thug that Pat had come to know. He didn't bother to retaliate.

The phone was on the loudspeaker, and Teresa heard the conversation.

'I think you should ring O'Neill to keep up the pretence that we trust him,' she said, anxiously putting her hand on his arm.

'All right then,' he said, bringing up the number on his mobile.

'Hello John.'

'What's happening?'

'I'm picking up stuff for them in Paris on Thursday, all going well.'

'Now that Birmingham is gone that must be where their new supply is coming from. I didn't know they had contacts over there,' said O'Neill, sounding thoughtful.

'When I get back with the load, I'm to meet the big fella.'

'Were getting nearer to getting them, and they'll spend a long time locked up. Watch yourself, they'll not go down easily that gang. Ring me as soon as you get back.'

'OK, I'll do that.'

'If we didn't know what he is about, you would think that he felt worried about us,' said Teresa knowing that they were entering the most dangerous phase in their dealings with these crooks. She said a silent prayer that Pat would be safe.

'It's hard to see through him. I'd better ring the Inspector.'

It impressed him how quickly the Inspector answered the phone.

'Hello, who's there?'

'The coffin maker. The crooks were in touch, and I'm collecting the next load in Paris on Thursday.'

'Have you told O'Neill?'

'Yes, he knows all about it.'

'Good, contact me when you get back.'

'It's strange but if I didn't know better I'd say the Inspector was the crook and that O'Neill was the good fella,' said Teresa, walking across the kitchen and sitting down at the table.

'He doesn't say a lot, but I think he knows what he's about,' said Pat, sitting down across from her.

She had her own bombshell to drop, and his reaction might not be good. The news might devastate him, and that's why she hesitated, waiting for the right time to tell him. Although she felt with all the struggles in his life that moment might never arrive.

Hurting him was not her choice, it tore at her heartstrings, but she didn't have any choice, he needed to know, and she would have to tell him. As she looked at his strained face, she decided not to heap any more misery on him today. Although time was running out, and she would have to tell him before they got to Paris, and say *c'est la vie* to their relationship. She was so familiar with the language that sometimes her thought came to her in French.

'I suppose the best way to get a place for us to stay in Paris is the internet.'

'I'll sort it out. The Irish College is probably the cheapest place'

'I'm blessed to have you, or I'd lose myself over there without a word of the language.'

'With your memory we'll change all that. I'd better contact them, the place fills up fast.'

With the false-bottomed coffin in the back of the hearse, they drove down to the Europort port in Rosslare. From there they took the ferry to Le Havre. Now they were well on the last leg of the journey: the road to Paris.

He was aware that Teresa was not the usual chatty and bubbly young woman he knew. She looked self-absorbed and thoughtful, as if she was working something out in her head. Whatever it was, it was certainly troubling her. Each time he spoke to her, she answered him in a detached and mechanical way like a robot. For a while, that was OK, but it was going on for too long, since they left Dublin.

If it was one of these problems that kept going around and around in her head without her finding a solution it might help to talk to someone, and why not him. He might be able to help and he wasn't stupid like they told him at school. She had almost knocked that negative thinking out of him, and he was grateful to her for that. It was now time to act, give something back and ask her what was troubling her.

'I could do with a cup of coffee to wake me up. Will we pull in at the next stop?

'Ok.' She was hardly aware of him at all, or so he thought. Whatever was worrying her must be big in her head as it was almost blotting out everything else.

Five or six kilometres later he pulled in to the roadside café and they joined the coffee queue. With full polystyrene cups in their hands, they sat down at one of the outside picnic tables. After a few quick sips, he took a deep breath and said, 'Teresa what's worrying you?'

She looked at him sadly and started to cry,

'This is the end of our relationship,' she said. She picked up a serviette and covered her eyes to catch her tears. Her shoulders were rising and falling with each tearful sob.

He felt stunned. This was so sudden. He thought they were getting on well and there was no clue in her manner up to now that she wanted to leave him. What did he do to bring this on?

'What's wrong Teresa?' he said, leaning over to touch her on the arm.

'You won't want me now.'

'I don't believe that for a minute. '

'I'm pregnant.'

Taken aback by what she said, he replied too quickly for it to sound sincere, but it was.

'I'm delighted to hear it. It's brilliant news.'

'Do you mean that or are you just saying it to appease me?'

'Of course I mean it. I'm overjoyed that I'm going to be a dad. Come here.'

They hugged for a long time.

'I was so sure you would want rid of me when you heard that news,' she said into the shoulder of his shirt, wet with her tears.

'Anything but, sometimes you can be so daft'

'This is one of the best days of my life. It's the sign I needed. I now know that God has forgiven my past when he allowed me to get pregnant, and that you are so pleased about it.'

'Of course the good Lord has forgiven you.'

'I'll marry you now if you still want me?'

'Nothing would please me more, but I have a surprise of my own.'

Still holding on to him, she moved away to arm's length to look up at him with eyes red from crying.

He laughed,

'It's nothing bad.'

'I don't care. Nothing is going to spoil my day.'

'Before we left, I got all the paperwork for us to marry in Paris. I was hoping you'd change your mind on the way.'

She hugged him again. 'And I have.'

'Do you think we can marry while we are over here?' he asked.

'Usually they have to put up the banns, but I think they might have abolished that here. It's Paris, after all, the city of *Amour*,'

If it wasn't a contradiction in terms, for the rest of the day, this was a joyous hearse, and they soon reached the outskirts of Paris.

With help from the satnav, they found their way to the Irish College and stopped outside the front door. It looked no different to the surrounding buildings resembling a warehouse with windowless granite walls facing on to the street. The black prison-like door was the only relief from this grim finish, and it didn't offer much in the way of design.

'Believe it or not, this is an expensive area of Paris; that is if you're thinking of buying. When this door opens, the elegance of the inside courtyard will surprise you,' said Teresa, halfway out of her seat to ring the doorbell.

'Hold on – in your condition. I'll get the doorbell.'

She heard him, but she didn't give him any heed. She got to the door before him and rang the bell.

A smaller door opened in the centre and the porter stuck his head out. They addressed each other in French and, following a short discussion, she returned to the hearse with Pat following her. He closed the car door behind her when she got into the passenger seat.

'You'll have to take care of yourself now, no rushing around. Leave all the heavy lifting to me,' he said, concern in his voice.

'I'm listening,' she said, thinking that men will never understand pregnancy. If he had his way, he would probably send her back to the convent for safe-keeping until their baby's birth.

It took a few minutes until the porter opened the door, and Pat drove into the courtyard. He looked around and while it may have faded a bit over time its origins as a French luxury villa from the Middle Ages were clear.

'Well do you like it?'

'I couldn't have imagined this from the awful kip it looked like from the outside,' he said, slowing down to admire the building.

The large rectangular courtyard was surrounded by four storied high buildings on all sides with open French windows leading out to decorative balconies. The long curtains blew hither and thither in the warm breeze, blowing from the south that he imagined coming all the way up from Africa. Well, why not, even though it was a long way.

Later, he was to learn that most of the rooms were bedrooms except for the bottom floor which housed lecture rooms, the library, the church, kitchen, dining room and a communal room.

The porter waved for them to follow him across the courtyard and pointed to a secluded parking spot in an alcove.

'The Luxemburg gardens are right across the way. I must take you to them before we go back,' said Teresa admiring the paintings on the wall as they climbed the stairs to their second-floor bedroom.

'Stretching our legs wouldn't do us one bit of harm,' he said, thinking there was a lot to do before they returned to Dublin. They might have to set priorities, selecting what they must do and forgetting the rest. He didn't mention that to her as he didn't want to say anything that might lower her mood.

'I would love to go to Notre Dame Cathedral and say a few prayers. I need to thank God for all he is doing for us. It's not a long walk.'

'That's fine with me.'

Before they could start, his phone rang, a new number he hadn't seen coming up on the screen before. Then a rough Irish voice said, 'Hello. I'm your contact here, and I'll get back to you in a few days when the stuff's ready. The big fella knows all about it.'

He went off the line before Pat had time to get more information, though it didn't matter, they were going to have an extended stay in Paris.

'It looks like we are going to have lots of time here. You're the tour guide, take it away,' he said, putting the phone back into his fleece jacket pocket and zipping it up. Normally losing a phone and not finding it again was awkward but to lose this one now would be a disaster. It was the only way their contact knew how to remain in touch with them.

'That's good. We'll take the scenic route to Notre Dame,' she said, linking arms but taking the lead.

Punctuated by regular coffee stops they toddled along the banks of the river Seine and under the romantic bridges following one trail after another from the tourist guide. They paid fleeting visits to such famous places as the Louvre and Musee d'Orsay, took the train up to Sacre Coeur and, later in the day they took the lift to the top of the Eiffel Tour to look out across the city.

'I wonder how many people have been up here since they built it,' said Teresa, feeling nauseous. Heights did that to her, and her pregnancy didn't help. She didn't tell him she was feeling unwell. Now that he knew about her pregnancy he would go on full alert.

If she threw up, he would think she was dying, she might make it to a loo before she let that happen. She heard somewhere Diet Coke would settle a sick stomach. He was talking.

'Over two hundred and twenty million people have visited this place, since they built it in 1889,' he said, thinking that if they had that many people on Achill, there wouldn't be room for anyone to move. Talk about cheek by jowl.

'That's a lot of people. If we got a Euro from each visitor, we'd be multi-millionaires. There's a stand over there, I'd love a coke.' Her stomach was churning, and she hoped against hope that this cure would work.

'Do you want any particular type of Coke?'

'Diet, but any type will do to slate the thirst.'

He joined a long queue, and it seemed like forever until he returned. They sat on a bench and sipped the cokes. When they finished drinking and much to her embarrassment, she burped loudly several times. It seemed everyone was looking at her. Pat laughed, and she could have killed him for enjoying her discomfort, but she knew his attitude was right. It was no big deal no one died.

They sat for ten minutes and to her surprise when they got up to go her stomach had settled. Their last visit of the day was to Notre Dame, and there she knelt down and gave thanks. He followed her example. The river Seine cruise would have to wait for another day.

Two tired travellers returned late to the Irish College in the evening, and the tourist trail around Paris had given Pat thinking time.

An idea had formed in his head, and he went in search of one of the many Irish priests staying in the College.

Next morning they were the first in the queue, even before the Germans at the other side of the bridge from the Eiffel Tower for a cruise on the Seine.

'This is almost sinful,' said Teresa, stretched out on a chaise lounge, eating pancakes and sipping her glass as they drifted past some of the most iconic sights of Paris.

'We're celebrating,' said Pat, aware that while they may look like a couple of tourists enjoying the Paris experience, they had another agenda. He had a nagging thought in his head the crooks might have lured them here to finish them off. If the thugs had arranged to have them murdered here in some back street in Paris it would look like a random killing. It was easily explained, they were in the wrong place at the wrong time in a strange city. The trail back to the thugs in Ireland would be difficult to prove.

He wasn't going to discuss his concerns with Teresa, but thankfully, he had another task, which was a pleasant one.

'I have a surprise for you,' he said, reaching forward and putting his empty glass on the table.

'I like nice surprises, what is it?'

'After you went to bed last night, I talked to one of the Irish priests about our marriage,' he said, struggling to wipe some of the sticky maple syrup from his fingers with a napkin.

'What did he say?'

'I showed him our papers. They are in order and he is willing to marry us any time.'

'You mean right now here in Paris?'

'Yes.'

His phone rang, and he fished it out of his pocket. On the screen, he saw the incoming call was from a local number.

'Hello.'

'Your load is ready. Where are you staying?'

'The Irish College.'

'Not tomorrow but the day after. At ten o'clock, park outside the front door and follow me, I'll be in a red Renault.'

'Is that in the morning?'

'You must be the thickest fool in Ireland. That's what I said.'

He didn't like the sound of that phone call, and he would keep the Glock pistol to hand wherever those thugs took him.

'Pat, we have only tomorrow for getting married. We'll be going home the following day. There's too much to arrange we couldn't possible manage it in that time, and we'll have to go back because we'll have a corpse in the hearse,' said Teresa, sitting up and placing her glass away from her on the table.

'I have another surprise for you.'

She stared at him with a worried look on her face, unsure of what to expect.

'I told everyone in the sitting room last night about our wedding, and they are arranging everything. We have a best man and bridesmaid. The ceremony is at seven tomorrow evening in the chapel. You know the girls that talk a lot about design?'

'I do, they're working in a couture house.'

'Well they are going to borrow bridal wear for you and the bridesmaid.'

'Can they do that?'

'They did it before for somebody else. All they have to do is tell the manager.'

'You were a busy little bee. I thought I was the organiser in this family,' said Teresa no longer stretched out and relaxed but sitting up engrossed and energised.

'The café the college use is throwing in a wedding cake, and we pay for the meal and the wine.'

'Sounds like a good deal to me,' said Teresa. 'I have to say you are full of surprises.'

The phone call had broken the romantic spell of Paris for Pat, and both he and Teresa were tense for different reasons. Organising the wedding was troubling Teresa, and what the crooks had set up for them was causing Pat many concerns. He was no longer on his home patch, and he didn't even speak the language; talk about being disadvantaged. When the trip on the river finished, they hired a taxi back to the Irish College, stopping at a jeweller to buy his and hers wedding rings.

The image of the quiet wedding Pat had in his mind evaporated when they reached the college. The students had been active and 'getting married' bunting and streamers were hanging from the wall inside and outside the college. There was a carnival atmosphere everywhere with musicians practicing their pieces for the reception in the café, and two harpists sitting on stools beside the chapel altar playing their selection for the wedding ceremony.

The designers whisked Teresa away to try on the wedding dress, and they followed that with a trip to the hairdresser's.

This gave Pat the opportunity to slip away to the hearse parked in the alcove and, undisturbed, he unclipped the Glock and loaded it with the bullets the Inspector had given him. He didn't like leaving a loaded pistol in the hearse overnight, but he might not have time in the morning to make it ready for use. Of one thing he was sure, he wasn't going to meet those crooks tomorrow without it.

At seven o'clock that evening everything was in place for the wedding and there was an air of expectation in the college chapel as they waited for the bride. The priest was dressed in vestments, and standing in front of the altar facing the congregation. Pat and the best man, who he had just met, were standing facing him.

The harp music filling every nook of the chapel, suddenly changed from a haunting Irish air to 'Here comes the bride'. Everyone looked around to get a glimpse of Teresa as she walked up the aisle. On one hand Pat felt he was the luckiest man in the world now that he was marrying Teresa but then there was the other problem casting a dark shadow on everything: his involvement with the crooks.

His father often said to him that hindsight is an eye-opener, and in Pat's case it was. If he could go back it would be different. Hate was the driving motive when he involved himself with the thugs. He wanted to get even with them for causing Marie's death. He knew even then, although he wouldn't allow it to come into his mind that revenge never achieved anything good, and it never would. None of what he was doing would bring Marie back but could get them killed. He should have left it to the Garda to deal with the drug men.

Teresa, standing beside him, touched his arm and brought him back to the present, to their marriage ceremony. She cried throughout the service. He wasn't far from tears himself; the singing, the harp music, and the wedding had made him emotional. He couldn't allow himself that luxury of crying in public; a coffin maker must show a tough skin always, or so he thought.

They reached the stage in the rite when the priest said, 'With this ring, I thee wed,' and held out his hand for the ring.

Pat took the velvet box from his pocket and handed it to the best man who took it with trembling hands and sweaty fingers. He opened the box, took out the ring. It slipped from his wet fingers on to the floor where it bounced a few times before rolling under the kneeling board of the front pew. The scramble to find it was similar to a non-contact rugby scrum as people dropped on all fours frantically searching.

The ring had probably dropped through a crack in the floor boards and would remain there until sometime in the future when they rebuilt the college. That could be a long wait. Someone suggested that they borrow a ring from a married couple, and they were just about to when Pat remembered they had bought two rings in the jewellers. He nodded to the priest and slipped his own ring on to Teresa's finger.

The priest gave a final instruction, 'You may kiss the bride.' The wedding was over, and they left the church and walked around the block to the restaurant.

Half way through the evening Teresa whispered to him, 'This is perfect, Pat. All of it, the wedding cake, the meal, the music and dancing.'

'And don't forget the wine,' he said having drunk two glasses and feeling a bit light-headed. Since his past misfortunes, he normally didn't drink wine or any other alcohol but what the hell, it was his wedding day.

'Don't know about that. In my condition, I'm not allowed any alcohol, but then I was never much of a drinker. Doing without is no hardship,' she said, feeling bloated with overeating but who could deny themselves the confectioneries of France. That was her excuse and she was sticking to it, even if it did mean she would suffer in the morning from a sick stomach.

'I feel tired Pat, what time is it?'

'No wonder, it's half past four in the morning.'

'Oh my God, where has the night gone? I know we are the guests of honour but do you think we could slip away without anyone noticing us?'

'Sure we can. They won't notice us going. With all the wine, they are having a good time.'

They walked slowly back to the college and the old buildings with the moon shining on them looked as if they too, were sleeping getting ready for the hustle and bustle of a new dawn. Pat was not looking forward to the new day; it was coming too soon. Without a night's sleep, would he be awake and bright enough to stay one step ahead of the crooks when he met them at ten o'clock in the morning.

26

Before ten o'clock the next morning, Pat and Teresa were sitting in the hearse parked outside the front door of the college waiting for their contact to arrive.

'I'm so sleepy,' she said yawning and leaning her head back against the seat.

'You could have stayed in bed. I could have met these crooks on my own.'

'Not a chance. No matter what happens from now on, wherever you go, I go.'

'Right, we'll see. Good God my head is splitting. I had forgotten what a hangover is like,' he said, pressing his hands against his head as if trying to squeeze out the pain.

'You're dehydrated, have we any water with us?'

He rummaged around in the door pocket and found two bottles. He offered her one.

'No, I'm ok, later maybe.'

'Why don't you doze for a while?'

'I might just do that,' she said, pulling down the sun visor and closing her eyes.

He unscrewed the top of the bottle and put it to his lips, gulping it down. She was right. He needed that. Minutes later in the rear mirror he spotted a red Renault coming up behind them. This must be their contact. The driver wore a baseball cap on his head with a hoody underneath. Pat gave Teresa a gentle nudge.

'Wake up, we have company.'

'I was just about to fall asleep,' she said, looking over her shoulder.

'With the gear he has on, he could be the President or the Pope, and we couldn't tell,' he said, trying to make light of their situation, but he wasn't feeling that way about their predicament. The opposite would be a more accurate description of how he felt. Not for the first time this morning, he considered calling off this escapade and driving back to Dublin.

'He is neither of those,' she said without mirth.

The red car drove cautiously past them with the driver examining the hearse for any signs of a double-cross that would land him in a French prison. Convicted drug dealers received lengthy sentences in most countries, and France was no exception. Satisfied, the criminal gestured for them to follow him.

'Make a note of where he's taking us. We can tell the Inspector later,' he said, struggling to keep up with the red Renault as it sped through the narrow back streets. A hearse wouldn't be his first choice of a vehicle for this chase.

'I will. The Gendarmerie can then put this lot out of business,' she said, searching in the glove compartment for a pen and paper.

To keep up Pat was travelling too fast, he was going to slow down and drive well within the speed limit. That might keep the unwanted attention of the police away from them. Apart from that, he had another reason to try and take control of this mad dash. He needed to take his power back from this thug and not let him be in command.

He slowed down, and the Renault disappeared from view ahead of them. When they came around the next corner, the red car had stopped half way along the street waiting for them to catch up. It roared away again when the hearse came in sight. Pat followed slowly. A few kilometres the Renault was waiting for them again. This time he didn't drive away from them. It was a small victory, but seemed like a significant one. In reality, it was only a power skirmish, the real battle was still to come with the odds stacked against them.

'Where is he taking us?' asked Pat, lost in this maze of back streets.

'Don't know this part of Paris that well, but I think a lot of immigrants live around here. They are mostly from North Africa, and that figures. There's rumours that the drugs come from over there.'

Finally, the red car slowed, and the driver put his hand out through the open window and signalled to them to stop. They were outside a dilapidated building with a sign over the entrance. With two industrial doors in the front, it looked like a typical back street car garage.

'What does the sign say, Teresa?'

'It means funeral undertaker. I don't like it Pat, maybe we should keep driving,' she said her voice, quivering with fear.

'We've come this far and I think we should see it through,' he said, following directions given by the Renault driver to back up to the doors. Then the red car took off at speed and disappeared into the distance. Strange how the mind works? He felt more secure when the red car was there; now a feeling of aloneness descended on the hearse.

They waited for what seemed an age before the doors opened. He reversed the hearse into the building, and kept going back until a raised hand stopped him. They were inside a dirty unkempt morgue with four men standing around waiting. A body lay on a marble slap.

Before leaving the hearse, he unclipped the Glock pistol from under the dashboard and stuck it into the waistband of his trousers. This lot would see it, and that might be enough to prevent any strong-arm stuff. It seemed to work as all eyes went to the pistol when he stepped out of the hearse.

'Teresa, sit in the driving seat and go when I tell you,' he said. Thank heavens she didn't start an argument about leaving him behind if things got difficult. Perhaps it hadn't hit her yet, but it might come to that.

One of the crooks came forward and said in broken English, 'We have a body for you.'

He looked sullen and untrustworthy, the type that would blow your head off in an instant. That still might be his agenda.

'No body, just the cargo,' said Pat. He didn't want the difficulty of having to dispose of another body when they got back to Dublin. If they got back.

He had never felt such fear. He was shaking, and his shirt felt wet with sweat. Not only did he have to watch this crook in front of him but he also had to be aware of what the others were doing in the background.

The terrible twin would have no difficulty in this situation, but he wasn't available any more. There are men for every job and his twin excelled at battering crooks into submission. Pat could not and would not accept his violence, and he was glad the terrible twin was gone forever. Even in this predicament, Pat's mind didn't stop distracting him.

The crook shrugged his shoulders and said something in French to the others. Hopefully it wasn't, 'shoot them.'

A side door opened, and two figures emerged dressed from head to toe in protective clothing. They looked like a forensic team on a crime field inspection. The room they came out of was in total contrast to the morgue. It was clean and clinical with an assortment of laboratory equipment on rows of stainless steel benches. This was the processing room for cutting the cocaine they sold to crime lords like the big fella. They had stacked the shelves along the wall with plastic bags of white powder.

The men took the coffin out of the hearse, placed it on trestles and removed the lid and false bottom. They lined the inside of the coffin with a plastic sheet and sealed the edges with a hot-wire gun. On top of the plastic, they laid two layers of aluminium foil. Then they filled the bottom with the bags of cocaine and covered them over with the plastic and the foil. Next they screwed down the coffin lid, sealed it with silicone and placed it back in the hearse.

When it came to drug smuggling they were professional. The protective clothing would prevent the coffin and hearse getting contaminated with drug residue the port sniffer dogs would find. The aluminium foil would prevent the scanners from seeing inside the coffin.

'Very, very good stuff,' said the English-speaking thug.

Pat didn't reply. He was on full alert, and nothing was going to knock him off-guard. With the tailgate closed, he shouted to Teresa,

'Drive out slowly.'

Pat put his hand on the butt of the pistol and backed out after the hearse, keeping a watchful eye on the thugs. No one moved, the gesture of putting his hand on the pistol was a threat enough. He closed the door behind him and dropped the four by two wooden bolt into place. It would take them some time to break down the doors, and by then he and Teresa would be well away from this place. Crying and shivering, she moved back into the passenger seat. He jumped in behind the wheel and drove away as quickly as he could.

'It's all over,' he said, briefly laying a hand on her arm.

'Oh my God, my stomach is churning, and I thought I was going to faint. I was praying for you through it,' she said through tears.

'We are out of it now,' he said, thinking this was no place to be and particularly not for a pregnant woman. Heaven only knew what effect it was having on their baby. He didn't have time to dwell on that as they weren't fully safe until they were on the ferry. A distraction might be the best way to get Teresa's mind away from their plight.

'Set the satnav for Le Havre, or we'll never find our way there,' he said.

'Ok, my hands are shaking,' she said taking the satnav off the dash. It took a few minutes adjusting the controls to set their course.

He knew she was good with electronic gadgets and in a few minutes, she placed the satnav back on the dash. An arrow came up on the screen map showing their current location, and a voice began to call out the most direct route to Le Havre.

'Thank the Lord for the satnav, without it, I don't know how we would manage.' She had calmed down a bit, and he was thankful for that.

'We have a map, but I don't think I could work it out.'

'Why do you say that?'

'I don't think I could read the words.'

'We should make this the last.'

'Yes it's near time to stop this carry on,' he said concentration on following the directions from the satnav.

He was so engrossed that he didn't notice she had gone silent and when he looked over, she was asleep and snoring quietly. From experience, he knew that tiredness often followed fear, and rest was the best thing for her. He wouldn't wake her. Given half a chance he would sleep on himself. To stop himself, he selected a CD and turned it on at a low volume. That and following the directions from the satnav would keep him awake.

The miles dragged on. He felt pleasantly surprised when drivers adopted a mannerly approach to the hearse, giving way at junctions and roundabouts, and showing no irritation when caught behind it in traffic.

Teresa slept throughout the journey and didn't wake until they were driving into the ferry car park at Le Havre.

'Where are we?'

'Pulling in to the boat car park.'

'I slept a long time. I should have stayed awake and kept you company.'

'Somebody felt tired,' he said, smiling.

'I must have been. My neck is stiff, and my back hurts.'

'It might help to get out and stretch our legs. We have time before they call us to board.

They walked around the perimeter of the car park and among the parked vehicles most without their drivers who were in for a snack in the café. All the vans and trucks were destined for Ireland, and some had travelled from as far away as Moscow. Haulage companies had no barriers to sending their trucks long distances if they could make a profit. Over the loudspeaker, a female voice called out in five languages, English, French, German, Spanish and Russian, for drivers to return to their vehicles and prepare to get on board.

The hearse was the first to get waved on, and before they got to the ramp a customs official walked towards them and raised his hand for them to halt. Pat's stomach churned, how could he explain away a coffin full of drugs?

He stopped a few metres from them and looked into the hearse and hesitated for a few seconds before waving them on. Pat loosened his black undertaker's tie; that was too close for comfort. A deck hand directed them to the front of the hold, and into a secluded corner where he covered the hearse with a tarpaulin.

In the café, they ate their first real food of the day, and before they finished the boat had sailed. Pat relaxed; they were safe now from any drug-dealing pursuers.

'I was ravenous. I can't remember when I was so hungry. I'm even going to have a sweet,' said Teresa, pushing her plate away from her.

'It's a sign of health, my father used to say and maybe he's right.'

'I think it's pregnancy in my case,' she said, tucking into a large wedge of black forest gateau.

'I can't use that excuse,' he said, feeling tired - exhausted, in fact - after what they had been through.

Meal finished, he was relieved when Teresa suggested that they should go to their bunks. He was asleep in minutes.

The clanking and banging as the ferry docked at Rosslare woke them and minutes later a voice came over the loudspeaker,

'Would the drivers make their way to the car deck for immediate disembarkation?'

'I'm too comfortable to get out of here,' said Teresa in the bottom bunk, rolling herself up tighter in the duvet.

'They'll take us back to France then. I thought you couldn't get out of the place fast enough,' he said jokingly.

'I'm asleep. I can't hear you. Will we have time for a bite of breakfast?'

'Of course, the hearse is the last to get off the boat.'

They dressed quickly and headed to a busy café doing a brisk trade. The drivers were ignoring the call to go to the car deck.

After a leisurely meal, they took the lift down to an almost deserted car deck. The deck hand removed the tarpaulin, and since there were few around to see the hearse. They were ready to go.

'This ridiculous carry-on of hiding the hearse to keep it out of the public eye is enough to give anyone a complex,' said Teresa, biting into an apple.

They were in the hearse and driving down the ramp.

'It doesn't seem to have affected your appetite much,' said an amused Pat.

'You know what they say, I'm eating for two,' she said, taking another chunk out of the apple.

'You must have good teeth to take a bite like that,' he said, feeling his own teeth tingling.

'That's another thing about pregnancy the foetus can take all the calcium from the mother's teeth.'

'Too much information,' he said as he braked hard to avoid hitting the customs officer that appeared in front of them out of nowhere.

'Damn, I nearly hit that silly eejit,' he said, rolling down the window and shouting, 'Hello.' This should just be a stop and go, a routine stop from the Irish Customs.

'Could I see your documentation?'

'Sure, no problem.'

He handed over the sheaf of papers, and the customs officer inspected it thoroughly. Officious, and in his late thirties, this fellow had the air of a man motivated to get to the next step up the promotion ladder. For a quick getaway they had met the wrong person, this gentleman had his eyes set on a big haul.

'Where are you coming from?'

'Paris.'

'Not a usual place for an Irish hearse to come from?'

'People die everywhere,' he said, wishing he hadn't said it that way. Unless he was mistaken this fellow would take offence easily.

'Would you mind getting out of the hearse, and opening the coffin?' This had got ugly. Pat walked around to the back of the hearse and opened the tailgate. Often when people see a coffin in its naked glory near to them, they have had enough and back away. He hoped and prayed this man would feel the same.

'OK, open it up. We haven't got all day,' he said standing beside Pat with his pencil poised over his clipboard.

'Well there's a problem, have you any children?' said Pat turning towards the him.

'What has that got to do with anything?' This fellow wasn't going to show his soft side easily.

'The young student in there died of meningitis,' said Pat.

'He had a virulent strain of bacterial meningitis and that's one of the most contagious diseases going,' Teresa cut in, covering her mouth with her scarf for effect.

'You may have noticed the lid on the coffin is sealed down with silicone, and I'm not breaking that seal. If that bug gets out, we could have an epidemic on our hands,' said Pat, backing away a little from the open hearse.

The customs officer wasn't sure any more, and his belligerent manner softened as he digested the information.

'I'll tell you what, talk to your superiors, get them to contact the medical officer of health. We'll need to close the port if you have to think about it for much longer,' he said pulling up his gloves to keep his hands covered.

He closed down the tailgate, hoping he hadn't overdone it. He was banking on this customs officer being afraid of looking foolish in front of his superiors for not knowing the protocol. They had to wait for an agonising few minute before he said,

'Drive on.' He looked even surlier as he walked away from them.

They didn't speak until they were well away from the port.

'How did we get away with that?' she said, gazing over at him.

'By the skin of our teeth.'

'The meningitis was a master stroke.'

'I don't know if they have a procedure for dealing with it or not. I was hoping he didn't know either.'

'And here am I, a convent-educated young woman telling lies as if reared to it.'

'You're learning.'

'Man of the World no less,' she said. 'You're one to talk.' They were enjoying the banter, and he was glad to be on the open road. Next stop Dublin.

27

Rested after the Paris trip, Pat telephoned the mobile number given to him by the drug dealer. He answered the call immediately,

'Have you the goods?' On the line was the same thug as always, and Pat decided to put on a tough act.

'I want to talk to the mechanic not the grease rag.'

'If I had my way you'd be toast long ago.'

'I'm shaking in my boots. When do I meet the big fella?'

'When this is over, I'll make sure to sort you out.'

'Promises, promises, you're wasting time, and I'm switching off in a minute.'

'In the Greenore Inn car park tomorrow night at seven, bring the goods and don't bring that stupid biddy…'

Pat switched off the phone.

'I'm always praying when you're on the phone to these people. It scares me to hear you talking like that,' she said, twisting a piece of tissue tight around her finger.

'Prayer won't do any harm, and I hope it will soon be over,' he said.

It was all a game, albeit a serious one. He knew this thug was no real threat to them. He wouldn't lift a finger to harm them unless ordered to do so by the big fella. The greatest fear always wins out and that is especially true for the shadowed underworld where the threat of assassination by friend or foe is always present.

If the big fella sanctioned their demise, this thug would enjoy taking them out. It didn't help to dwell on such things. Anyway, the big fella wouldn't get rid of them yet - they were too useful to his drug smuggling.

'Who are you going to ring first?' she asked.

'I think we should give the Inspector a buzz. He'll advise us,' he said, dialling the Inspector's number.

'Hello.'

'Pat the Coffin Maker here.'

'Well, what's going down?'

'I'm back from Paris, and I'm meeting the big fella tomorrow evening.'

'Where's it happening?'

'Seven O'clock, the Greenore Inn car park and then the bungalow. That's unless they take us somewhere else?'

'Did you tell Detective O'Neill yet?'

'No.'

'Oh, tell him, I'll see you there.' With that he was gone.

'That was brief. I was expecting to hear more from him,' she said, eating again, this time yoghurt.

'As my father was fond of saying,' "Short and sweet as a horse's gallop."'

'We better do as he says and ring O'Neill. And don't give yourself away.'

'Yea we can't let him know about the Inspector.'

When he rang O'Neill's phone, he answered immediately.

'Detective O'Neill here.'

'John, it's the Coffin Maker here.'

'You got back safe. I was a bit worried about you.'

Pat felt like saying 'pull the other one,' but he didn't.

'We have the goods. The big fella is seeing us tomorrow evening at seven.'

'Where?'

'At the bungalow in Greenore but they're going to meet us first in the Inn car park at seven, same as before.'

'I think we have him. I'll be there with a few of the lads.'

'Ok then,' said Pat, feeling confident that he had given nothing away to alert O'Neill that they were on to him.

'Drive carefully.'

'It always amazes me how sincere and concerned he sounds,' she said, throwing the empty yoghurt carton into the rubbish bin.

'Any time he leaves the Gardaí, he can take to the Abbey stage,' he said, but there was something else on his mind: how to find a way to leave Teresa behind without offending her when he went to Greenore.

Teresa was ahead of him in her thinking. She knew him well enough to figure out that he was trying to conjure up such a scenario in his head. A preventive strike might get her the outcome she wanted. It was not her mother's way. She was always advising her to use her feminine wiles, whatever they were, in dealing with men.

'Pat, tomorrow I'm going to be sitting here, out of my mind with worry if I don't go to Greenore, and stress and worry is the worst thing for our baby. The doctors warned me about it.'

He almost said 'it's better than getting killed,' but he stopped in time. No sense in planting that thought in her head. He had to accept there was danger ahead in Greenore, but he expected the Inspector to have a squad of armed Garda with him to protect them. At this stage, it was about the Garda sorting it out. In many ways, he and Teresa were now onlookers in what he hoped was the final drama: the arrest of the big fella.

If he were honest about it, he was trying to find an excuse for taking her with him, but it wasn't easy to get past the reality of it. They wouldn't shoot her here in the safety of her home but there was every chance of it happening in Greenore, even by a stray bullet.

If he left her behind, she would probably follow in the VW, although he could disable it easily enough by taking out the rotor arm. At that point, she would likely hire a taxi. With her determination, she was capable of renting a helicopter if nothing else worked. It was over the top, but he wouldn't put it past her to do that. Apart from locking her up in prison, there was little he could do to stop her getting to the showdown.

That's what you get for marrying a strong woman, but they were all like that nowadays. His father had it sussed long ago when he used to say jokingly, 'I knew they'd be trouble when they gave women the vote.'

The safest thing was to take her with him and keep an eye on her.

'OK, but you will have to guarantee me that you'll stay in the car no matter what happens?'

'I'll do exactly as you say,' she said, knowing that it was unlikely she would follow such an order. She didn't want to push it with him now that she had her way. Maybe it was a precursor to the rest of their life together, and she wondered if she had used her feminine wiles on this occasion?

Pat didn't sleep well. The coming confrontation was on his mind. He had played it out many times during the night coming up with different endings and none of them good. The thought was strong in his mind as it had been in Paris that he should cut bait and run, but that wasn't his way. Pig-headed they often described him on the island and he didn't know if that was a good or a bad thing. He would see it out. Whenever he felt troubled, his mind took him back to the island. To that time in his childhood when he felt so secure with the only parents he knew.

When morning came, he didn't tell her he had agonised all night over their dilemma. Now he was trying to do the opposite - pretending he felt unworried about the trip to Greenore. It was nothing, just another drive through the north Dublin countryside, but she would know it was far from that.

When they drove into the car park of the Greenore Inn, it was filling up with people coming to take advantage of the early-bird menu. There was no place to hide the hearse and, as always, no one ignored it. Although, in this small community, he would say that no one present guessed they were smuggling drugs.

Teresa looked translucently pale from fear.

'Are you scared?' he asked, not knowing what else to say.

'I'm going to be honest and say yes. Not so much for me but for you and our baby. I think we should turn around and get out of here. I have a bad feeling about it,' she said, nervously peering out through the windscreen.

He wouldn't dismiss her advice without considering it deeply. In many ways she was right. They should get the hell out of here. This wasn't acting in a gangster movie. This was real life.

'Would you consider waiting in the pub for me? It would be safe for both of you,' he said, looking into her troubled face.

'Can't do that, Pat, I'm going to stay by your side,' she said, reaching over and gripping his hand tightly in hers.

The arrival of a motorbike, stopping in front of the hearse, cut short their discussion. The rider signalled them to follow. It was game on; their chance to escape from this nightmare had gone and, worryingly, there was no sign of the Gardaí. Would they arrive when it was all over? He wouldn't think about what that meant. People the world over accused their Police of deliberately coming late to violent encounters, to pick up the pieces when the carnage was over.

The motorbike rider led them up behind the cottage. He stopped outside the first trailer and dismounted. He pushed up the visor from his face and, with both hands, removed his helmet and placed it on the pillion. He stood there waiting.

Pat took off his jacket and tucked the pistol into his belt for everyone to see before he opened the hearse door.

'Be careful, Pat,' she said, placing her hand on his arm.

'I will,' he said, gently removing her hand.

He stood behind the door and rested his elbows on the top of it, like the American cops he had seen on TV in a shootout. Though they tended to crouch behind the car door and fire through the open window. It wasn't that dramatic here yet, but he didn't know how it would develop.

'The big fella is on his way. We'll wait for him here,' said the thug, struggling to remove his biker gloves.

Pat nodded. They seemed to wait for hours. The air was still, and he felt surrounded by silence. Nothing stirred except the glint of the moon on the waves in the harbour. He could smell the sea, and that reminded him of the island. He wished he was there now, safe.

'Here he comes,' said the thug as a large black car drove in behind the hearse, blocking their exit. He should have thought of that. The back door opened, and a heavy figure in dark clothing emerged. Pat didn't recognise him for a second until he stepped into the light: the Inspector.

'You're the big fella,' he said, astonished. He'd expected to see O'Neill.

'That surprised you, coffin maker. You escaped from Paris, and they shouldn't have allowed that to happen. You're a tricky little bugger. Anyway I'm going to deal with you myself,' he said, taking a gun from his pocket.

Teresa jumped out of the hearse. 'You won't get away with it,' she said, rushing towards the Inspector. Before she could get near him one of the thugs grabbed her. Pat used the diversion to take out his pistol and point it at the Inspector.

'Let her go unless you want a bullet.' He obeyed.

'Get back into the hearse and stay there,' he said and without saying a word, she did what he said. He was hoping that O'Neill would arrive at any moment, and he would try to keep the Inspector from shooting him until he did.

'It's between us now, and neither can afford to shoot first.'

The Inspector gave a dry sarcastic laugh.

'I don't think so, coffin maker. The gun I gave you only fires blanks. Try it if you like,' he said, putting his gun down by his side.

'How can you be sure it's the same gun?'

The Inspector hesitated, and before he could speak another man walked into the light holding a gun. He pointed it at the Inspector. Pat recognised him immediately, one of the criminals he was supposed to have shot.

'This gun has real bullets in it. It's payback time. I owe the coffin maker a lot. He saved my life, and he has forgiven me for the death of his wife.'

'Don't shoot. We can work this out. It'll be like old times. You with your job back, and I'll give you a cut of the load in the coffin,' said the Inspector, fear in his voice. He knew what this man was capable of.

'Say your prayers, asshole. The world will be a better place without you,' he said, squeezing the trigger. Pat saw a flash followed by a bang, and a hole with a red border appeared in the Inspector's forehead. He looked shocked and staggered slightly before falling forward with a resounding thump.

Then a breathless O'Neill rushed into the light with his men.

'Drop your weapon.' He shouted the command several times.

'Goodbye, coffin maker. I don't want to be locked up in Mountjoy for the rest of my life,' said the shooter, ignoring the order as he kept walking towards O'Neill with his pistol raised. One of the advancing Gardaí fired, and he spun around and fell forward.

Teresa came out of the hearse, and Pat gathered her into his arms as if to protect her. O'Neill came towards them, followed by a tall man in a braided uniform.

'Commissioner O'Conner, this is Pat and Teresa that I have told you about.'

'I'm real pleased to meet you. What a great job you did for us, risking your life like that. John kept me up to date on what was going on, but for operational reasons, we couldn't tell you everything. We've been trying to catch the Inspector for years, but he was too clever for us. God knows you deserve the award coming your way for bravery.'

'No awards. With Teresa's help, I have avenged Marie's death, and that's what I wanted.'

'Are you sure about that, or do you want time to think about it?' said the Commissioner.

'I'm sure,' said Pat and Teresa squeezed his hand to let him know that she was happy with the decision he had made.

'By the way, this is now Inspector John O'Neil. I have just promoted him.'

Pat and Teresa congratulated O'Neill.

'The Gardaí emptied the coffin while we were talking, and you can get under way any time you like. If you ever need any help from us don't hesitate to contact me,' said the Commissioner, grasping both their hands in turn in a strong handshake.

'God, am I glad all that's over. I'm lucky I didn't have a heart attack,' said Teresa, clipping in her seat belt as he reversed the hearse back from the container. The Garda had already taken away the Inspector's car.

'You can say that for both of us. I think we'll celebrate and have a big meal somewhere on the way home?' he said, driving away from the bungalow, certain that it was one place he never wanted to see again.

'That would suit me nicely,' said Teresa, smiling.

She was thinking of their child. It didn't matter if it was a boy or a girl, but she knew he would prefer a boy. Men were like that, they preferred sons. She knew if it was a boy, he would most likely want to call it Pat, and if it was a girl it would have to be Teresa. Solid, determined and predictable is what you got with him. She could easily convince him to change his thinking if she wanted to. Maybe she had discovered her womanly wiles.

She was a bit scared of giving birth with all the horror stories she had heard, although most of them were probably untrue. That was some time away, and she would put it out of the head.

Pat was thinking of business and what he was going to do with his new property in Galway. Sell it was one solution, but then house prices were at rock-bottom. Better to put it up for rent and keep it until the market improved. Then, there was another approach which he favoured - expanding his business and opening another undertaker's in Galway. He could employ someone to manage it for him. He would discuss it with Teresa but not now. This was a family night for relaxation and enjoyment.

Lightning Source UK Ltd.
Milton Keynes UK
UKOW040608060313

207195UK00001B/19/P